Changbai Mountain

John Pritchett

ISBN: 9798333575487
Library of Congress Control Number: 2024916334

DEDICATION

To my dear friend Susan,

Your unwavering support has been the cornerstone of my writing journey. This book, like so many others, is a testament to your encouragement, patience, and keen insight. Your steadfast belief in me has been a guiding light through every challenge and triumph.

Thank you for being my rock, my confidante, and my greatest cheerleader.

With deepest gratitude and love.

TABLE OF CONTENTS

CHAPTER 1

MONTLAKE PARK

The academic term drew to a close at the University of Washington. The last moments of the semester played out in a quiet, almost ceremonial fashion. Doreen, the last student to finish, approached with deliberate grace, setting her exam booklet on Professor Josh Cooper's sleek wooden desk. The room seemed to hold its breath as she did so.

Professor Cooper looked up and met her gaze. He recognized in Doreen the hallmark traits of his most diligent pupils: dedication, precision, and a relentless pursuit of excellence. Confident in her meticulous approach, he accepted her booklet with a nod of acknowledgment, adding it to the orderly stack that symbolized the culmination of his inaugural semester as an educator.

Doreen lingered at the threshold for a moment, a soft smile playing on her lips. "Wishing you sunny days ahead," she said, her voice carrying a warmth that matched the late afternoon light streaming through the windows. Her words, simple yet heartfelt, left an indelible mark on Professor Cooper. As she turned and walked away, the classroom felt just a little emptier, her presence a lingering memory that would inspire him in the days to come.

Josh stood alone in the hushed classroom. The room, a relic from a bygone era, whispered tales through its classic decor. Dark wooden panels, rich with the patina of age, adorned the walls, framing venerable chalkboards borne witness to countless scholarly exchanges. The chalkboards, now dusted with faint, ghostly remnants of lessons past, stood as silent sentinels to the knowledge shared within these walls.

The classroom exuded an undeniable grandeur. Adorned with ornate molding and high arches, the lofty ceiling contributed to an air of spaciousness, making the room feel majestic and open. The historical allure and profound heritage of the room were palpable, each detail telling a story of the past. The room's dignified ambiance and rich legacy inspired Josh's insatiable thirst for knowledge and the thrill of discovery. In this hallowed space, he felt a deep connection to the generations of scholars who had come before him, their intellectual pursuits echoing off the walls of the classroom.

Josh's gaze swept across the now-empty seats that had once brimmed with eager students. Each vintage desk, meticulously positioned in neat rows, bore secret engravings—initials, doodles, and cryptic symbols etched into the wood by generations of students. These marks, seemingly insignificant, told stories of youthful exuberance, quiet rebellion, and the timeless tradition of learning. The desks, polished to a soft sheen by the hands of time, reflected the soft, golden light filtering through expansive, arched windows.

The windows themselves were like portals to another world, offering glimpses of the lush campus foliage and the majestic Gothic architecture beyond. Sunlight streamed through, casting a warm, dappled glow that danced across the polished hardwood floors, each beam adding to the room's ethereal ambiance. The polished hardwood floors, rich with the patina of history, reflected the sunlight in a soft, shimmering dance, adding to the room's timeless elegance.

At the front of the classroom, a traditional teacher's desk stood as a proud sentinel. The solid wood construction and craftsmanship of the traditional teacher's desk spoke of an era when education was revered and teachers were the keepers of wisdom. The desk, though modest, held a commanding presence, symbolizing the countless lessons and profound insights shared over the years.

In the quiet of the empty classroom, Josh's thoughts drifted back to the genesis of his academic journey—an echo from a similar setting years prior. It had been a time marked by both loss and revelation. Following his father's untimely passing, Josh had discovered a hidden legacy that would forever alter the course of his life.

Amidst the sorrow, he had learned of a significant trust his grandfather had established in his father's name, a beacon for aspiring geology enthusiasts. This endowment, steeped in familial pride and purpose, aimed not only to honor his father's memory but also to propel Josh along a path of academic and personal discovery. The trust represented more than just financial support; it had been a testament to his father's passion for geology and a guiding light for Josh's future endeavors.

As he stood in the hallowed silence of the classroom, the weight of this legacy had settled over him like a mantle. His grandfather's foresight and his father's love for the earth's mysteries had intertwined to create a destiny that

Josh now embraced with unwavering dedication. The endowment had not been merely a financial boon—it had been a profound connection to his heritage, a driving force that fueled his thirst for knowledge and his commitment to honoring the legacy left behind.

Josh's reminiscence carried him back to the pivotal moment he had met Emily, his future wife. Their paths had converged during the whirlwind chaos of college class registration—a serendipitous encounter that would forever change their lives. The campus had buzzed with the frenzied energy of students scrambling to secure their schedules, but amidst this administrative turmoil, Emily had stood as a pillar of calm and efficiency.

As an undergraduate advisor, Emily had been a steadfast pillar in the storm, her demeanor both warm and composed. She had deftly navigated Josh through the labyrinth of paperwork and course timetables, her expertise and reassuring presence making an otherwise stressful process seem almost effortless. Her eyes, filled with a mixture of patience and understanding, had met his with a knowing smile, and in that instant, a connection had sparked.

What had begun as a simple advisory meeting quickly developed into something far more profound. They lingered in conversation long after addressing practical matters, drawn together by shared interests and a mutual curiosity. Emily's intelligence and kindness captivated Josh, while his passion and determination left an indelible impression on her.

That serendipitous encounter had marked the beginning of a deep and abiding relationship, one built on a foundation of mutual respect and shared dreams. As Josh stood in the quiet classroom, the memory of meeting Emily brought a smile to his face, a reminder of the extraordinary journey they had embarked upon together, beginning with that fateful day amidst the hustle and bustle of college registration.

Her beauty had struck him deeply, the memory etched indelibly in his mind. Her complexion, a flawless canvas of soft ivory, seemed to emit a gentle luminescence, casting a serene glow that had caught his attention from the moment he laid eyes on her. Yet, it had been her captivating green eyes that truly ensnared him. They were a mesmerizing blend of intensity and tenderness, like twin emeralds radiating warmth and mystery.

Her eyes acted as beacons, irresistibly drawing him into her world. They revealed a depth of emotion and understanding that spoke directly to his soul, silently promising the profound connection they would share. In that fleeting yet eternal moment, he saw beyond her surface beauty and glimpsed the essence of the woman who would become his lifelong partner. Her eyes were portals to her soul, offering a tantalizing glimpse of the love, wisdom, and companionship within.

Every detail of that encounter remained vivid in his memory—the way the light had danced on her skin, the soft curve of her smile, and the quiet grace with which she had moved. It had been a moment of pure enchantment, a perfect confluence of time and emotion that had marked the beginning of a love story that would span a lifetime. As Josh reflected on that moment, he felt a renewed sense of gratitude and wonder for the extraordinary woman who had become his steadfast companion and the center of his world.

Interrupting his reverie, the commanding presence of Professor Joseph Stanley—the esteemed head of the Earth Sciences Department and Josh's boss—had filled the room. His resonant voice, rich and authoritative, had echoed through the empty space, breaking the silence with a sense of purpose and gravity.

"Josh, there you are," Professor Stanley intoned, his voice carrying the weight of years of wisdom and experience. The older man's eyes, sharp and discerning, swept across the classroom before settling on Josh with a mixture of approval and curiosity. His entrance, much like his persona, exuded a blend of scholarly gravitas and paternal warmth, a reminder of the profound influence he had wielded in shaping Josh's academic journey.

"Reflecting on the semester, I see," he remarked, a knowing smile tugging at the corners of his lips. His resonant voice carried a note of camaraderie, bridging the formalities of their respective roles with a genuine sense of friendship.

In that moment, the quiet classroom pulsed with renewed energy. The shared history and mutual respect between them infused the space with a palpable sense of purpose and direction. Josh felt a surge of gratitude for the guidance and support that had brought him to this point. His reverie seamlessly transitioned into the present as he prepared to engage with his boss, a cornerstone of both his professional and personal life.

"Well done, Josh," Professor Stanley proclaimed, his voice resonating with pride and warmth as he extended a handshake. Concealed in his palm was a familiar item—an emblem of scholastic excellence that carried profound significance within the academic community. As Josh grasped his boss's hand, he felt the polished surface of a red wooden apple, a symbol steeped in tradition and meaning.

Among the faculty, it was a cherished tradition to bestow a red wooden apple upon each new professor. This gesture symbolized the enduring bond among educators, a tangible reminder of the legacy of knowledge that transcended generations. The apple, meticulously crafted and imbued with history, represented not only the recipient's entry into the esteemed ranks of academia, but also the shared commitment to fostering intellectual growth and nurturing the minds of future scholars.

Josh's eyes widened with a mix of surprise and gratitude as he accepted the apple. The weight of the small token in his hand was more than just physical; it carried the collective respect and acknowledgment of his peers. The deep crimson of the apple gleamed in the soft light of the classroom, its polished surface reflecting the dedication and passion that had brought him to this moment.

"Thank you, Professor Stanley," Josh replied, his voice thick with emotion. His eyes shone with paternal pride, and the handshake lingered for a moment longer, sealing the bond between them.

As Professor Stanley released his grip, he added, "This apple is a symbol of our trust in you, Josh. May it remind you of the responsibility you bear and the noble path you walk as an educator."

In that quiet, poignant exchange, the classroom seemed to hum with a sense of continuity and purpose. The red wooden apple, a small yet powerful emblem, now rested in Josh's hand, guiding him forward on his journey. The gesture, simple yet profound, underscored the timeless connection between those who teach and those who learn, weaving Josh into the rich tapestry of the academic world he so cherished.

"Congratulations," Professor Stanley reiterated after presenting the apple to Josh. "Your father would have been proud."

Professor Stanley transcended mere collegiality; he served as a guiding light, steering Josh along the path to honor his father's legacy. With heartfelt gratitude for the unwavering support, Josh and Professor Stanley exchanged farewells as they departed the classroom, each heading toward their respective offices.

Back at his office, bent over his desk, bathed in the gentle glow of his monitor, Josh's attention wandered from the stack of exams before him. A pang of remorse surfaced as he reviewed the final grades. Despite his unwavering commitment to academia, a nostalgic yearning for the days of field research persisted—a stark contrast to his current role as an educator.

The lecture hall had become his domain, students his attentive audience. Yet, it failed to ignite the same zeal he had known amidst untamed landscapes. Teaching carried its own prestige and gratification, but it fell short of the thrill that came with unraveling geological secrets hidden beneath the earth's crust.

Leaning back, eyes closed, Josh immersed himself in contemplation. The call of geology had once drawn him to the wilderness, but now, the confines of academia felt restrictive. With a resigned exhale, he made a choice. He would fulfill his professorial duties for the rest of the summer, but thereafter, he'd return to his true calling—the boundless frontiers of fieldwork. This epiphany sparked excitement, rekindling his sense of purpose.

Josh powered down his computer, gathered his belongings, and a smile spread across his face. Present disappointment faded against the prospect of future adventures. Each step toward the exit lightened the burden of expectation, replaced by the allure of what lay ahead. For him, this wasn't an end; it was the prelude to a new chapter of discovery.

Renewed determination in his stride, Josh headed home. His residence, conveniently nestled near the vibrant heart of the University of Washington's campus, stood just a stone's throw from the historic Montlake Bridge. This iconic structure gracefully arched over the channel where Union Bay's calm waters merged with the shimmering expanse of Portage Bay. The area epitomized a harmonious blend of academic hustle and tranquil lakeside repose—a picturesque scene where verdant campus greenery met the blue hues of the bays.

Tucked away in Montlake Park, the charming single-family house stood as a tribute to Josh's grandfather's belief that the beginning of his educational path warranted a residence far from the aroma of beer and locker rooms. A generous bequest from his late grandfather. The house was a lavish gift—yet one easily afforded by a man who had been a prominent figure in the local forestry-products sector.

Renovated inside and out, the property blended vintage allure with contemporary style. Its facade boasted pristine white plantation shutters and a meticulously crafted stone porch. Inside, modern sophistication reigned: a blackened steel fireplace, a high-end chef's kitchen, and expansive glass walls with generous windows that offered an unobstructed waterfront view of the Montlake Cut—a waterway separating the peninsula, bridging Union Bay to the east and Portage Bay to the west. More than mere wood and stone, the residence served as Josh's sanctuary—a nurturing ground for dreams and academic ventures.

Upon his return home, Josh's wife, Emily, and their sons—Johnny, age six, and Jimmy, age four—greeted him. Clad in swimwear, their faces bright with anticipation, they reminded him of the promised swimming lessons at semester's end. Emily conveyed their eagerness; they had taken his word to heart. With a hearty chuckle, Josh assured them the lessons would begin soon. Emily had offered many times to take the boys to swimming lessons, but they were determined to have their dad accompany them.

Sensing their mild disappointment, Emily started an impromptu water fight. Laughter filled the air as they doused each other and wrestled on the lawn. Drenched but elated, they retreated indoors, where Maya, their devoted housekeeper, maintained her strict no-mud policy, directing them to the house's mudroom entrance.

In the warmth of their home, surrounded by familial joy, time seemed suspended. Sunlight bathed them, and they hugged, momentarily lost in each other's embrace. Maya's call for lunch drew them back to reality. On the terrace overlooking the lush University of Washington campus, they dined. Sun-dappled evergreens cast patterns on the wooden floor, and the hint of salt from nearby Puget Sound lingered in the air. Occasional seagull calls punctuated their conversation.

Emily, in a sky-blue sundress, watched as Maya set the table with a fresh salad—organic greens from the local farmers' market, topped with a tangy vinaigrette. Josh leaned on the balcony railing, sipping a craft beer from a nearby brewery. His eyes crinkled with joy as he observed Johnny and Jimmy chasing each other around the yard. Johnny, sandy-haired and curious, pursued Jimmy, who erupted in giggles.

As they were having lunch, they felt the world slowing down, only to be interrupted by the sudden ringing of the phone. A speaker mounted on the exterior wall served as a link to the outside—a necessary intrusion, reminding them that life's demands were never too distant. Emily, a nurse at the local birth center, had insisted on the speaker for quick accessibility if needed.

Josh retreated into the house, drawn by the insistent ring of the telephone. Unlike most calls, this one wasn't for Emily; it was for him. His father-in-law, Roger, a Navy Captain stationed at the Pentagon, urgently requested Josh's presence. Roger's intelligence team had taken an interest in a mysterious volcano, and they needed Josh's expertise. Over the phone, Roger remained tight-lipped about the specifics.

After Josh agreed, conditioned on Emily's approval, Roger pressed for immediate action. "Make it here by Monday," offering that travel arrangements and crucial documents would follow. Josh's groan echoed through the room as he contemplated the gravity of the situation.

The sun-kissed deck framed Josh's revelation to Emily. Amidst their sons' exuberant shouts, he approached her with deliberate steps. Emily met his gaze, sensing the gravity of his news. Her eyes mirrored a blend of calm and curiosity, the tranquil scene poised on the brink of change.

"What was the call about?" Emily's inquiry held steady yet inquisitive tones.

Josh didn't hesitate, relaying the urgent directive from her father: a summons to the nation's capital. His task? Assessing a volcanic threat for the Pentagon.

Emily's features furrowed in concern, her mind racing with questions. "Which volcano?" Emily leaned forward, seeking answers. "And why specifically you?"

Josh's response came, a mix of professional pride and defensiveness. "I'm a volcanologist," he asserted.

"Of course you are," Emily conceded, "but surely there are other experts."

Josh nodded, acknowledging that his skills weren't unique. Yet, seizing the moment, he underscored the mission's critical nature. "I must leave by Sunday," Josh disclosed.

The revelation hit Emily like a bombshell, momentarily shattering her composure. "Sunday!" Her surprise was palpable.

Josh, momentarily taken aback by Emily's reaction, could only reiterate the importance that Roger had conveyed. Emily, now standing with a resolute posture, directed Josh to explain the change of plans to their sons regarding the postponed swimming lessons.

"Josh," Emily said, "I know I could take them, but they really are insistent that you be there."

"We can start them tomorrow," Josh offered, his voice carrying a mixture of relief and understanding as their conversation concluded.

Retreating to the quiet of his study, the soft light from the desk lamp cast a warm glow around him. Josh took a moment to steady his nerves before calling his department head to inform him of the upcoming trip. The atmosphere crackled with anticipation as he punched in the number, each ring amplifying the significance of the impending conversation.

Professor Stanley, a pillar of wisdom and steadfast support within the department, assured Josh of his complete backing. His only request was practical: could Josh grade the final exams before leaving?

"Leave them at my home before you set out," Professor Stanley instructed, his voice exuding both confidence and authority. "I will take the steps to ensure that the registrar promptly records them."

Josh's answer was immediate and firm. "Absolutely."

CHAPTER 2

YMCA

As dawn painted the sky, Saturday buzzed with anticipation. Johnny and Jimmy vibrated with excitement, eagerly awaiting their swimming lessons. Seattle, nestled between the briny clasp of Puget Sound and the pristine waters of Lake Washington, was a water-lover's paradise. Beyond its picturesque backdrops, the city transformed water into a thrilling platform for aquatic adventures—sailing, kayaking, paddle boarding—or leisurely strolls along scenic waterfront parks and piers.

Johnny and Jimmy's neighborhood appeared to float on water, cradled by the Montlake Cut and the inviting banks of Portage Bay. Their proximity to these waters added weight to their swimming lessons. Emily's harrowing encounter with a riptide off Virginia Beach highlighted this significance. Fortunately, her near-drowning experience had taken place during childhood—a time when resilience and adaptability were on her side. Children recovered more quickly from trauma; their brains were more malleable. Adults, like Emily, might linger longer in fear's grip. As the boys grew older, Emily's apprehensions resurfaced, amplified by the water's easy accessibility near their home. Josh hoped their growing swimming proficiency would ease her persistent worries.

In the kitchen, Josh found Emily and Maya embroiled in a lively debate over the ideal pre-swimming meal. Maya, ever cautious, had delayed breakfast for the boys, risking their swimming lesson timetable. Emily, the diplomat, countered Maya's traditional wisdom with modern science: eating before swimming was safe. Scientists had debunked the old belief that food caused cramps by diverting blood from muscles. Emily argued that a light meal provided essential energy. Acknowledging Emily's health knowledge, Maya retreated to prepare a wholesome breakfast for the boys.

Maya emerged once more, presenting a breakfast spread that delighted the boys: a pancake buffet adorned with an array of toppings. She also crafted Emily's favorite treat—Belgian waffles topped with generous helpings of fresh strawberries. Meanwhile, Josh savored his preferred breakfast combination: hearty burritos paired with the trendy allure of avocado toast. As was her custom, Maya had already eaten, finding satisfaction in curating the morning's medley.

Nestled within Seattle's historic Pioneer Square district, the Downtown Seattle YMCA stood just five miles to the south. Their destination was the venerable stone Seattle Federal Office Building—an 11-story edifice that commanded an entire city block. Its imposing form and dignified air seemed to underscore the task's importance.

Inside the aquatic center, Kim, a seasoned swim instructor, greeted them. The adults recognized swimming proficiency as a vital skill—one that significantly reduced the risk of drowning, a leading cause of fatality among young children.

The conversation shifted to the optimal age for swim instruction. Kim explained that by age four, most kids could learn fundamental water safety techniques: buoyancy, water treading, and navigating toward an exit. By age five or six, children mastered the front crawl stroke.

Kim peered down, observing Emily clutching a set of water wings—those colorful inflatable cuffs often dubbed floaties—intended for the young boys.

"I'm afraid we don't use these here," Kim articulated with polite firmness. She explained that swimming instructors discouraged such devices because they impeded a child's natural movement in the water, fostering a rigid and upright posture counterproductive to mastering the art of swimming.

Emily's concern surfaced swiftly. "But wouldn't they sink?" she asked, her voice tinged with worry.

Kim reassured Emily, explaining that the YMCA's teaching philosophy focused on guiding children to harness their core strength and controlled breathing to achieve buoyancy.

"We wouldn't let them sink," Kim concluded with conviction.

With confidence, Emily and Josh placed their sons under Kim's expert tutelage and retreated to the bleachers. Emily still held onto the unused floaties, now a symbol of her newfound understanding.

At the prime of their youth, Johnny and Jimmy stood on the cusp of a new adventure in the world of swimming. Clad in matching crimson swim trunks and equipped with large-framed goggles, they were a vibrant sight to behold. The boys, eager and spirited, plunged into their aquatic lessons. Before long, with Kim's help, they floated atop the water with the ease and grace of ducks, their laughter echoing across the pool.

As the swimming lesson ended, Kim offered a firm reminder to Josh and Emily. She emphasized that while swimming lessons significantly enhanced safety, they did not render children immune to drowning. Unwavering vigilance remained necessary whenever children were near water. Emily and Josh welcomed this guidance with gratitude, understanding its critical importance for their children's well-being.

Upon returning home, Emily and Maya enlisted the boys to prepare a light lunch. They had discovered that involving the boys in the process made them more excited to eat. The boys, eager and cooperative, took turns assembling turkey and cheese roll-ups. They skillfully layered slices of turkey with savory cheese, crisp lettuce, and cucumber for a satisfying crunch. Next, they carefully arranged a cornucopia of carrots, bell peppers, and celery sticks alongside creamy hummus, ready for dipping.

While the boys were deeply immersed in their culinary escapade, Josh sought fleeting serenity. He ascended to his home office, delving into digital correspondence. Amidst the virtual stack, he discovered the expected message from his father-in-law. A cursory glance at the government flight reservation elicited a groan; enduring economy-class confinement on a five-hour transcontinental journey was unappealing for his tall frame. However, fortune favored him—his stepfather, Frank, a travel agency owner, might secure a more comfortable arrangement.

Redirecting his attention to the email's attachments, Josh found the Standard Form (SF-86) Questionnaire for National Security Positions form. Seeking clarity, he contacted his father-in-law, Roger, to inquire further. Roger explained that completing the SF-86 was imperative for Pentagon access to classified sectors where he worked.

"Is there more I should know?" Josh probed.

Roger mentioned the need for Josh to submit fingerprints.

"Good heavens," Josh exclaimed.

"Oh, and remember, you may not bring any personal electronic devices on the premises," Roger added, concluding with a stern reminder about providing accurate and honest information, especially if a polygraph examination is required.

"A polygraph?" Josh balked.

Josh meticulously tackled the detailed application, a labyrinth of questions demanding an exhaustive recounting of his life story. Work experience, places of residence, academic background—all woven into a tapestry of pertinent sections. For Josh, detailing his employment and past addresses was straightforward. His sole professional journey had unfolded within the university's walls, and aside from his boyhood residence across the bay on Mercer Island, he had lived in his present domicile.

Enumerating references and kin, Josh navigated through the remaining inquiries. A chuckle escaped him as he responded to questions probing into financial strife and digital security competencies. A modest inheritance from his late grandfather ensured financial stability, and his technological acumen fell short of executing the cyber exploits the form inquired about.

As Josh worked through the questionnaire, he noticed that the further he delved, the less relevant the queries became. He affirmed no involvement in terrorist acts, nor did he align with any groups intent on disrupting the American government. With the document completed, he affixed his signature, digitized the form, and dispatched it to his father-in-law.

Later that evening, the family gathered around the television, immersed in the latest installment of the beloved American martial arts-themed comedy, Kung Fu Panda. Laughter echoed through the room as the film seamlessly blended humor, heart-pounding action, and artistic animation. Between mouthfuls of popcorn, Johnny and Jimmy reenacted their favorite scenes, their little bodies mimicking the panda protagonist's kung fu moves. Observing their antics, Josh suggested to Emily that perhaps karate lessons would channel their boundless energy more effectively than swim lessons.

CHAPTER 3

SEWARD PARK

As dawn tiptoed over Montlake Park, the sun cast its first tender rays upon the deck. Emily's fingers traced the rim of her coffee cup, its porcelain warmth a promise of comfort and familiarity. Josh, his eyes crinkling with morning light, leaned back in his chair, savoring the moment. The air, crisp and invigorating, whispered secrets of saltwater and pine.

Seattleites cherished their daily elixir, as coffee wove itself into the city's DNA and coursed through Josh and Emily's veins like a shared memory. Their first date—an invitation for coffee after student orientation—had set the stage for their intertwined lives. In his new Montlake Park home, Josh encountered a challenge with the intricate built-in coffee maker, which featured ten bewildering brewing options and a touchscreen.

Overwhelmed by its complexity, he watched as Emily adeptly used her phone to access the operating instructions. With the web app's guidance, she navigated the settings and successfully brewed two perfect latte macchiatos.

Since that fateful day, the coffee machine had transcended mere appliance status. It brewed comfort, whispered encouragement, and witnessed their quiet moments. Josh and Emily sipped their creamy concoctions, laughter dancing between them. The machine, with its digital heart, had become a trusted friend in the rhythm of their mornings.

As the sun ascended, casting its benevolent glow, Josh and Emily clung to their cups, savoring more than coffee. They tasted beginnings, shared vulnerability, and found solace in the hum of technology—a love story steeped in latte macchiatos.

Maya stepped onto the deck, accompanied by the two groggy boys. She greeted them with a delightful, kid-friendly breakfast: English Muffin Breakfast Pizzas. Splitting and toasting whole-grain English muffins, she allowed the boys to top them with tomato sauce, shredded cheese, and their favorite toppings—diced bell peppers, cooked sausage, or sliced olives. A quick stint under the broiler melted the cheese, and voilà!

Mini breakfast pizzas were ready.

Meanwhile, Maya offered to take the boys to church, leaving Josh and Emily to enjoy a quiet breakfast together at home. Josh surprised Emily by reappearing on the deck with a bag of bacon cheddar chive bagels from Blazing Bagels. The label proudly proclaimed them as the Best Bagels West of New York. Emily appreciated the thoughtful gesture; it reminded her of their first coffee date many years ago. After savoring the bagels and another cup of coffee, Emily silently led Josh back inside and upstairs to the bedroom.

Soft morning light bathed the room, casting a warm glow on the rumpled sheets. Their shared history, memories of countless mornings like this one, hung in the air as they closed the door behind them. Without a word, they embraced, their lips meeting in a tender kiss. The world outside faded away, leaving only the two of them entwined in each other's arms.

Josh stirred from his repose, roused by the distant sounds of the boys returning home with Maya. The clock ticked, reminding him of his impending flight from Seattle-Tacoma International Airport, bound for Washington, D.C. But before embarking on his journey, he yearned to savor precious moments with his sons. Sundays were their sanctuary—a time to forge memories and traditions that would fortify their family ties for years to come.

On a sun-kissed Sunday morning, shoelaces secured, the boys set forth. Seward Park, nestled nearby, beckoned with allure. Josh guided the boys through winding trails, their curiosity ignited by flora, fauna, and natural wonders. The park, flanked by water on three sides, bestowed vistas of Mount Rainier and Lake Washington. Ancient forests enveloped them, teeming with wildlife. Here, Josh and his mother had once strolled with their faithful black Labrador, Ace. It was also the place where she had confided her intention to remarry, a decade after the tragic loss of Josh's father.

Their laughter danced through the air as they raced along the forest path. As they ventured deeper, leaves crunched underfoot, and sunlight filtered through the leafy canopy. Armed with magnifying glasses, the boys transformed into nature detectives, scrutinizing bugs, leaves, and mysterious footprints. Their giggles erupted when they stumbled upon a squirrel's hidden acorn stash.

A wooden bridge spanned a babbling stream, and Josh hoisted the boys to peer into its crystal-clear waters. Jimmy, the younger of the two, exclaimed, "Fishies!" Nearby sticks became swords, and the brothers engaged in epic battles, with Josh playing the role of a dragon. Their laughter echoed across the water, etching joy into the fabric of their shared experience.

As the sun reached its zenith, they retraced their steps, Josh carrying a tired yet content Jimmy—his curly brown locks resting against Josh's shoulder. In that magical moment, Josh cherished the unbreakable bond he held with his sons.

In the quiet of their home, Emily awaited Josh's departure for the airport. The terminal lay just fifteen miles away, and she hoped Sunday traffic would be forgiving. After heartfelt kisses with their boys, they entrusted them to Maya's care, along with their eagerly anticipated lunch. They climbed into Josh's BMW—a generous gift from his late grandfather after his old car had given up—the untimely check engine light had once threatened to derail one of their first dates. That memorable journey had taken them to a sprawling six-hundred-acre ranch nestled sixty miles north of Seattle in the lush Skagit Valley.

Now, years later, Josh knew it was time to replace the aging car, but sentimentality held him back. He couldn't bear to part with this token of his grandfather's deep affection.

As they arrived on schedule, Josh skillfully guided the creaking BMW to the Departure Drop-Off Zone, conveniently close to Alaska Airlines' terminal entrance. The morning's flurry of events caught up with them, and they embraced. Yet time was not theirs—a Port of Seattle Police Department officer, clad in a sharp black uniform and cap, badge proudly displayed, politely signaled for them to move their vehicle along.

Inside the spacious, light-filled main terminal, Josh approached the Alaska Airlines counter and politely presented his tickets to the agent, inquiring about any reservation changes. After checking her terminal, the agent informed Josh that Alaska Airlines had upgraded his flight to First Class. Grateful, he made a mental note to thank his father-in-law for the upgrade once he landed in Washington. His six-foot-plus frame would certainly appreciate the extra space and generous legroom. Unsure of the trip's duration, he packed and checked in two bags before heading toward security.

Reflecting on past flights, Josh mentally accounted for each significant moment. From meeting Emily's family in Norfolk, Virginia, to their honeymoon flight to Hilo via Honolulu, and even attending a workshop in Sicily focused on Mount Etna, each journey had left its mark. Now, as he boarded the flight to Washington, D.C., he wondered what this new chapter would bring.

CHAPTER 4

THE PENTAGON

Josh's plane descended, its wheels kissed the runway at Ronald Reagan Washington National Airport. Landing to the south, Josh could see the Pentagon out the right-side aircraft windows, proudly standing on the west bank of the Potomac River on the edge of Washington, D.C. The clock hovered just before 10 p.m., and anticipation hummed through his veins. As he stepped into the terminal, a familiar figure stood waiting: Roger, resplendent in his khaki Navy uniform. Roger's eyes crinkled in a smile, and without missing a beat, he shared how he'd hopped on the Metrorail from the Pentagon to reach the airport.

Roger's voice carried relief as he greeted Josh. "You made it just in time."

Josh furrowed his brow, puzzled by the urgency. After all, their flight had landed on schedule.

Roger leaned in, explaining that the airport imposed strict nighttime noise restrictions after 10 p.m. With bags in tow, they climbed the escalator to the Metrorail station, joining the stream of travelers. The Blue Line train stood ready, whisking them northward on a brisk five-minute ride to the Pentagon City Metrorail station. Roger playfully reassured Josh, saying, "Don't worry, Josh—the Metro stays open until midnight."

As the brief trip unfolded, Roger confided that, for the first time in his career, securing nearby housing on post had proven elusive. Forts Myer and McNair, the closest quarters to the Pentagon, boasted limited government housing options, saddled with a six- to eighteen-month waiting period. Other more distant installations, weighed down by Roger's demanding work schedule, were impractical. So, he and Emily's mother, Megan, took matters into their own hands. They secured a cozy two-bedroom apartment conveniently nestled just across the street from the Pentagon's southern flank. Tonight, this choice proved serendipitous—the Metrorail station lay within easy walking distance.

Past ten p.m., they arrived at the apartment complex. The full moon cast its silvery glow, illuminating the community. To the south, lush greenery stretched out, while the Potomac River flowed to the east. Right outside the doors, an expansive open-air row beckoned with shopping, dining, and entertainment options. Inside, Megan (who preferred the affectionate moniker "Meg") greeted them. After a heartfelt embrace, she eagerly offered Josh a personalized tour, while Roger slipped out of his navy uniform.

The modern apartment exuded an airy ambiance, with its bright white walls and expansive windows that captured both sunlight and moonlight, casting a luminous glow throughout. Bedrooms and the living room lined the southern side, while the northern expanse housed the bathrooms, kitchen, and dining room. From the cozy living room, the Pentagon loomed large, its angular silhouette etched against the skyline, embodying the heart, soul, and brain of the military. Beyond it, the Washington Monument stood sentinel, a distant yet reassuring presence.

Meg, his gracious host, proudly unveiled the complex's amenities. Six tennis courts awaited racket-wielding enthusiasts, while three rooftop decks promised panoramic views of the cityscape. For aquatic aficionados, there were two swimming pools—one for leisurely laps, the other for spirited splashing. And for those seeking to sculpt their physiques, two fitness centers stood ready, dumbbells gleaming under fluorescent lights.

"Josh, are you hungry?" Meg's voice carried through the open space.

Josh shook his head and whispered back, "No, not really."

Roger chimed in, practical as ever: "Then you should turn in. Breakfast is at six thirty."

Josh dialed home. Emily's soothing voice soon echoed over the phone. Despite the late hour, she granted the boys a reprieve—they could stay up a little longer. It was an unfamiliar dance: Josh away from his sons, and the boys navigating their first separation.

Emily had coined the term "sleep days," and Josh reminded Johnny and Jimmy that they had seven sleep days left. Together, they counted down, anticipation building with each passing night. And when the magic number arrived, Johnny's voice echoed through the apartment: "Zero!"

Emily had shared with Josh that as children mature, they develop trust in the return of those who leave. By using the concept of "sleep days," parents created a concrete reference point, easing separation anxiety.

Emily, ever resourceful, orchestrated playdates with friends and scheduled a midweek visit with Josh's grandmother and Emily's sister Ellen, who had followed in Emily's footsteps and just completed her nursing program at the University of Washington. The boys loved their grandmother and their aunt. Josh felt reassured—the boys were in capable hands.

As Josh relayed the early breakfast timing to Emily, he expected her gentle plea: "Hang up and rest."

Their joint exchange, a lifeline across distance, concluded with a heartfelt "Love you."

As dawn's light crept across the room, Josh stirred to the melodic rhythm of Meg's voice—a gentle summons to breakfast. For an ephemeral heartbeat, her voice transported him back home, the cadence of her voice reminiscent of Emily's familiar tones.

"I'll be right there," Josh assured Meg, untangling himself from the remnants of jet lag.

Josh showered and dressed, shedding the sleepy fog that clung to him. Emerging, Josh squinted against the brilliant morning sun streaming through the dining room windows.

Seated at the table, Meg presented a classic breakfast tableau: eggs, their golden yolks winking, nestled alongside crispy hash browns and a generous serving of bacon. The aroma enveloped him—a comforting embrace to start the day.

Josh observed the metamorphosis in Meg's demeanor. Clad in a charcoal business suit, her crisp white blouse radiated professionalism. As a financial advisor at a prominent national brokerage firm, Meg deftly navigated the unique employment challenges faced by military spouses. The firm's expansive reach equipped her with adaptability, flexibility, and portable skills—essential tools for her ever-shifting life alongside Roger's duty stations.

Roger, donning the same uniform style as the night before, epitomized the quintessential United States Navy officer. His khaki shirt and matching trousers clung to his frame, pressed and tailored. Black dress leather oxfords, their soles gleaming, completed the ensemble.

Emily had once shared her father's reverence for well-buffed shoes—the subtle message of unpretentiousness conveyed by self-polished leather. On his shirt collar, the metal rank insignia—an eagle with wings outstretched—proclaimed his status as a captain. Ribbons cascaded from his left breast pocket, each fabric strand weaving a narrative of naval service: campaigns fought, commendations earned, and sacrifices etched in memory. Tradition, honor, and unwavering duty converged on his appearance.

This morning, Roger's steely blue eyes mirrored the weight of responsibility he carried—reflecting the path ahead.

Outside the apartment, the pair strolled northward along Army Navy Drive, their destination set on the iconic Pentagon, famous for its unique design. The walk was brief, a mere ten minutes. As the colossal building loomed before them, Roger seized the opportunity to enlighten Josh about the building's storied past. He recounted that this immense five-sided structure stood as the U.S. Department of Defense's headquarters, boasting an astonishing six million square feet of floor space—an architectural titan among office buildings worldwide.

With a tinge of regret in his voice, Roger shared that construction began on September 11, 1941—six decades before the tragic 9/11 attacks—when a hijacked plane slammed into the Pentagon, claiming one hundred and eighty-four lives and damaging the edifice. The duo continued their journey in silence until they reached the main entrance, nestled on the southeast side, next to the Pentagon Metrorail station. There, Roger ushered Josh through the initial security screening where a uniformed police officer, wearing a silver Pentagon Force Protection Agency badge with the motto "we will never forget," greeted him.

Once the officer verified Josh's credentials, father- and son-in-law stepped across the threshold, passing through massive wooden double doors into the Pentagon's interior. Josh's initial excitement waned as Roger directed him to yet another security checkpoint. Here, a clerk photographed him and issued him a temporary Pentagon visitor badge, its photo capturing a fatigued version of himself—a stark contrast to his usual appearance.

Josh attempted to regale Roger with a tale of how he had once rescued himself from using an unflattering Washington State Driver's license photo for his student ID by following Emily's suggestion that he replace it with a more flattering image from his Facebook page. However, Roger's demeanor had shifted, growing more serious as they neared the heart of the Pentagon. Josh sensed Roger was now all business. Together, they ascended a stainless-steel escalator, climbing to the second-floor concourse.

Inside the Pentagon, Roger guided Josh across the bustling concourse. Josh craned his neck, taking in the mini-shopping mall atmosphere that catered to the thousands of Pentagon civilian and military employees.

Josh's eyes landed on a flower shop, prompting an inquisitive glance at Roger.

"That shop is a lifesaver," Roger explained. "It's been my go-to for birthdays, anniversaries, and Valentine's Day."

Roger and Josh walked past the flower shop and up an inclined ramp that led past the center ring of the Pentagon toward the large, windowed doors that led to the Pentagon's massive courtyard.

As they stepped outside, the fresh summer morning air enveloped them, and the vivid blue skies and greenery momentarily distracted Roger from his usual focus. A modern food court stood in the center of the open space.

Roger recounted its history: during the Cold War, this area, known as "Ground Zero" was an assured target if a nuclear war broke out. Some even believed that Soviet satellite reconnaissance closely monitored the spot, once occupied by a humble one-story gazebo hot dog stand, mistaking it for a top-secret meeting room.

Construction crews replaced the original hot dog stand with a more contemporary food facility in 2006. A wooden owl decoy from the original stand, placed atop the new structure, served as a subtle nod to "Ground Zero's" past.

As they approached the other side of the Pentagon, where Roger's office awaited, he shared navigation tips.

"First, locate the corridor you need among the ten," Roger advised and explained that sometimes cutting across the courtyard was quicker than following the interior hall. Next, he continued, identify the ring (labeled A to E, starting with the interior ring) within that corridor. Take the stairs or an elevator to the designated floor and find the room number.

"Clear as a bell, right?" Roger chuckled. Roger then explained how the building's unusual five-sided design allowed quick access to any part of the building, the farthest spot from any other part of the Pentagon, within seven minutes.

Back inside, Roger led Josh down corridor eight, descending a set of stairs deep inside the Pentagon to the basement level that housed the offices of the Defense Intelligence Agency (DIA), home to Roger's current assignment. They stood before double doors marked with a simple sign: "J-2 Directorate for Intelligence."

Pausing, Roger leaned in toward Josh. "Inside these doors, refer to me as 'Captain Banks' or 'sir,'" he instructed. Josh nodded, and Roger added, "And for you, Professor Cooper. Your title will make them respect you more. Use it."

Satisfied, Roger swiped his pass over a security card reader and entered his security PIN. Josh, feeling a mix of anticipation and curiosity, found himself once again in the waiting arms of a senior Pentagon security officer. Roger explained the officer would be Josh's guide through the final stages of in-processing.

"See you in a bit," Roger offered with a friendly nod.

Guided through a labyrinth of echoing hallways and corridors, Josh stepped into yet another modern security office. The room buzzed with activity, and the air carried a faint scent of disinfectant. The first order of business: fingerprinting. Josh had mentally prepared for the traditional ink-and-paper process—the kind often dramatized on television and in movies—but his handler quickly dispelled that notion.

"Since 1999," the handler informed Josh, "most government agencies had transitioned to an advanced electronic fingerprint identification system." He noted that this modern approach had allowed for more efficient processing of fingerprints. Josh's fingertips were now captured using state-of-the-art equipment, a far cry from the old ink smudges.

The security manager quietly wondered about Josh's background. He recognized that the adjudication and vetting of clearances took twelve to eighteen months. What he did not know was that the government had granted Josh an immediate interim clearance—an exception reserved for cases where facts and circumstances aligned with national security interests.

Following fingerprinting, Josh willingly consented to undergo yet another session of having his photographs taken. Unfortunately, the outcome wasn't much better than the earlier ones—he still resembled a deer caught in headlights. With the security process complete, he received the second of his two badges. The second badge, a blue Intelligence Community badge, bore the same unimproved image.

Josh clipped the badges to the black lanyard provided by the security officer, who handed him over to an escort.

The escort guided him back to the J-2 offices, offering helpful advice: "If you ever get lost within the Pentagon, just ask for directions to the Market Basket—some affectionately call it the BC Café because of its location in the basement corridor." The escort assured Josh, "The café is right across from the entry to the J-2 spaces."

Now it was Josh's turn to swipe his security badge at the entrance to the J-2 spaces and test his issued security PIN. Inside, he encountered his

Roger, who offered him a fresh cup of coffee. Guided by Roger, Josh made his way to the conference room where the briefers awaited him.

CHAPTER 5

J-2

The Directorate for Intelligence (J-2) provided crucial support to high-ranking officials, including the Chairman of the Joint Chiefs of Staff, the Secretary of Defense, the Joint Staff, and Unified Commands. As the national-level hub for crisis intelligence, it assisted military operations, offered indications and warning intelligence within the Department of Defense (DoD), and addressed Unified Command intelligence needs.

Seated beside his father-in-law at the head of the table, Captain Banks introduced Professor Cooper to a diverse audience of civilian and military analysts. Roger proudly presented Josh as one of the nation's leading volcanologists. He explained that Professor Cooper was there to tackle their "volcano problem" and encouraged everyone to bring him "up to speed on the scenario."

The conference room came alive as Captain Banks introduced the first briefer, Li Liu, a civilian China analyst. "Professor Josh," Li began, "you may or may not be aware that U.S.-China relations have been complex and contentious for years. Let's delve into the factors driving this complexity."

Li pointed to a bulleted list that covered trade disputes, technological competition, human rights issues, military tensions, geopolitical rivalries, pandemic fallout, economic decoupling, and cybersecurity. Josh's attention waned; these topics held little relevance for him.

Sensing Josh's disengagement, Captain Banks intervened.

"Dr. Cooper, you're probably wondering how any of this relates to volcanoes."

He then clarified that Li's presentation aimed to illustrate the convoluted state of U.S.-Chinese relations.

"Context matters," he emphasized.

With a nod from Captain Banks, Li continued her briefing. She turned directly to Josh and revealed that China's ambassador had recently reached out to her U.S. counterpart, expressing interest in a bilateral meeting between the two countries' presidents.

"Given the strained relationship," Li explained, "the request genuinely shocked our ambassador."

"And then, almost as an afterthought, China's ambassador also extended an invitation for a U.S. team to visit Changbai Mountain." Li turned to Josh, her expression curious. "Are you familiar with it?" she asked.

"Yes," Josh replied, his memory jogging. He recalled it was a stratovolcano, positioned right on the Chinese–North Korea border. "If I remember correctly," he continued, "it features a large crater lake—"

"Heavenly Lake," Li interjected, completing his sentence. Josh nodded in agreement.

Captain Banks got straight to the point, voicing the question that had been nagging at him since his initial call to Josh: "Is it dangerous?"

Josh hesitated, aware that the entire assembly hung on his every word. "I'm not entirely sure," he admitted. "I'll need to study the most recent data."

"Well, Dr. Cooper," Captain Banks said, leaning forward, "that's precisely why we invited you here. Let's get you set up."

Finally, Josh thought to himself, he had a name for the enigmatic volcano that had brought him to Washington, D.C.

With this cue, Li pushed herself away from the oak conference table and caught Josh at the doorway. "Dr. Cooper, please follow me and I'll get you set up at a desk."

The J-2 spaces occupied a sizable steel enclosure known as a Sensitive Compartmented Information Facility (SCIF). These SCIFs, or vaults as intelligence officers referred to them, were purpose-built to safeguard classified information of the Sensitive Compartmented Information (SCI) level. Because of the operational security (OPSEC) risks they posed, security officers prohibited personal cell phones, smartwatches, computer flash drives (commonly referred to as "thumb drives"), and any other personal electronic devices (PEDs) within SCIFs. Cameras, whether analog or digital, were also off-limits unless they were U.S. Government property and used under stringent guidelines. Roger had earlier advised Josh to leave behind any electronic equipment.

Inside the SCIF, a labyrinth of office cubicles stretched out, each section designated for specific functional or geographic purposes. Signs hung above each area, revealing its intended use. Li led Josh to the section labeled "China" and directed him to an unoccupied seat within the four-person quad.

Li introduced Josh to his new teammates. Among them were the team lead Army Major Rick Stevenson and Chris Wyatt, a civilian analyst. Li added that Major Stevenson had recently returned from a tour at the U.S. Embassy in Beijing and Chris from a rotational assignment at the National Security Council (NSC). Li then guided Josh to an empty desk in the cubicle, explaining that Valarie Smith, who had taken Chris's place at the NSC, usually occupied it. Josh glanced at the array of equipment on the desk. Pointing to the computer, Li introduced the JWICS terminal—a secure intranet system for housing Top Secret/Sensitive Compartmented Information (TS/SCI). She then gestured toward a black box supporting the monitor.

"This switch box," Li said, "connects you to NIPRINet, our unclassified gateway to the internet." Li promised the IT team would come by after lunch to handle the setup. Josh's stomach growled at the thought of lunch. Li must have heard it and promised Josh that they would go to lunch soon.

Li turned to the last piece of equipment, a simple brown bag on the floor. It held classified documents for destruction. "We don't put any paper in the regular trash," she explained, pointing to the nearby gray metal container. "All paper goes in the burn bags." Joshua nodded, grateful for Li's guidance in this complex environment and the promise of lunch.

Li guided Josh through the bustling hallway next to the J-2 spaces. The fluorescent lights hummed overhead, casting a sterile glow on the linoleum floor. Freshly brewed coffee wafted from the Market Basket café, enticing them both.

"Look, Josh," Li exclaimed, her almond-shaped eyes brightening. "They have Peet Coffee!"

Josh, a resident of Seattle, appreciated Li's enthusiasm. She had associated Peet's Coffee with his home. He decided not to correct her. Contrary to popular belief, Peet's Coffee wasn't a Seattle creation. Its roots lay in Berkeley, California, where Alfred Peet had founded the company decades ago. The headquarters remained there to this day, a testament to its West Coast origins.

The café menu surprised Josh. Instead of the usual greasy fare, it offered healthy options. He chose a chicken parmesan hot sub with breaded eggplant and marinara sauce—a departure from the typical fast-food choices. Li opted for a medium garden salad, a vibrant mix of fresh greens, ripe tomatoes, crisp cucumbers, and green peppers.

As they settled into their seats, Josh seized the opportunity to delve into Li's background. Her story intrigued him—a blend of intellect, duty, and dual identity.

Li hailed from Taipei, Taiwan, a city rich in both tradition and modernity. Her parents, both accomplished scholars, instilled in her a passion for learning and a deep sense of duty toward her country. As a child, their tales of China, their ancestral homeland captivated her. Mathematics and computer science soon captured her imagination, and her analytical mind earned her admiration from teachers and mentors alike.

Her educational journey took her through prestigious institutions. Li completed her undergraduate studies at National Taiwan University (NTU), majoring in Computer Science and International Relations. There, she delved into research projects related to cyber threats and network security. Taiwanese intelligence agencies recognized her potential, and she earned a scholarship to pursue a master's degree in Cybersecurity and Intelligence Analysis at Stanford University. Li honed her skills in data analysis, cryptography, and threat assessment.

But her quest for knowledge didn't stop there. Li pursued a doctoral program at Long Island University (LIU), focusing on Intelligence Studies. Dr. Kimberly R. Cline, the university president, mentored her during her doctoral research. Li's dissertation explored the intersection of cyber warfare and national security—an area of growing importance in the digital age.

Her dedication extended beyond academia. Li interned with the Taiwanese Intelligence Agency (TIA) during summer breaks, tracking cyber threats originating from China. Her linguistic aptitude—fluent in Mandarin, Taiwanese, and English—made her an asset in cross-border investigations. Later, after gaining her American citizenship, she took part in an exchange program with the Central Intelligence Agency (CIA), spending a year at Langley, Virginia. There, she collaborated with analysts, gaining firsthand experience in intelligence operations.

After completing her doctorate, Li found herself at a crossroads, with multiple job offers from intelligence agencies vying for her expertise. She joined the Defense Intelligence Agency (DIA), where her unique blend of cyber threat knowledge and cultural insights proved invaluable.

Li's analytical prowess and unwavering commitment to safeguarding national security quickly earned her respect among her colleagues. Her capabilities impressed Josh. As they sat in the bustling Market Basket café, Li turned to him, her eyes sharp.

"Okay, Dr. Cooper," Li prompted, her tone businesslike. "You're up."

Josh hesitated. He was reluctant to share his personal history, especially with someone as accomplished as Li. But before he could respond, Major Stevenson approached their table, interrupting their lunch. The major informed Josh that an IT team member awaited him to set up his computer access—an urgent task.

Relieved to escape the personal inquiry, Josh turned to Li. "Next time," he promised, and then he chased Major Stevenson back to the J-2 vault, leaving Li to contemplate the mysteries that surrounded them both.

CHAPTER 6

KNOW KNOWNS

Josh sat at his new desk, contemplating how to convey information about the volcano to his J-2 colleagues. He turned to Li, seeking guidance. Li proposed using a Johari Window to communicate his findings. Unfamiliar with this technique, Josh asked Li for an explanation.

Taking a seat next to Josh, Li sketched out the four-quadrant model on a pad of paper. She began with the "Known Knowns" quadrant, which represented information that both analysts and others were aware of—facts, data. This quadrant allowed analysts to organize existing knowledge about a specific situation, threat, or issue.

Then, Li labeled the second quadrant as "Known Unknowns," representing data analysts suspected to be relevant but hadn't yet collected or verified, and therefore represented gaps in an analyst's understanding. Next, Li explained the information that was unknown to them but known to others, representing hidden information "or secrets," as she put it, that needed investigation.

Completing the model, Li introduced the "Unknown Unknowns," a quadrant for information neither known to them nor known to others—a realm of potential surprises, emerging threats, or novel developments. She encouraged Josh to explore additional sources to reduce the size of this quadrant. Impressed, Josh recognized the value of the Johari Window approach and promised Li he would try it. Li, appreciative, pledged to assist him in organizing his research into a presentation when he was ready.

Josh, bolstered by the model Li had shared, flipped the switch below the monitor to the unclassified NIPRINet. His fingers danced across the keyboard as he gathered notes, the phrase "Known Knowns" turning over and over in his head. Geography, he mused, was an easy known known to start with.

As Josh studied the mountain, just how little scientists knew about the mountain surprised him. Unlike the well-known volcanoes he had studied in the U.S., few outside of China were aware of the volcano.

Adding to his notes, Josh discovered a massive bowl-shaped volcanic depression, a caldera formed by the collapse of the top of the volcanic cone, that once capped the mountain. This cataclysmic event occurred during its largest volcanic eruption over a thousand years ago, now known as the Millennium Eruption. Since that fiery outburst, the mountain's caldera had filled with water, forming a seven-square-mile crater lake known as Tranchi Lake by the Chinese government or popularly known as Heavenly Lake.

Turning his attention to the "Known Unknowns," Josh pondered the gaps in his understanding of Changbai Mountain. At 9,000 feet, this solitary giant was the tallest peak both in Northeast China and on the Korean Peninsula. It had remained elusive for so long because it rested in a remote region of Asia and straddled the border between two countries—China and North Korea—that had lived in near-complete isolation throughout much of the 20th century.

Only after China had opened to the outside world in the 1980s and 1990s did scientists gather information about this enigmatic peak. Josh's focus shifted to the Millennium Eruption that had rocked the mountain in the 10th century. Volcanic eruptions, he knew, provided valuable insights into a volcano's inner workings.

Magma, rising from deep within the Earth, not only sculpted the volcano's form but also dictated its eruptive behavior. As the magma ascended, detectable earthquakes signaled the volcano's growing restlessness. Ground deformation, unusual heat flow, and changes in groundwater and spring water properties served as clear harbingers of impending eruptions.

Josh sat at the conference room table, his once-steaming cup of coffee now a lukewarm memory. The question posed by his father-in-law during that morning's briefing echoed in his mind: "Is it dangerous?" His research led him to a perplexing revelation. Despite being labeled as dormant, Mount Changbai carried a reputation as one of the most perilous volcanoes on Earth and the most hazardous in China. Josh felt compelled to unravel this apparent contradiction.

Changbai's eruptive history played a pivotal role in its dangerous status. The frequency and magnitude of past eruptions had provided crucial insights into the volcano's risk level. Although Mount Changbai did not erupt frequently, it compensated for this lack of frequency with sheer power when it erupted. Its 946 AD eruption had ranked among the largest explosive events in the last 10,000 years. The 969 AD eruption had dwarfed the famed Krakatau eruption of 1883, spreading an ash cloud eastward across an expanse as vast as the Korean Peninsula, reaching all the way to Japan.

Josh understood the nuances of volcanic behavior. Mount Changbai, a stratovolcano, had unleashed explosive eruptions that released ash, gases, and pyroclastic flows. These eruptions posed greater hazards because of their potential for widespread destruction. Pyroclastic flows—hot, fast-moving clouds of ash, gas, and rock fragments—could devastate entire regions. Lahars, mudflows triggered by volcanic activity, posed another threat.

But it wasn't just the explosive potential that made Mount Changbai treacherous. The mountain's crater lake added an extra layer of danger. Held back by the mountain's caldera walls, the lake's waters could become a catalyst for massive mudflows. If a significant eruption occurred, the mix of volcanic debris and water would threaten the over one and a half million Chinese and Korean citizens living within sixty miles of the volcano.

Josh had witnessed firsthand the aftermath of volcanic eruptions during the eruption of Mount Rainier. Ashfall had disrupted air traffic, damaged crops, and affected human health.

Although slower-moving lava flows posed less immediate danger, they still destroyed structures and vegetation. Closer to the volcano, volcanic gases emitted during eruptions could harm both humans and animals.

Mount Changbai's proximity to populated areas played a crucial role in assessing its potential danger. Beyond the people living near Mount Changbai, an eruption would have severe consequences for the broader region. Ashfall would halt air travel, damage crops, and even affect electronics. The potential impact on the climate remained difficult to determine.

Comparing it to the 1893 Krakatoa eruption, where the volcano had propelled ash, known as tephra, about fifty miles into the air, Mount Changbai's potential impact intrigued Josh. The massive amount of tephra and debris released during such an eruption acted as a solar radiation filter, reflecting sunlight and reducing the amount of solar energy reaching the Earth's surface. Global temperatures dropped by as much as one degree Celsius for an entire year after the Krakatoa eruption.

As Josh continued his quest to unravel the geological mysteries of Changbai Mountain, he could not shake the feeling that ancient secrets lay hidden within its rugged slopes. What other surprises might this enigmatic volcano hold?

Li, eager to assist Josh, checked her sources. After a quick trip to the printer, she returned to present Josh with a stack of papers. "Dr. Cooper," she said, "this is the latest classified information on the volcano from Chinese sources that I could find."

"Please call me Josh," Josh said, as he thanked her and began sifting through the pile of reports. According to the reports, the Chinese government labeled Changbai as China's most dangerous volcano and the one most likely to erupt. The next section summarized the twenty-five-year seismic history of the area. Josh appreciated that seismic activity played a crucial role in understanding volcanoes, providing valuable insights into their behavior and potential hazards. Except for a period from mid-2002 to mid-2005, during which the area experienced a seismic crisis with a swarm of earthquakes (none greater than magnitude 3.7) recorded, the region had been quiet.

Josh knew that swarm earthquakes near volcanoes were not uncommon. These closely clustered seismic events, often with two hundred earthquakes occurring in a day, were usually short-lived and associated with geothermal activity—such as fluid movement and pressure changes in the subsurface around a volcano.

However, more concerning was the survey data from 2000 to 2007, which revealed horizontal displacement or bulging of the volcano.

As a volcanologist, Josh had encountered this type of data before. Prior to the cataclysmic eruption of Mount St. Helens in 1980, the bulging of its north flank by nearly four hundred and fifty feet had served as a clear sign of impending volcanic activity. This bulging had shown that magma was rising toward the summit, and pressure was building up. It had been a critical warning sign, reflecting intense geological activity beneath the surface. Contemplating the current state of the Changbai Mountain, Josh wondered if perhaps the Chinese government had valid reasons for concern.

Soon, Li returned, her excitement clear in her eyes. "Josh, look at this," she urged, placing a stack of fresh reports on his desk. "This might explain why the Chinese government is so concerned about Changbai. They believe that North Korea's nuclear testing could trigger Changbai Mountain to erupt."

Josh remained skeptical. While nuclear explosions had caused minor earthquakes, he doubted that the energy released by such tests could lead to a volcanic eruption. The distance between the test site and the mountain—about fifty miles—had strengthened his conviction that nuclear testing was an unlikely trigger. Josh shared his conclusion with Li, who remained undeterred.

"Josh, it doesn't matter what you think. What matters is what the Chinese government believes," Li explained. She then outlined the delicate balance between reality and perception in the intelligence world.

"In your scientific realm, reality is everything," Li noted. "But in our line of work, government perception holds immense value—even if it's not always grounded in reality. We strategically leverage misperceptions and misinformation to our advantage."

Josh raised an eyebrow. "So, lying?" he asked. Li shook her head.

"It's not about lying, but recognizing that truth can be relative. If the Chinese government believes nuclear testing will cause the mountain to erupt, and that belief benefits us strategically, then so be it," Li concluded.

Josh grappled with the ethical implications. "Sounds like a dilemma," he concluded.

Li agreed, adding, "Like you, we prefer reality, but we also seek advantages when possible."

As the workday neared its end, Li suggested they pause for now. She promised to consult her team chief and reach out to her Korean team counterpart for additional information. Encouraging Josh to look beyond his initial reservations, she urged him to examine the data. Josh pushed Li's reports aside and returned to his terminal, diving back into his research.

Immersed in his work, Josh lost track of time. Distractions faded away, leaving him focused. It was like playing a flawless melody without conscious effort. His father-in-law's arrival interrupted Josh's concentration. Roger asked about Josh's progress. Pleased with developments, Roger suggested they call it a day.

In the cozy apartment, Roger changed out of his uniform and joined Josh in the living room. There, Josh recounted the boys' inaugural swim lesson to Meg. "Josh," Roger declared with pride, "you're in for a delightful dinner treat tonight." The trio set off toward the nearby SkyDome restaurant, an iconic establishment conveniently within walking distance from their apartment. Perched atop the Hilton Crystal City Hotel, the restaurant revolved, granting panoramic vistas of the D.C. skyline. For Josh, the experience evoked memories of his hometown's Seattle Needle. As the restaurant turned, his thoughts wandered to his wife and boys, and he silently vowed to call them upon returning to the apartment.

"Six more 'sleep days," Josh murmured under his breath, savoring the anticipation.

CHAPTER 7

MOUNT CHANGBAI

Josh stirred Tuesday morning, the sky outside his guest bedroom painted in muted grays by dawn. Raindrops danced against the window, a gentle rhythm that seemed to echo the city's mood. Roger joined him after breakfast, and they stepped outside into the thick humidity. Their umbrellas unfurled, a shield against the unwelcome rain.

The bustling city, so vibrant yesterday, now held its breath. Commuters moved more slowly, seeking shelter from the downpour. At the Pentagon City Metrorail station, they caught the train—a mere one-stop journey to the Pentagon Metrorail station. Emerging from the mist, the Pentagon's wet limestone facade glistened in the faint morning light. Its civilian and military employees, undeterred by the weather, hurried inside.

In the secure confines of the J-2 spaces, Roger turned to Josh. "How much time do you and Li need to complete the presentation?" he asked.

Josh considered the question, aware that his father-in-law, accustomed to the rapid pace of crisis intelligence, would find forty-eight hours an eternity. Josh replied he needed another two days to complete his research and prepare a thorough report.

Li, waiting at Josh's desk, greeted him with a warm and friendly expression. Confidence and poise radiated from her. Beside her stood another analyst—Young Ho, from the Korean team. Josh recalled their earlier conversation; Li had promised to consult with the Korean team analysts.

Li suggested moving to a nearby conference room. Young needed space to spread out the maps he had brought. As they walked, Josh couldn't help but reflect on the whirlwind of the past twenty-four hours. The same conference room where he'd received his welcome brief now hosted this unexpected collaboration. Life at DIA was proving to be anything but predictable.

Inside the conference room, Li's deft hand flicked the wall switch, illuminating a digital sign at the head of the room. Its letters glowed: "Top Secret SCI." The signal was clear—a warning to anyone entering that the conversation about to unfold held immense sensitivity.

Josh turned to Li, the dependable guide he relied on. "I understand Top Secret," he said. "But please help me with SCI."

Li stepped closer. Her smile conveyed warmth and encouragement, while her raised eyebrows showed attentiveness and concentration. She explained while Top Secret (TS) security clearances represented a classification level controlling access to classified information, SCI—Sensitive Compartmented Information—was different. It wasn't a classification level in itself; rather, it was a specialized category. SCI granted access to specific types of sensitive information: intelligence sources, methods, and analytical processes—all referred to as compartmented information.

"Don't worry, Josh," Li assured him. "Your clearance includes SCI access if you need it. And once Young is done, I think you'll understand why you need it."

Intrigued, Josh settled into his seat, anticipation building. He waited for Young's presentation, ready to uncover the secrets hidden within the compartmented information.

Young, a seasoned analyst at the Defense Intelligence Agency (DIA), meticulously unfurled a map across the conference table. The map bore cryptic classification markings, hinting at secrets hidden within its contours. Beside it lay a scroll, a timeline chronicling North Korea's nuclear ambitions. Young's weathered finger traced the path of history, connecting dots of clandestine tests and geopolitical tensions.

His gaze settled on a marked spot: "Punggye-ri Nuclear Test Site," nestled in the rugged terrain of North Korea's northeastern mountains, a place of covert significance. Li leaned in and whispered to Josh, "It's only seventy miles from Changbai."

Young's narrative unfolded. On October 9, 2006, they detected the first nuclear test—an underground test that yielded between 0.7 and 2 kilotons or 700 to 2,000 tons of explosives.

"A fizzle," Young reflected, comparing it to the devastating bomb dropped on Hiroshima in 1945, which had a yield of about 15 kilotons.

But, as he explained, North Korea was relentless. Within three years, a second test produced 2 to 5.4 kilotons. By early 2013, their efforts escalated to yield 6 to 16 kilotons, followed by approximately 12.2 kilotons later that year. The crescendo came in late 2017—a massive detonation registering between 140 to 250 kilotons.

Josh furrowed his brow. "That's quite a range," he mused aloud.

Young nodded, acknowledging the international disagreement over the explosion's true magnitude. With a touch of pride, he declared, "I'd stick with the U.S. estimate of 140 kilotons."

Josh leaned forward; eyes fixed on Young—the seasoned analyst who held the keys to North Korea's nuclear secrets. "And since then," Josh inquired, "what happened?"

Young's response was succinct, delivered with the weight of classified knowledge. "Cold," he said, his voice low. "The site went cold."

Intelligence reports hinted at a seismic shift—the mountain above the test site had collapsed, rendering it unsafe for further experimentation.

Li, always sharp-eyed, pointed to the map spread across the table. "What are these?" she asked, her finger tracing tunnels etched onto the paper.

Young leaned in, explaining that these tunnels—portals—were the arteries of the complex. Four major passageways snaked beneath the earth, each with its own secrets.

Li pressed further. "Did they all collapse?" Her gaze bore into Young's, seeking clarity.

"No," Young replied, his gaze unwavering. "Only the west portal where the tests occurred." The south and the north portals remained intact, potentially harboring the ghosts of future nuclear trials.

But there was a caveat—an uncertainty that hung heavy in the room. Korean President Kim Jong Un had announced an end to testing, but without external inspections, the truth remained elusive. Young cautioned we couldn't trust the North Koreans. The situation, like the tunnels themselves, was labyrinthine, filled with hidden dangers and complex twists.

Young's parting words echoed in Josh's mind: "Monitor every tremor, every whisper of activity. North Korea's nuclear capabilities still linger in the shadows."

Josh and Li expressed their gratitude to Young and returned to their desks. Once there, Li inquired of Josh whether he believed a nuclear test could indeed trigger an eruption of Mount Changbai.

"I'm not entirely certain," Josh replied, his brow furrowing and repeated what he had told Roger earlier. "I'll need to examine the data." He assured her he would provide an answer soon.

Josh, despite his confidence as a volcanologist, found this question to be unfamiliar territory.

However, upon reflection, he realized perhaps it wasn't new. After all, scientists had studied the relationship between earthquakes and volcanic eruptions. In their simplest form, the forces generated by a nuclear detonation were akin to those of an earthquake.

Josh understood earthquakes could occasionally trigger volcanic activity, but specific conditions had to be met. Foremost, there needed to be enough eruptible magma—molten rock—within the volcanic system. The critical question was whether Mount Changbai harbored a significant reservoir of molten rock beneath its surface.

To find the answer, Josh delved into his notes and scoured the internet. Seismic mapping revealed that the volcanic plumbing system beneath the mountain included a magma reservoir at a shallow depth compared to similar volcanoes. Historical estimates showed past Mount Changbai eruptions had involved over seven cubic miles of dense magma. A quick comparison revealed that this was indeed a substantial volume. For context, the 1991 Pinatubo eruption in the Philippines expelled twelve cubic miles of material, the 1883 Krakatoa eruption in Indonesia ejected about eleven cubic miles of materials, and the 1980 Mount St. Helens eruption in Washington state yielded 0.6 cubic miles of debris.

Josh also understood that determining the level of pressure within the magma storage region was a crucial variable. Tectonic stress resulting from the collision of continental plates in the Earth's crust provided the force for volcanic eruptions. However, there was a consensus among scientists that if a volcano was already under pressure due to stored magma, the additional seismic activity from an earthquake could indeed trigger an eruption. The intriguing question that occupied Josh's mind was whether the force generated by an underground nuclear explosion could exert a similar effect.

Returning to his notes, Josh encountered a plethora of open-source reports suggesting that nuclear testing near Changbai had caused the mid-2002 to mid-2005 swarm of earthquakes. However, he dismissed these press reports as unreliable. Seeking a more authoritative source, he stumbled upon a peer-reviewed article in a scientific journal. This article argued that strong ground motions resulting from nuclear explosions might agitate Mount Changbai's magma chamber, potentially speeding up volcanic activity. It concluded that underground nuclear testing near an active volcano posed a direct threat to the volcano itself.

Now, a critical question lingered for Josh: What magnitude of nuclear test would be necessary to generate sufficient pressure to threaten Changbai?

Leaning over to Li, Josh asked her, "What did Young mention about the size of their largest test?"

Consulting her notes, Li responded it had registered between 140 and 250 kilotons.

Josh returned to the journal. The report showed that a threshold of 100 kilotons near an active volcano could indeed pose a direct threat to a volcano. However, this threshold remained theoretical, as the scientist had not specifically applied it to Mount Changbai.

Josh sat hunched over his workstation, eyes fixed on the screen. The data he'd unearthed lay sprawled across spreadsheets and charts, a digital landscape of seismic activity and magma storage regions. His criteria—two distinct thresholds—loomed large: a sufficient volume of magma and a plausible explanation for the mounting pressure within the molten depths.

"Josh," she said, her tone brisk yet friendly, as she held out a tuna wrap and a cup of coffee, "I noticed you skipped lunch. I hope you don't mind—I grabbed these for you."

Josh's gratitude was evident as he accepted the food. He'd been so engrossed in his research that time had slipped away unnoticed. Now, with the savory aroma of lunch filling the room, he felt a renewed surge of energy.

Li leaned against the edge of his desk, her gaze direct. "Let's make the most of this break," she suggested. "We should start drafting the briefing."

Josh nodded, appreciating her practical approach. He thanked her, then shifted his chair closer to her workspace.

"Josh," Li began, "writing for the intelligence community is a whole different beast compared to academia. The difference lies in how we structure our information. Brevity, clarity, and urgency—those are our guiding principles."

"For example, we use BLUF," Li explained.

"BLUF?" Josh echoed.

"Yes, BLUF," Li confirmed. "It stands for 'Bottom Line Up Front.' It's a communication principle that emphasizes delivering the most critical information or primary message right at the beginning of a conversation or document. By doing this, the audience grasps the key details immediately, facilitating efficient understanding and decision-making."

Josh shook his head in agreement and found himself amused to find himself back in the student's role. Li was an excellent teacher, he thought to himself.

Li leaned forward; her pen poised over a notepad. "Josh," she said, "let me introduce you to the inverted pyramid."

Josh raised an eyebrow. "Inverted pyramid?"

Li nodded. "Imagine an upside-down triangle," she began, sketching the shape in quick strokes.

Li continued. "At the widest part—the top—we place the most substantial, interesting, and crucial information."

Josh interrupted, pointing at the drawing. "The BLUF—the central message."

Li smiled. "Exactly. The top section of the pyramid contains the BLUF—the key takeaway that organizes all the information. As you move down the triangle, details become less critical, illustrating that other material should follow in order of diminishing importance."

"One more thing," Li urged. "No summaries. Our reports don't end with a summary; they start with one—the BLUF."

Josh grinned. "I think I understand."

"Great," Li said, her smile widening. "There are a few more tips to keep in mind."

"First," she continued, "use active voice. It makes your writing clearer and more direct. Instead of saying, 'The report was reviewed by the committee,' say, 'The committee reviewed the report.''

"Next," she added, "avoided jargon and technical terms. She reminded them of the K.I.S.S. principle—Keep It Simple, Stupid. Their audience might not have been familiar with specialized language, so they kept it straightforward and accessible."

"Also," Li went on, "be concise. Every word should serve a purpose. Cut out any fluff or unnecessary details that don't add value to your main point."

"And," she emphasized, "always check your facts. Accuracy is crucial in our line of work. One wrong piece of information can lead to incorrect conclusions and poor decision-making."

Josh nodded, absorbing her advice. "Active voice, clear language, conciseness, and accuracy. Got it."

Li nodded in approval. "Exactly. And remember, clarity is key. Your goal is to communicate your message effectively and efficiently."

Josh leaned back in his chair, feeling more confident. "Thanks, Li. This is helpful."

Li gave him an encouraging smile. "You're welcome, Josh. Just keep these principles in mind, and you'll do great."

Josh glanced at one of the several clocks mounted on the walls of the SCIF. Surprised by the lateness, he thanked Li for the lesson, logged off his computer, and headed toward his father-in-law's office. Exhausted, Josh hoped Roger would be ready to head back to the apartment. The day's revelations echoed in his mind, and he looked forward to preparing the briefing tomorrow with Li.

Roger and Josh stepped out of the Pentagon; their faces bathed in the brilliance of a summer sky. The earlier clouds and rain had vanished, leaving behind a clear, blue expanse. Roger's footsteps seemed lighter as he crossed the Pentagon parking lot, buoyed by the insights Josh had shared in his office before their departure. The briefing, scheduled for Thursday, was well on its way to being ready.

Together, they strolled back to Roger's apartment, the sun's warmth infusing their tired bodies. Inside, sunlight streamed through the windows, casting elongated shadows on the floor. Roger, ever the adventurer, proposed a refreshing swim in the complex's rooftop pool. Josh, borrowing Roger's extra pair of swim trunks, followed him.

For Josh, swimming was more than exercise; it was a meditative escape. As he stepped into the pool, water enveloped him, cradling his body like a cocoon. Weightless, he surrendered to the rhythm of each stroke, allowing the day's worries to dissolve. The world beyond the water's surface faded, replaced by the soothing pulse of his own breath.

Later, in the apartment's kitchen, Josh glanced at the microwave's built-in clock. The three-hour time difference between Washington, D.C., and Seattle tugged at his thoughts. It was too early to call home to Emily and the boys. Excusing himself, he retreated to the guest room, stretching out on the bed. Sleep claimed him swiftly, wrapping him in its soothing embrace.

Josh awoke to a gentle rap on the bedroom door—the sound of Meg's soft knocking at the door coaxing him toward dinner. Still groggy, he stumbled into the dining room, cheeks flushed with embarrassment at having slept so long. Yet, there was something magical about waking from a nap to find himself more rested than after a full night's sleep. It was a sweet surprise, like stumbling upon a hidden treasure.

Perhaps it was the invigorating swim—the water's embrace had worked wonders. His body felt lighter, thoughts clearer, as if the fatigue that clung to him earlier had dissipated. Meg had prepared a simple spaghetti and meatballs dinner, and Josh attacked it with surprising gusto, his appetite reawakened.

After the meal, Meg invited Josh to join her and Roger in the living room for a movie. She had chosen a dramatic volcano film, and while Josh appreciated the gesture, he knew he'd spend the evening critiquing its inaccuracies. For Meg, however, this shared movie time held a special place in her heart—it was a nostalgic callback to their first lunch with Emily and Josh. Back then, Josh had been a wide-eyed freshman geology student, eagerly sharing insights about the tectonic forces shaping Earth's continents and oceans. As the credits rolled, Josh excused himself and retreated to the guest room.

As he settled into the guest room, he couldn't help but reflect on the movie they had just watched. The dramatic volcano film, while entertaining, was riddled with scientific inaccuracies. Josh mentally noted each exaggeration and error: the unrealistic eruption timelines, the overly dramatized seismic activity, and the implausible survival scenarios.

Despite these flaws, he appreciated Meg's choice. It was a thoughtful attempt to bond over something connected to his field of expertise. He smiled, remembering how Roger and Meg had engrossed themselves in the storyline, their faces illuminated by the flickering screen.

Josh also realized that the movie night had deeper significance for Meg. It was a cherished tradition that harked back to their early days of friendship. He remembered how, during their first lunch together, he had enthusiastically shared his knowledge of geology, capturing everyone's attention with his passion for the subject.

As he prepared to call Emily, Josh felt a wave of gratitude. The evening had been a perfect blend of nostalgia and fresh memories, a reminder of the strong bonds he shared with those around him.

He dialed Emily and the boys, his voice filled with excitement. His update on the progress he had made had Emily beaming. "I might fly home on Friday," Josh told her. He recounted the rooftop swim with her dad and the volcano movie that Meg had roped him into watching. Emily handed the phone to the boys, but not before warning Josh: they'd learned a new song. "It's called 'Chewy Puff Coconuts,'' Emily explained. Apparently, Maya had tucked these snack bars into the boys' swim bag after lessons and then she taught them the song. "They've been singing it nonstop ever since," she added.

And so, over the phone, Josh heard their little voices, harmonizing to the tune of "I Can't Help Myself (Sugar Pie, Honey Bunch)" by the Four Tops:

Chewy Puff Coconuts.
Chewy Puff Coconuts.
You know I love you.
I love you.
I can't help myself.
I love you and nothing else.
Chewy Puff Coconuts.

CHAPTER 8

POWERPOINT RANGER

On Wednesday morning, Li arrived at Josh's desk. She assured him that today he would earn his "PowerPoint Ranger badge." Josh, furrowing his eyebrows, tilted his head in puzzlement.

Li explained that a "PowerPoint Ranger" was someone skilled at creating briefings using Microsoft PowerPoint. "It's all in good fun," Li assured him. "We're quite adept at using these slides to communicate and share information." She then proposed they start by identifying their bottom line.

Josh acknowledged her suggestion with a nod. "Right, BLUF: Bottom Line Up Front."

After a moment of contemplation, Josh grabbed a marker and wrote on the dry erase partition that separated their desks: "Recent Chinese Government Changbai Mountain concern based on fear that North Korea nuclear testing could cause mountain to erupt."

Li countered with her own succinct statement: "China Fears Volcanic Eruption Because of North Korea Nuclear Tests."

"Okay," Josh said, leaning back, "what's next?"

Li explained that before diving into the substance of their brief, they needed a transition to guide the audience. This transition, akin to a debate format, should present their claim (in this case, their BLUF) followed by the elements of their argument.

Josh listened intently; he relished the art of argumentation. One of his earliest college courses focused on effective writing and argumentation skills.

After a few minutes, Josh scribbled on the board: "A=B+C," and underneath it: "Fear = Testing + Eruption."

Li nodded approvingly. "Exactly. Now let's build our argument around this equation. We'll need simple points to support each element, showing how testing leads to fear of an eruption."

Josh felt a sense of accomplishment as they outlined their briefing. The collaboration with Li was invigorating, and he was eager to put their skills to the test in the upcoming presentation.

In their ongoing tag team collaboration, Li took the reins, poised to add a draft transition statement to the whiteboard. "Recent Chinese Government invitation for the team to investigate Changbai volcano likely stems from fears that North Korea's nuclear testing could trigger an eruption," she wrote.

But Li, ever the discerning analyst, swiftly erased it. "Too wordy," she informed Josh. "Give me a minute." Moments later, a more concise version emerged: "China's invitation to study Changbai volcano due to North Korea nuclear test concerns."

Josh nodded in agreement, impressed by her ability to distill the message so effectively.

Stepping back from her work, Li scanned the evidence before her, eyes sharp and focused. Leaning forward, she appended an asterisk and the word "likely" to the critical statement. Precision mattered—especially in the realm of intelligence analysis.

Turning to Josh, she explained the necessity of revisiting their judgment with this crucial caveat. Josh's head tilted in a gesture reminiscent of a curious puppy.

Li recognized this as a pivotal moment. "Josh," she began, her voice steady, "we lack the luxury of perfect information. Uncertainty looms like a persistent fog." Her words carried weight. Analytic judgments always bore a measure of uncertainty; it was an unavoidable truth.

"But how much uncertainty?" Josh's question hung in the air.

Li delved into the nuances. Likelihood assessments hinged on factors like source reliability, gaps in knowledge, and the currency of underlying information. The spectrum spanned from almost no chance to likely, even approaching near certainty.

As the morning wore on, Li and Josh meticulously built their case. China's concern about the volcano tied to North Korea's nuclear testing became a complex puzzle they were determined to solve. Drawing on Young's intel and Josh's research, they crafted an interesting argument. The risk of a volcanic eruption, potentially triggered by nuclear activity, loomed large. It became increasingly clear that China's worries about Changbai might be well-founded.

Approaching lunchtime, Li shifted her attention to Josh, who sat hunched over a pile of notes. "Josh," she said, her voice gentle yet firm, "we've been at this for quite some time. Let's take a break and recharge our brains."

Josh nodded, fully aware that fresh insights awaited them after a well-deserved pause. He inquired whether they had time to visit the Pentagon gift shop.

"Of course," Li replied.

Together, they retraced their steps through the courtyard and made their way to the main concourse, where the "Fort America" gift shop awaited.

Li seemed just as enthusiastic as Josh about sorting through the mementos, both on a mission to find an age-appropriate gift for Johnny and Jimmy.

After some collaborative deliberation, they settled on matching "Pentagon - established in 1943" emblazoned army gray T-shirts.

With their mission accomplished, they returned to the café for lunch, savoring the much-welcomed break before diving back into their work.

After lunch, Li guided Josh on how to incorporate effective visual information to clarify their analysis. She explained visuals should enhance their findings and data, making complex information more accessible.

"Josh, we use visuals to convey spatial or temporal relationships more effectively than we can with written text. Think of tables, flowcharts, and images," she said.

"You mean like when a picture is worth a thousand words?" Josh replied.

"Exactly," Li agreed with a smile.

Li looked up at the whiteboard where they had captured their work and smiled with satisfaction until she spotted the asterisk.

"Josh, what about our early caveat of 'likely'?" Li asked.

Josh considered it for a moment, reflecting on the information they had gathered. "I understand why China might want to know more about the volcano," he said. "What I'm less comfortable with is the correlation between nuclear testing and a volcanic eruption."

Li addressed the issue by noting that their assessment was based on China's fear and motivation for requesting the team, not on whether this fear was rational.

"Truth and fear are relative," Josh teased.

Li didn't take the bait and instead concluded the conversation by asking Josh to inform Captain Banks that they would be ready to brief tomorrow.

Roger breathed a sigh of relief upon learning that the team had scheduled their briefing for Thursday. Glancing at his watch, he realized that amidst the pressure of preparing the brief; he had spent little time with his son-in-law. Roger suggested they take the rest of the afternoon off.

After a quick stop at the apartment to change into civilian clothes—what Roger called "civvies"—the pair hopped on the metro. After a twenty-minute ride on the Yellow Line from the Pentagon City Metrorail station to the Gallery Place—Chinatown Metrorail station, they took a short walk to the Rocket Bar, a funky downstairs pool room nestled in the Penn Quarter neighborhood.

Roger's choice of venue did not surprise Josh. Roger and Meg had maintained a pool table in various military quarters. Despite Meg's complaints about the hassle of moving the table from one location to another, she loved the pool table, and cherished the time the family spent around it. During one of Josh's first visits to Emily's parents, shooting pool on the full-size billiard table in the sunroom became a favorite activity. The only family member Josh defeated was Emily's younger sister, Ellen—though only after she scratched the eight ball on her last shot.

Washington, D.C. often earned the label of a bedroom community. People commuted into the city for work during the day and retreated to the suburbs in the evenings. As a result, D.C. quieted down, especially in residential neighborhoods. The bar had just opened at 4 p.m. when Roger and

Josh arrived. After Josh finally secured a win following four losses, he accepted the wisdom of quitting while ahead.

Meg arrived at the apartment around the same time as Roger and Josh. She was pleased to hear that they had spent quality time together. Knowing Roger didn't drink often, she planned dinner—a large salad with water-rich cucumbers, celery, and radishes to help rehydrate the pair after their evening of drinking.

After dinner, Josh timed his call perfectly to catch Emily just as she arrived home from spending the afternoon with Josh's grandmother and her sister. He shared the news that he had completed his work and, following the Thursday morning briefing, had rescheduled his Sunday flight to arrive on Friday. "I should get in at 9 p.m.," Josh reported.

Emily breathed a sigh of relief. Being a parent with young children while one parent was away on travel posed both challenges and rewards. Even with Maya's help, Emily took on the emotional strain of the boys missing their dad, providing extra comfort and reassurance. Yet, as much as she missed Josh, she cherished the one-on-one bonding time with her sons. She hoped this experience would foster their independence and resilience.

Emily handed the phone to the boys, who were overjoyed to learn that their seven days of waiting had been shortened to five.

Johnny eagerly recounted their afternoon with their grandmother and aunt. They had heard about Seattle's Underground Tour from the YMCA and convinced their mom that they were old enough for the adventure. The tour took them beneath the streets of Seattle's Pioneer Square neighborhood, through a maze of underground roads and basement-level storefronts. After securing a promise from their dad to take them again, Johnny passed the phone to his younger brother.

Jimmy picked up where Johnny had left off. "Dad, Aunt Ellen bride us," he began.

"Bribed us," Johnny said, correcting his younger brother, and explained that Aunt Ellen had promised to take them for ice cream if they endured a little more shopping. Josh understood.

Josh didn't mention to the boys that he had been to the Seattle Underground before and knew of its intriguing shops. Instead, he imagined the shopping journey his sons had endured. Changing the topic, he asked Jimmy about his ice cream flavor choice.

"Melted chocolate," Jimmy boasted, "and Johnny had salted car-mel."

His adorable pronunciation tugged at Josh's heartstrings. Emily then took the phone, anticipating Josh's next question. "Honey lavender," she said.

"What does that taste like?" Josh inquired.

Emily's voice dropped to a playful whisper. "Imagine the softest kiss, sweet and lingering, with a hint of floral temptation. It's like tasting a summer night, warm and fragrant, wrapped in silky smoothness."

The boys erupted into giggles at the mention of a kiss. Josh chuckled along with them, feeling the warmth in Emily's words.

With that, the call ended. Josh eagerly awaited his homecoming. Meanwhile, Johnny and Jimmy returned to their task of creating a welcome sign for Dad.

CHAPTER 9

STAFF BRIEFING

Josh woke on Thursday morning, his excitement palpable. His mind raced through the day's agenda: breakfast, followed by a trip to the Pentagon for a crucial staff briefing. Roger had drilled into him the importance of these briefings—they kept the team informed and in sync on critical matters. But where was Roger? Josh pondered this as he sipped coffee in the kitchen, waiting.

Meg stepped into the kitchen, her brisk steps echoing. "Josh," she began, her tone caring and compassionate, "Roger's boss, Colonel Walsh, summoned him to an early meeting. Roger thinks you can find your way to the office solo. Can you?"

Josh nodded, though he felt a twinge of uncertainty about navigating the path alone.

Meg reassured him, "If you get lost, just ask for directions to the BC Café or the Market Basket."

After breakfast, Josh reached his desk unaided—a minor victory. Waiting for him were Li and Young, their expressions focused as they reviewed their notes, pens scratching across paper. They refilled their coffee cups and headed to the conference room. Soon, other team members joined them, including Major Rick Stevenson, Chris Wyatt, and Young's team chief, Major Rich Stewart. Josh recognized everyone except Major Stewart.

Then, Josh's father-in-law, Captain Banks, and his boss, Army Colonel Bob Walsh, entered the room. Just as Captain Banks moved to close the door, an older gentleman with unruly silver hair took a seat next to him.

"Alright," Captain Banks signaled to Li, his voice authoritative, "if we're ready, let's begin."

"Earlier this week," she began, her voice unwavering, "Captain Banks entrusted us with unraveling the mystery of why China invited a U.S. team to visit Changbai Mountain." With confidence, Li asserted that China's overture related to concerns about North Korea's nuclear tests. She then introduced her esteemed colleague, Professor Josh Cooper, who would provide the essential backdrop on Changbai

Mountain before the group delved into their other discoveries.

Josh stepped forward, the overhead slide transitioning to reveal a detailed image of the mountain. "Behold," he declared, his tone professorial, "Changbai Mountain—a dormant volcano straddling the Chinese-North Korean border."

But before he could delve further, Colonel Walsh leaned forward, gesturing toward the image. "And that lake?" he pressed.

Josh's response was succinct: an eruption over a millennium ago had reshaped the mountain's summit, birthing the very lake they now scrutinized.

"Good Lord, that must have been one hell of an explosion," someone blurted out, their awe unmistakable.

Josh nodded. "It was." He summarized for the inquisitive soul that the eruption—named the Millennium Eruption—ranked among the most cataclysmic events in recorded history. The room buzzed with shared wonder.

Colonel Walsh then pointed to the yellow dashed line bisecting the image. "What's that yellow line?" he demanded.

Josh met his gaze. "Sir," he replied, his tone matter-of-fact, "that line demarcates the border between China and North Korea." A playful glint entered his eyes. "They split the lake in half, even Steven." Laughter erupted, the idiomatic phrase resonating through the room.

"Even Steven," the colonel snorted, wiping tears from his eyes. But then his expression turned serious. "Is the lake dangerous?" he asked, his curiosity unyielding.

Josh paused, considering the weight of ancient eruptions and the tranquil expanse of water before him. "Not now," he answered, "but beneath its serene surface lies a turbulent past—a reminder that nature's fury can reshape the world."

Gathering his thoughts, Josh continued, knowing the topic demanded precision. His wife often teased him about slipping into "professor mode," but today, it was essential. He leaned forward, projecting confidence.

"Crater lakes like this one," he began, his voice measured, "pose unique hazards. Their risks hinge on several factors." He gestured to the screen, where an image of the serene lake nestled within a volcanic crater awaited their attention. "Consider this: When magma interacts with water in such a lake, the consequences can be explosively dire."

The colonel leaned back, his expression serious. "What are the chances of an eruption?" he asked.

Josh had expected this question. During their briefing preparations, the team had dissected it, acknowledging the limitations of their predictive capabilities.

"The last eruption occurred in 1903," Josh explained. "While we estimate eruptions roughly every century, our predictive capabilities aren't precise. Accurate forecasts? We achieve about twenty percent accuracy, and usually only within weeks of any warning signs."

Colonel Walsh and Captain Banks nodded, signaling the end of Josh's spotlight. Now it was Young's turn to present.

Young stood, nerves coursing through him. He now recognized the older gentleman with unruly silver hair as Thomas Miller, the seasoned analyst from the non-proliferation team. Thomas' expertise in North Korea's nuclear program was unparalleled. Young mentally kicked himself; he should have involved Thomas from the start. Hindsight, however, was a cruel companion.

As Young advanced the slide deck, the screen revealed a graph—an intricate display of data points representing North Korea's nuclear tests. A horizontal line cut across the plot, marking the

100-kiloton threshold. Scientists speculated that crossing this line might trigger a volcanic eruption.

"This threshold matters," Young explained, his voice wavering.

"But wait—Pyongyang has already exceeded it," Thomas interjected, his hand shooting up in objection. "Doesn't that refute your argument?"

Young met Thomas' gaze. "Not necessarily," he countered. "The threshold is elusive. Estimates hover between 140 and 250 kilotons. Would 140 have sufficed?" The room held its breath, awaiting the answer.

Josh reentered the discussion, his resolve unwavering. "Clearly," he asserted, "this threshold remains theoretical. Scientists did not apply the model specifically to Mount Changbai."

Thomas' frustration grew. "Pyongyang ceased testing years ago," he noted.

Li, unable to resist, interjected, "Isn't the crux of the issue that the Chinese government believes a nuclear test could trigger an eruption? Perhaps they believe testing will resume." The room buzzed with tension.

"Good point," Captain Banks concurred. "That's precisely what we tasked you to address." With that, the briefing concluded.

As Captain Banks and Colonel Walsh exchanged gratitude with the briefers and filed out of the room, Captain Banks pulled Josh aside, closing the conference room door to secure their privacy. There, Roger shared the morning's revelation: China's tone had shifted from invitation to near-demand. The White House feared that Beijing now viewed the site visit as a precondition for any U.S.-China Summit.

"A team is assembling," Roger revealed, "at the Cascades Volcano Observatory in Vancouver, Washington."

The observatory was a mere three-hour drive from Josh's home. The United States had five volcano observatories: Alaska, California, Washington, Hawaii, and Yellowstone. Was the choice of the one so near his home a coincidence? Josh wondered.

"Josh," Roger continued, "we need you. Your volcano expertise, your familiarity with our challenges, and your newfound security clearance—it all makes you indispensable."

Alone with his father-in-law, Josh dropped formalities. "I can't go," he pleaded. He'd promised Emily no more fieldwork after nearly losing his life twice while in the field.

Roger rested his hand on Josh's shoulder. "Josh, I understand," he said. "Please take some time to think about it. Why don't you stretch your legs? I'll be here when you decide."

Josh heeded his father-in-law's advice, ascending the stairs—or more aptly, the "ladder," as his father-in-law's naval traditions would call it—and headed to the outdoor courtyard. The sun blazed overhead, its heat unyielding. The thick, humid air clung to Josh's skin, prompting him to retreat back into the cool, air-conditioned haven of the building.

Inside, Josh navigated past bustling shops in the concourse until he arrived at the "Hall of Heroes." The memorial honors over 3,400 recipients of the Medal of Honor—the highest military decoration in the nation. As he wandered through the corridors, Josh realized the Pentagon transcended mere office space. It was a living memorial, a museum of sacrifice.

Each corridor had a purpose. One honored each branch of the armed services. Another celebrated General MacArthur. Yet another paid homage to the forty signers of the Constitution, twenty-three of whom had fought for independence. Then, before him, stood the 9/11 Memorial, attached to the Pentagon chapel. It commemorated the lives lost when American Airlines Flight 77 crashed into the building on that fateful day, September 11, 2001.

The weight of service, sacrifice, and honor enveloped Josh. He knew his next steps. Rushing back to his father-in-law's office, he prepared to share his resolve.

"Great," Roger's father-in-law rejoiced upon learning from Josh that he would join the survey team. He assured Josh that he would inform the team of his participation and instructed him to fly home and spend the weekend with Emily and the boys.

"You can drive up to Vancouver on Monday," Roger declared.

Josh pondered how different, how much more direct, his father-in-law was in uniform compared to his demeanor at home—the uniform seemed to transform him.

Continuing in this authoritative tone, Roger issued a series of directives. He reminded Josh not to discuss his time at the Pentagon with anyone.

"No mention of J-2 or intelligence," he demanded firmly.

Next, he informed Josh that he could not disclose his destination to anyone outside the survey team.

"Where should I tell Emily I'm going?" Josh protested.

Roger paused for a moment. "Tell her what I told the other team members: their government has asked us to keep the destination confidential because they don't want to alarm the local population."

Josh nodded, absorbing the instructions. The gravity of the situation was clear, and he understood the importance of maintaining secrecy for the mission's success and safety.

CHAPTER 10

HOMECOMING

Frank, Josh's stepfather, owned a travel company, but he wasn't the only family member with airline connections. Roger pulled strings by reaching out to the Pentagon's Defense Management Travel Office to secure an earlier flight home for Josh.

On Friday morning, Josh dressed and savored the light continental breakfast set out by Meg. After bidding a swift farewell to Roger and Meg, he embarked on a brisk walk to the nearby Pentagon City Metrorail station, where he caught the Blue Line bound for Ronald Reagan Washington National Airport. The sun had just risen, casting a soft, ethereal glow over the city. Josh felt as though he were slipping away from Washington, D.C., under the cover of darkness, akin to a stealthy thief. The irony amused him, considering his father-in-law's strict directive not to discuss his Pentagon experiences with anyone: "No mention of J-2 or intelligence," he recalled.

The flight from Washington, D.C. to Seattle took just over five hours. As Josh stepped into the concourse, the morning sunlight streamed through large windows, painting the bustling area with a gentle radiance. Its golden hues cast playful, warm rays across the well-polished floors, energizing him. Scanning the expansive space, his eyes found Emily and his sons. With their arms outstretched, each boy held an opposite end of a homemade "Welcome Home Daddy" banner.

During the ride home, the boys, who had never flown before, bombarded their father with questions about the flight.

"How do planes fly? How do pilots steer the plane? Could you see the clouds from the window?" Josh answered each question as best he could.

Emily, wanting to give Josh a break from the questioning, asked the boys if they could fly anywhere where they would want to go. Jimmy shouted out, "Disney World!"

"Too short," Johnny added.

Perplexed, Jimmy turned to his mother for clarification. She explained you had to be forty-eight inches tall to ride the largest rides at Disney

World. Jimmy wanted to know how tall he was.

"Forty-three inches," Emily responded.

"And Johnny?" Jimmy asked.

"Forty-seven inches," Emily added.

"Too short!" Jimmy proudly proclaimed. Emily didn't know what she enjoyed more about Jimmy's response—his math prowess or his enthusiasm.

"Soon," Josh promised the boys. "Soon."

By the time they arrived home, it was almost noon. Maya had prepared homemade pizza for lunch. After she settled the boys at the table, Josh asked Emily to join him on the deck. For the young parents, the deck served as a place of solitude, free from the prying ears of their sons. They reserved it for their most sensitive conversations.

Once outside, Emily wasted no time asking Josh what was on his mind. Josh explained that the Cascades Volcano Observatory had invited him to monitor a volcano causing concern. When she asked which one, Josh hesitated, then told her he couldn't say.

"You can't tell me the name of the volcano?" Emily asked, her frustration growing.

"No," Josh replied. He explained that the foreign government requested secrecy to avoid alarming the local population.

"Foreign government?" Emily's frustration grew. "Are you telling me this secret volcano isn't even in the United States?"

Josh stood silently.

"Fine, tell me if it's dangerous," Emily demanded, becoming more assertive.

Josh avoided geologic jargon and promised her that, in this case, the volcano was not dangerous.

Emily reminded Josh of his promise not to conduct any more fieldwork. Josh implored her that this was different, reassuring her that this volcano, unlike the last one that nearly cost him his life twice, was safe.

Josh retreated indoors and ascended the stairs to the safety of his desk, giving Emily a chance to cool off. Her Irish temper resembled a dormant volcano, its rage concealed beneath a tranquil exterior. Unlike the fiery outbursts he encountered elsewhere, her anger smoldered.

At his desk, Josh breathed a sigh of relief as he surveyed his almost empty email inbox. Summer break was a blessing, he mused. He located the email he sought—a message from the Cascades Volcano Observatory in Vancouver, Washington. Sent by his college mentor, Joffre, who had once treated Josh, then a graduate student, to a tour of the observatory, the email welcomed Josh to the team. Joffre, also his late father's former colleague, had been present during his father's passing. Joffre expected Josh to arrive sometime on Monday, before lunch. The email concluded with the directive that the team should be "wheels up" by mid-week.

"Mid-week," Josh murmured to himself, contemplating how he would break the news to Emily.

After a quiet dinner, Maya and the boys stepped out the front door. Josh, curious, wondered where they were off to. Emily explained Maya had volunteered to take the boys to catch a movie. Josh considered two possibilities: either Emily had forgiven him and wanted an intimate evening, or she intended to continue their earlier discussion.

Later, as they lay in bed, Josh pondered how to make the most of his remaining time with his family before his departure. He knew the conversation with Emily was inevitable, but he hoped to balance it with some cherished moments together.

The following morning, after breakfast, Josh turned his attention to his sons. At the YMCA, Kim, the boys' swim instructor, welcomed them back warmly. Emily and Josh observed as she guided Johnny and Jimmy through their lessons.

Kim helped the boys relax in the water, teaching them to lie on their fronts, extend their arms, and keep their faces above water. "Relax. Trust the water," she repeated, her voice calm and reassuring. Next, she taught them the art of floating on their backs. Johnny and Jimmy reclined, gazing up at the ceiling. With knees slightly bent and arms extended to the sides for optimal balance, Kim encouraged them to keep their ears and eyes submerged, allowing their bodies to float. She gradually extended the duration of each float, praising their progress and reminding them to remain calm.

After the lesson, Kim quietly assured Emily and Josh that, with time, the boys would gain confidence and learn to trust their bodies and the water. When Johnny and Jimmy rejoined their parents, Kim celebrated their achievements, resting a hand on each of their heads. "They are doing really great!" she exclaimed, her pride clear.

Emily and Josh smiled, grateful for Kim's patience and encouragement. They knew these victories in the pool were steppingstones to greater confidence and independence for their sons.

Back home, the boys were famished. "Swimming takes a lot of energy," Maya acknowledged as she passed them a second helping of hot dogs and macaroni and cheese. In a repeat of Friday's performance, Emily gestured for Josh to come out onto the deck.

"Oh, Josh," she began, "if it's important to you, then I'll support you."

She then asked him when he had to leave, and how long he would be gone. Josh knew the answer to the first question and told her he would drive up to the observatory on Monday and the team would depart on Wednesday. Explaining how long he would be gone was more difficult because he didn't know. He explained the process involved several factors: the team assessed what monitoring instruments were already present, determined what additional instruments they needed, and then selected and installed them. The time required for site selection and installation would depend on the terrain, and after installation, the equipment would have to be tested and calibrated.

Emily cut him off and asked, "Best guess."

"Two to four weeks," Josh promised. "I'll keep you up to date on our progress."

"Well then, let's make the best of the time we have together this weekend," Emily concluded. Josh had foreseen this and suggested, given the boys' recent interest in planes, that they visit

Seattle's Museum of Flight on Sunday.

After arriving home from the movies with Maya, the boys went straight to bed. Emily and Josh waited until after breakfast on Sunday to share the exciting news about their planned outing. The museum, just a fifteen-minute drive south from their house, opened its doors as they arrived. With an impressive collection of over 175 aircraft and spacecraft, it stood as one of the largest air and space museums in the United States.

Inside the expansive three-million-cubic-foot, six-story exhibit hall, Emily and Josh struggled to keep pace with their enthusiastic boys. Johnny and Jimmy darted from one exhibition to the next, exploring both indoor and outdoor displays. Among the highlights were a Space Shuttle trainer, the legendary Blackbird, and a meticulously crafted replica of Air Force One.

Guiding the boys to the Kid's Flight Zone next to the main gallery of aircraft, Emily and Josh watched as Johnny and Jimmy transformed into junior pilots. Strapped into flight harnesses, they tested their piloting skills in hang gliding simulators. Later, they took turns sitting in the cockpits of a RotorWay Scorpion helicopter, a Thorp T-18 home-built aircraft, and a P-47D Thunderbolt replica, eagerly operating the controls.

As the morning rushed by, hunger set in. Emily and Josh led the boys to the Wing's Café, where Nathan's All Beef Hot Dogs and Beecher's White Cheddar Mac and Cheese satisfied the boys' appetites. Meanwhile, Josh and Emily, mindful of their own metabolism, opted for the quinoa power bowl—a healthier choice featuring crisp romaine, roasted corn, sweet potato, black beans, tomato, baby spinach, and a zesty chipotle-lime vinaigrette.

At the museum's gift shop, the boys deliberated before selecting a pair of P-40 Flying Tigers Warhawk plush toys. On their way to the car, they passed through the Vietnam Veterans Memorial Park. Dominating the space was a meticulously restored B-52G Stratofortress that had flown during Operation Linebacker II. This operation, also known as the "Christmas Bombing," took place in December 1972 and was one of the most intensive air campaigns of the Vietnam War, aimed at forcing North Vietnam to negotiate an end to the conflict. The B-52s played a crucial role, delivering massive payloads to strategic targets.

Plaques adorned the walls, bearing the names, military ranks, and other details of those who had served during the Vietnam War—a poignant reminder for Josh, whose memories of the Pentagon lingered in the background.

As they walked through the park, Josh reflected on the significance of service and sacrifice, feeling a renewed sense of purpose and responsibility. The day had been a perfect blend of education, fun, and family bonding, creating lasting memories for all of them.

CHAPTER 11

CASCADES OBSERVATORY

Monday morning unfolded in Seattle with extraordinary beauty. Accompanied by Emily, Josh rose early, eager to embark on their nearly three-hour drive to Vancouver, Washington. From their second-story bedroom window, the sun emerged from its nocturnal slumber, casting golden rays across the horizon. Though they could have lingered in bed, the morning beckoned them to seize the day.

Emily descended the stairs as Josh tiptoed to the boys' room. Through the door, the rising sun cast enough light for Josh to glimpse his sons, still nestled in their low-profile matching twin beds. Jimmy clutched his beloved P-40 Flying Tigers Warhawk plush toy. Josh savored the moment, knowing that one day his boys would want their own rooms.

Downstairs, even early riser Maya was still in bed. Emily had prepared a simple breakfast in the kitchen nook: toasted sourdough, fresh fruit, and coffee. The warm butter on the sourdough slices released a comforting aroma. The bowl held strawberries, sunburst-orange mandarin segments, and plump cherries, each bite bursting with sweetness. Cradling their coffees, Emily and Josh found solace in this uncomplicated pleasure.

At the threshold, Emily pressed a kiss to Josh's cheek, her well-wishes accompanying him as he embarked on his journey south. The United States Geological Survey's Vancouver, Washington office was a familiar destination for him. As a college freshman, he had attended an open house there—a moment of profound insight that clarified his career path. The office buzzed with real-time monitoring of volcanic activity, disseminating forecasts and alerts. Their research into volcanic processes served as a lifeline for communities preparing for potential eruptions.

Inside the red-bricked building, the receptionist guided Josh to Joffre's office. Once a visitor himself, Joffre now held the title of Scientist-in-Charge. He welcomed Josh with a firm hug.

"Glad to see you, Josh! But I'm curious—how did you end up here?"

Josh recounted the unexpected call from his father-in-law and his Pentagon experience, glancing over his shoulder to ensure privacy.

"Don't worry," Joffre said, using air quotes for the word "intelligence," "I've briefed the team on the latest 'intelligence' from the Pentagon."

Joffre then turned to Josh. "So, where do you think we should start?"

Drawing from his earlier conversation with Emily, Josh proposed a plan: assess the existing monitoring instruments and identify any gaps. Joffre nodded in agreement and assigned Josh the task of preparing a detailed report on Mount Changbai's current monitoring equipment and any coverage gaps.

As the morning unfolded, Josh delved into the intricacies of the Tianchi Volcano Observatory (TVO) near the Changbai volcano. Established in 1999, the TVO tracks seismic activity around Changbai using a network of seismic stations located 10, 15, and 30 miles from the volcano. These stations detect both natural seismic events, such as earthquakes and volcanic activity, and unnatural ones, such as those caused by nuclear tests.

Despite the gnawing hunger in his stomach, Josh persisted. He continued scrutinizing TVO's equipment list, noting the ground-based GPS devices used to measure changes in the mountain's surface. Reflecting on Mount St. Helens' eruption, he appreciated the critical role tracking a volcano's shape plays in predicting its behavior. The bulge that appeared on Mount St. Helens before its 1980 eruption was a significant indicator of volcanic activity.

Scientists closely monitor volcanoes for signs of impending eruptions. Before Mount St. Helens erupted, fresh magma rose within, causing the north side of the volcano to bulge outward by 0.6 miles. This protrusion was a clear sign that pressure was building inside. On May 18, 1980, Mount St. Helens erupted. The bulge collapsed and slid down the mountain, releasing 100 billion cubic feet of rocks at speeds up to 150 miles per hour, devastating a 24-square-mile area north of the volcano.

TVO went beyond ground-based GPS to track changes in the mountain's shape. They also employed InSAR (Interferometric Synthetic Aperture Radar) from orbiting satellites. This advanced technique allowed them to detect subtle changes in the volcano's shape, significantly enhancing TVO's understanding of its behavior and potential hazards.

At lunchtime, Josh joined the team in the break room. Joffre had chosen subs from Philly Bilmos

Cheesesteaks, stirring memories of Josh's inaugural visit to Vancouver when Joffre had introduced him to the same lunch spot. The team comprised seismologists, whose meticulous analysis of earthquake patterns, tremors, and ground vibrations helped predict volcanic activity; data scientists, who collected and integrated data from diverse sources; geographers who investigated volcanic system formation and behavior and gas geochemists, who analyzed gas samples seeping from the volcano to gain insights into its magma composition and ongoing processes.

Among the crowd, Josh was relieved to spot a familiar face. Dan, from the Jet Propulsion Laboratory, served as the team's IT and remote drone specialist. His innovative work in volcano monitoring had saved many lives, including Josh's. The group also included operational specialists responsible for daily operations, inventory management, and communication. However, it was Victor Müller, the acoustic imaging pioneer, who intrigued Josh the most. Armed with submersible vehicles equipped with hydro acoustic techniques (sonar), Victor planned to map Mount Changbai's lake floor for signs of volcanic activity, similar to his work with Ecuador's crater lake-capped Quilotoa volcano.

His expertise complemented their seismic studies—an impressive team, as Joffre had assured Josh.

As Josh finished his loaded cheesesteak wrap, Joffre inquired about the morning's progress. Josh's unexpected response was that the Chinese appeared well-equipped for volcano monitoring.

Joffre's baffled retort was, "Then why the hell do they need more?"

Josh pledged to delve deeper into the matter after lunch.

Throughout the rest of the day, Josh combed through various databases, assembling a comprehensive list of volcano monitoring capabilities that the team could offer to the Chinese government. While acknowledging TVO's robust network, Josh remained resolute in identifying areas for enhancement.

As the day drew to a close, Josh presented his findings to Joffre. Topping his list was gas emissions monitoring. Although TVO had some equipment, Josh believed they could benefit from additional resources in this area, as enhanced gas emissions monitoring would yield valuable insights into ongoing volcanic activity.

To unravel the enigmatic secrets of the volcano's crater lake, Josh proposed using Victor's pioneering acoustic imaging technology.

This innovation would provide crucial information about the volcano's behavior during both eruptive and non-eruptive phases.

Josh also emphasized the importance of his former colleague Dan, the team's IT and remote drone specialist. He noted how Dan's capabilities had played a pivotal role in monitoring the last eruption in the United States. Josh convinced Joffre that upgrading the Chinese data transmission systems would improve real-time monitoring with minimal effort.

Joffre thanked Josh for his thorough list, recognizing that these additions and enhancements would significantly help TVO scientists deepen their understanding of the volcano.

"I just hope we can navigate the Department of State and Department of Commerce export controls," Joffre mused aloud. These regulations governed the export of defense products to safeguard national security interests, prevent the proliferation of weapons of mass destruction, and curb the accumulation of conventional arms.

"Share the list with the team, and I'll have our operational specialist start the export permissions process." With that, Joffre declared it a day.

As Josh was about to leave, Joffre stopped him. "Where are you staying?" he asked.

"I'm planning on staying at a hotel down the street," Josh replied.

"Oh no, that won't do. You're staying with me," Joffre insisted.

Josh stepped into Joffre's cluttered bachelor apartment, where the air smelled of old books and forgotten takeout containers. The mismatched furniture bore the marks of countless moves and late-night conversations. As the sun dipped below the horizon, Joffre fired up the well-worn grill, filling the air with the sizzle of burgers, laughter, and shared memories. Leaning against the railing, they watched the lights twinkle in the distance, finding sanctuary on the deck—a place where workplace concerns vanished, and time slowed.

Back inside, the mess told its own stories. Piles of papers spilled from overstuffed drawers onto the floor, and Joffre's laptop blinked with notifications, evidence of his tireless work as the center's scientist-in-charge. Josh chuckled, knowing that this chaos was Joffre's creative canvas.

They ate their juicy, slightly charred burgers on mismatched plates, accompanied by cold beer and flowing conversation. The night air carried their laughter. After a burst of competing yawns, Joffre excused himself and headed to bed. Josh sat on the worn-out couch and called Emily, who had also had a long day. She shared that her sister Ellen, who had recently completed her nursing program at the University of Washington, had applied for a position at the birth center where Emily worked.

"Wow," Josh acknowledged, "that would be amazing."

Emily and Ellen shared a deep bond, and through their relationship, Josh glimpsed another dimension of his wife. As the night deepened, Josh realized that messy apartments and well-worn grills held a magic of their own.

CHAPTER 12

PACKING DAY

When Josh woke up on Tuesday morning, he felt surprisingly refreshed, despite having spent the night on a couch. Joffre's rhythmic, low-frequency snoring punctuated the quiet morning air, resembling a distant idling engine or a soft, repetitive growl. Each snore's vibrations resonated through Joffre's bedroom door, creating an amusing effect. After shaving and showering, Josh tiptoed toward the kitchen, intending to surprise Joffre with breakfast. However, it was Joffre who surprised him, shuffling half-asleep to find Josh rummaging through the refrigerator and pantry.

"Josh, you'll never find breakfast in there," Joffre laughed, explaining that he always ate breakfast out. "Give me a minute, and I'll take you to my favorite greasy spoon," he promised.

Fifteen minutes later, they climbed into Joffre's faded blue Saab—a car adorned with rust spots, dings, and a missing hubcap. The Saab had witnessed cross-country road trips, volcano climbs in the Cascade Range, and countless late-night drives. With a hint of sentimentality, Joffre called it a loyal companion. The engine grumbled to life, emitting a nostalgic cloud. It wasn't a roar, more of a throaty sigh—a here-we-go-again sound. The Saab's steering wheel wobbled, but it seemed to know every neighborhood pothole.

"She might not be sleek or glamorous, but she's got character," Joffre added.

The quaint 1949-style diner exuded nostalgia, a family-owned establishment known for its hearty, home-cooked meals. Jenny, the hostess, recognized Joffre as one of their most loyal patrons and led them to a cozy booth. Josh admired the vintage décor, taking in the checkered floors and retro memorabilia.

Jenny, with her habitual friendly manner, asked Joffre, "What will you have?"

"The usual," Joffre replied.

Jenny knew Joffre's usual order: three scrambled eggs with bacon, accompanied by shredded hash browns. Turning to Josh, she inquired, "And what about you, honey?"

Josh found the endearing phrase reminiscent of his grandmother. He perused the menu and opted for a garden omelet with peppers, mushrooms, spinach, tomato, and onions—skipping the shredded hash and toast.

Upon reaching the observatory, the team sprang into action. They began loading equipment onto a waiting flatbed truck, equipped with winches for handling bulkier items. Operational specialists had planned ahead, reserving a white passenger van for the team. Josh watched as they skillfully winched two pallets, each containing twenty-four cases of Meals Ready to Eat (MREs), onto the flatbed. His curiosity piqued, he turned to Joffre for an explanation.

Joffre emphasized their reliance on these self-contained, shelf-stable meals. In their current situation, where traditional food service wasn't available, MREs were a lifeline.

"Josh," Joffre explained, "we've had team members suffer from diarrhea because of local food. It's not that the food is necessarily bad; it's just that our digestive systems aren't accustomed to it. When something foreign hits your stomach, abracadabra—diarrhea."

Joffre continued to extol the virtues of MREs: they were lightweight, portable, easy to store, and had a long shelf life. Plus, they provided a balanced mix of protein, carbs, fat, and electrolytes. Noticing Josh's curiosity, Joffre promised to grab a couple of packs for them to try during lunch. Josh eagerly awaited the experience.

As the team pressed forward with their preparations, Joffre carefully reviewed the terrain maps crafted by the geographers for their upcoming expedition. These cartographic treasures served a crucial purpose: enhancing the team's understanding of the area they were about to explore. Among the maps was the initial location map, illustrating four distinct routes to the mountain. The North Slope, West Slope, and South Slope routes all lay within China, while the East Slope route extended into North Korea.

Drawing from a comparison between the existing monitoring equipment deployed by Chinese scientists and the gear Joffre's team planned to bring, the geographers produced specialized maps. These visual aids highlighted critical areas, guiding the team's fieldwork strategy. Following these, a series of topographic maps revealed elevation contours, landforms, and terrain features. Geological maps documented rock formations, fault lines, and other volcanic characteristics.

Curiosity tugged at Josh, and he couldn't resist asking, "How are we getting there?"

Joffre reassured him that the operational specialists were still ironing out the details. Once they had a plan, the geographers would lay it all out.

Satisfied, the two friends-turned-colleagues set off for lunch, anticipation humming in the air. During their midday meal, Joffre presented Josh with an array of MRE (Meals Ready to Eat) options, meticulously chosen based on what he knew the team favored. Josh's eyes widened as he surveyed the choices: the zesty Chicken Burrito Bowl, the hearty Santa Fe Rice and Beans, the protein-packed Southwest Beef and Black Beans, and the classic comfort food, Chili with Beans.

Opting for the Southwest Beef and Black Beans, Josh eagerly tore open the tan-colored package. To his delight, it revealed not only the main dish but also an assortment of accompanying items. There were apple pieces in spiced sauce, a moist applesauce pound cake, a savory Teriyaki beef stick, and Chipotle tortillas—perfect for wrapping the beef and beans. But that wasn't all! A cheddar cheese spread awaited, ready to be slathered on the tortillas for an extra burst of flavor.

The thoughtful meal prep service had gone above and beyond, including additional treats.

Josh discovered a mocha cappuccino drink mix, perfect for a caffeine boost, and an accessory packet containing sugar-free beverage powder, sugar-free chewing gum, a towelette, salt, a spoon, and tissue. It was a well-rounded meal experience, complete with all the essentials—even in the heart of the workplace hustle.

As Josh inventoried his MRE, he turned to Joffre. "Okay, how do you cook it?" he inquired.

Joffre pointed out the one package Josh had overlooked—the flameless ration heater, also known as an MRE heater. This ingenious self-heating system contained a plastic bag filled with magnesium and iron powders, along with table salt. Demonstrating the process, Joffre placed Josh's Southwest Beef and Black Beans into the container, added water, and started a chemical reaction. The water boiled, heating the food with no visible flame or external heat source.

Curious about breakfast, Josh asked, "And what's the plan for that?"

Joffre's response was firm: "Yeah, don't even think about it." He was determined to savor one last meal at his favorite diner before their departure for China.

Joffre and Ben, with Josh observing silently, reviewed the itinerary for the journey from Vancouver, Washington, to China's side of

Changbai Mountain—a seamless blend of air and ground travel. The itinerary began with a direct, non-stop flight lasting eight and a half hours from Portland to Changbaishan Longjia International Airport, the closest major airport to Changbai Mountain. Once through customs, the team would embark on a three-hour chartered bus ride to reach Changbai.

Ever the pragmatist, Joffre cut to the chase. "And what about our equipment?"

Ben, the team's senior operational specialist, assured Joffre it would follow later. Ben elaborated, explaining that unloading cargo from an aircraft onto waiting trucks was a meticulous process. The ground crew scrutinized the cargo manifests and adhered to security protocols, including verifying seals on containers. Their specialized or oversized cargo would require even more time—perhaps three hours.

"Ben," Joffre demanded. "We don't budge without our gear. Stay with the equipment. Without it, we're mere tourists."

Eager to change subjects, Ben offered to have one of his operational specialists help Josh check his equipment, emphasizing that repacking Josh's gear using their standard travel configuration was essential.

Josh accepted Ben's offer with a quick "Certainly!" After retrieving his bags from his car, Ben introduced Josh to Dawn. "You can trust her, Josh. She's the best packer we have and also the team's medical specialist."

Dawn promptly directed Josh to dump his gear out on the floor. "Trust her, trust her," Josh repeated in his head as he spilled his clothing out onto the hanger floor.

Dawn separated Josh's clothes, promising to repack each item in separate transparent vacuum-sealed pouches. The team expected comfortable weather on the mountain—no snow, but rain.

Satisfied with Josh's selection of several pairs of jeans, t-shirts, and a windbreaker, Dawn continued combing through the pile. "Two pairs of hiking boots. Smart," Dawn commented and then offered Josh two sets of United States Geological Survey-issue Gore-Tex rain gear. Gore-Tex was an amazing fabric made from polytetrafluoroethylene (PTFE), better known by its trademark name Teflon. It effectively stopped water from passing through while allowing moisture vapor to escape from within, providing excellent breathability.

Dawn continued her inventory of travel essentials, focusing on Josh's passport. His response—that he didn't have it—caught her off guard.

"Where is it?" she demanded, her concern clear.

Josh explained that upon learning about the trip, he had airmailed his passport to A.J., one of their operational specialists. A.J. had promised to add it to the team's other passports for fast-tracking the team's visas.

Relief washed over Dawn's face. "Okay, if I know A.J., he took them directly to the Chinese consulate-general office in San Francisco. I'll check to see when his return flight is."

Moving on, Dawn asked Josh if he had any medical prescriptions.

"None," Josh assured her.

Dawn then explained that there were no specific vaccine requirements for travel to China. However, the Centers for Disease Control and Prevention (CDC) recommended being up to date on routine vaccines, including Hepatitis A and B, the flu, and COVID-19.

Josh considered his vaccines for a moment. "All good," he said, "except for the flu shot."

Dawn reassured him, noting that none of the team needed one, as the flu season had already peaked in Southern China.

Dawn demonstrated the team's standard medical pack. The travel health kit had two compartments. As Josh looked down at the floor, Dawn directed his attention to each item.

The first compartment held essential first-aid supplies: antibacterial wipes, hand sanitizer, an instant cold pack, pain relievers, scissors, self-adhesive wrap, a thermometer, and tweezers. In the second compartment, skincare essentials included aloe vera gel, antibiotic ointment, antiseptic spray and wipes, a variety of bandages, and calamine lotion. Completing the kit were gauze pads and rolls, along with medications for stomach issues—such as antacids, anti-diarrheal tablets, and rehydration salts.

Pointing to the diarrheal medication, Dawn's tone turned serious. "Josh, I know people in the United States treat diarrhea like a minor inconvenience, but it can indeed become life-threatening when traveling overseas," she urged.

Continuing in the nurse-like tone Josh was used to hearing from his wife Emily, Dawn explained how diarrhea could lead to fluid loss, especially in warmer climates or if you weren't drinking enough water. "Severe dehydration can be fatal," Dawn warned.

But Dawn wasn't done. Like Joffre's caution during the MRE demonstration, she explained that overseas, you might encounter different bacteria, parasites, or viruses that cause diarrhea.

Infections could be more aggressive and resistant to treatment. Left untreated, prolonged diarrhea prevented nutrient absorption, leading to malnutrition and weakness.

Finally, to Josh's relief, she concluded by emphasizing that consuming contaminated water or food was a common cause of traveler's diarrhea. "We bring our own water. Don't drink the local water. Don't brush your teeth with it. Keep your mouth closed in the shower," Dawn demanded.

"One more item," Dawn promised. "I need your cell phone before we leave."

Josh demanded an explanation, and Dawn clarified, "Too much of a security risk. We'll give you one of ours on the plane." The phone would contain all the team's contact information, as well as key officials' details at the U.S. Embassy in Beijing and the U.S. Consulate General in Shenyang, located 180 miles away from Changbai.

As the conversation shifted to embassies, Dawn handed Josh a brown envelope, her attention divided between the task at hand and the envelope's contents. She continued packing items into two black military-style carry bags—the kind often seen on television. Manufacturers designed these heavy-duty nylon bags to withstand extreme conditions.

Josh couldn't resist a playful remark. "Is it bulletproof?"

Dawn smiled but returned to her packing without missing a beat.

Meanwhile, Josh focused on the envelope. It bore the seal of the United States Department of State and contained a Travel Advisory for China. The contents were far from reassuring. The State Department had designated China as a Level 3 threat: Reconsider Travel—a level below the highest advisory level, Level 4: Do Not Travel. Outlined in the advisory were several risks, each of them sobering.

The People's Republic of China (PRC) government enforced local laws arbitrarily, often issuing exit bans on U.S. citizens and citizens of other countries without a fair and transparent legal process. The U.S. Department of State determined that there was a risk of wrongful detention of U.S. nationals by the PRC government in China.

But that wasn't all. The advisory warned that U.S. citizens traveling in the PRC might face detention without access to consular services or information about their alleged crimes. Interrogations and detention without fair treatment under the law were actual possibilities.

PRC authorities held broad discretion to label documents, data, and materials as state secrets, potentially leading to detainment and prosecution of foreign nationals for alleged espionage. Josh's earlier concerns about diarrhea seemed trivial in comparison.

As the team wrapped up their preparations for the trip, Josh caught up with Joffre. Despite the late hour, their appetites remained undeterred, and Joffre inquired about dinner plans.

Josh's unexpected response caught his friend off guard: "KFC." The memory of the iconic red and white KFC chicken barrel in Joffre's refrigerator from the night before had lingered in Josh's mind.

Back at their apartment, Josh and Joffre settled down with their meal, accompanied by a cold beer. They indulged in one of those cheesy end-of-the-world volcano movies that Joffre loved collecting. The scene was almost comical: two volcanologists perched on Joffre's worn-out couch (soon to be Josh's bed), dissecting the film's scientific inaccuracies. Volcanoes seemed to follow them everywhere—even the Rainier Beer they sipped featured a volcano on its label.

As the movie concluded, Joffre bid Josh goodnight. Alone, Josh dialed home to speak with Emily. Her tired voice revealed a long day at the birth center. Josh kept the call brief, sharing that the team would depart in the morning.

"Hopefully, only two weeks," Josh assured Emily. She said their boys were fast asleep and would be disappointed to miss his call, but Josh promised he would reach out again in the morning.

CHAPTER 13

MOVING DAY

Once again, Joffre's couch proved to be as comfortable as ever, leaving Josh refreshed and eager to start his day. After a quick shower, he was undeterred by his previous kitchen mishap and brewed two steaming cups of black coffee. The rich aroma filled the air, offering a comforting promise for the day ahead.

After his shower, Joffre joined Josh in the kitchen, dressed and ready for the day. He took a polite sip of his coffee, then leaned in, his voice low and conspiratorial, "How about we head back to the diner for a proper cup of coffee?"

At the diner, Jenny greeted Joffre with a familiar smile, leading them to the well-worn leather booth they had occupied just twenty-four hours earlier. Turning to Joffre, Jenny asked, "What will you have?" Her eyes sparkled as she directed the same question to Josh, amused by his surprise.

"My usual," Josh declared, and Jenny jotted down their orders. Soon, she returned with a replica of the previous day's meal—a comforting consistency in a world of uncertainties.

Midway through their quiet breakfast, a sudden call disrupted the calm. Josh glanced at Joffre. "Everything alright?"

"Yeah," Joffre replied, his tone steady. "Dawn informed me that A.J. delivered the passports. Let's roll."

Fifteen minutes later, Joffre and Josh arrived back at the Cascades Volcano Observatory, unsure when they would see it again. They made their way to the waiting passenger van, already filled with their team. Dawn exchanged their personal cellphones for official ones, handing the personal devices to a staff member who would stay behind. With this administrative task completed, Joffre and Josh boarded the white passenger van, joining a convoy of trucks and flatbeds headed for Portland International Airport.

The convoy took a swift thirty-minute drive south, crossing the Columbia River. At the airport, they bypassed the bustling passenger terminal and headed directly to the cargo center located beside the main runways. The team members stood at attention, their anticipation palpable.

Dawn leaped out of the van and strode into the customs office, clutching the team's passports and the meticulously prepared cargo manifest. The minutes that followed were tense, each second ticking by like a heartbeat. When she returned, passports in hand, her expression showed a hint of dissatisfaction.

Curious and alert, Joffre rolled down the passenger window. The crisp air, tinged with the faint scent of aviation fuel, greeted him. "What's up, Dawn?" he inquired, his voice carrying a mix of concern and impatience.

"Export controls," Dawn replied, her tone matter-of-fact. "They haven't cleared our gear yet."

Stepping out of the van, Joffre sought refuge from the unrelenting morning sun beneath a nearby Douglas-fir tree. Dawn joined him, and together, they huddled over their phones, working to untangle the bureaucratic knot.

Meanwhile, Dan, the team's IT and remote drone specialist and Josh's former field colleague, explained the delay to Josh. His words wove an intricate web of regulations—a labyrinth governing the transfer of scientific equipment across borders. These export controls aimed to prevent sensitive technologies from slipping into the wrong hands, especially those of unfriendly foreign governments.

"And what about our equipment?" Josh pressed, concern etched on his face.

"It should be exempt," Dan said, though his confidence wavered.

Emerging from the shade, Dawn and Joffre acknowledged that the Department of Commerce had fumbled the paperwork, and resolution would take time.

As a minor consolation, the cargo flight company had granted permission to park the vans in a nearby hangar while they awaited word from the Department of State and the Department of Commerce regarding the export paperwork.

"Yeah," Joffre remarked, glancing out of the passenger window. "It lacks the glamor of the arrival terminal across the way, but it's better than baking in the sun." Feeling the pressure from that morning's coffee on his aging bladder, he added, "And they have restrooms."

Josh called home.

"Hello, Cooper residence," Emily answered, her voice tinged with uncertainty as she glanced at the unfamiliar number on the caller ID. "Sorry, honey, I almost didn't answer because I didn't recognize the number."

"Understandable," Josh replied, carefully sidestepping the security concerns tied to personal phones in China. Dawn had briefed him on the risks—spyware, data theft, and hardware vulnerabilities—but he chose not to burden Emily with those details. Instead, he explained everyone had switched to official travel phones.

Emily put the boys on the speakerphone, and their warm chorus of "Love you, Dad!" enveloped the call.

"Love you too. Be good for your mom and Maya," Josh implored his sons.

Emily, always a calming presence, shared that the recent trip to the aviation museum had eased the boys' minds. They now understood better what it meant when Dad went on a plane ride. She added, "Jimmy thought you were flying in a P-40 Flying Tigers Warhawk."

The shared exchange of "I love you" signaled the end of the call.

Josh sprawled out on the hangar's cool concrete floor, the surface absorbing his body's heat. A refreshing chill seeped through his clothing, soothing his muscles and offering respite from the morning's heat. It was a grounding experience, connecting him to the solidity of the earth beneath. The cool floor beckoned contemplation—a moment to pause and perhaps find solace in its simplicity.

Soon, Joffre and Dawn appeared before the team, bearing news from Washington, D.C.: customs officials had cleared their equipment, and they could board the plane once the air handlers finished loading their gear. Joffre and the rest of the team watched as the crew meticulously stowed their equipment aboard the leased Air China Boeing 777. The wide-body twin-engine aircraft proudly displayed Air China's iconic bold red stripe along its polished fuselage, symbolizing its national identity. The airline's logo—a majestic phoenix—adorned the tail section.

As the loading neared completion, the team stood ready to board. The process unfolded unconventionally—no boarding passes, no zone instructions. A female flight attendant, dressed in a 1950s-style traditional red Chinese dress, guided each team member to their seats. They were free to choose from the thirty-six business-class seats. Beyond the curtained-off business section, over three hundred and fifty empty economy seats awaited their journey.

With everyone settled, the flight attendant closed the main cabin door. The sun hung high, casting its warmth upon the plane. Gracefully, it taxied along the taxiway, heading toward its assigned departure runway. The twin engines hummed with anticipation; their massive fan blades poised to propel the aircraft skyward. Sunlight danced on the wings.

Aligned with runway 26R, the tarmac stretched ahead—a ribbon of asphalt vanishing into the distance. Finally, the engines spooled up, their power building. Josh, seated in the front row, felt the vibration through his seat. As the pilot pushed the throttle levers forward, the engines roared to life, thrusting the massive aircraft forward. The force pressed Josh against his seat. Peering out of his window, he saw the city of Portland sprawled below—the harbor, the mountains, and the lush greenery. The Pacific Ocean glimmered in the distance.

The 777 climbed, the cityscape shrinking until a breathtaking, boundless blue sky replaced it. And so, the journey to China and the unknown began.

CHAPTER 14

TIANCHI OBSERVATORY

Josh and Joffre's team embarked on a nearly nine-hour flight from Portland to Changbaishan International Airport, covering almost five thousand miles. Their route traced a great circle northwest to Alaska, skirting the Aleutian Islands and crossing the vast expanse of the Pacific Ocean before descending along the eastern coast of Russia and China. As Josh settled into his business class seat, the flight path displayed on the screen near the bulkhead drew his attention. To his surprise, it mirrored the northern segment of the Ring of Fire—a volcanic chain encircling the Pacific Ocean. This fiery geological marvel harbored half of the world's active volcanoes and generated ninety percent of global earthquakes.

The Ring of Fire owed its existence to the restless dance of tectonic plates—massive slabs of

Earth's crust that jostled and collided like exuberant dancers on a crowded floor. Unlike fixed entities, these plates continually shifted atop the solid and molten mantle rock layer. Their interactions birthed both volcanoes and seismic events, shaping the planet's surface over eons.

As the conversation turned to Changbai, Josh shared an intriguing revelation: this mountain range defied the norm. Unlike most mountains formed through plate tectonics, Changbai's origin was unique. It had emerged from ancient fault lines rather than plate collisions. Josh emphasized that these fault troughs—large depressions caused by fault movement—had played a pivotal role.

Curious, Joffre probed further. "What are the implications for Changbai?"

Josh continued, explaining that a shallower magma chamber was significant. Its proximity to the surface meant that pressure could build up more quickly, leading to highly explosive eruptions. He noted that the dual magma chambers contributed to the complexity of Changbai's volcanic activity. The interactions between these chambers could lead to varying eruption styles, from effusive lava flows to catastrophic explosive eruptions.

Joffre pressed on. "And how deep is Changbai's chamber?"

"Two chambers," Josh replied. "One lay at a depth of three miles, while the other rested five miles below Heavenly Lake."

"Ah, Heavenly Lake," Joffre acknowledged.

"Exactly," Josh confirmed. Their geological discussion continued, fueled by the mysteries of Changbai's unconventional origins.

As they awaited lunch service, Joffre turned his attention to the in-flight movie selection. He found a film titled "Skyfire," a Chinese volcano disaster movie set twenty years ago, where an unexpected volcanic eruption wreaked havoc on Tianhuo, a fictional volcanic island off the Chinese coast. Josh laughed out loud. "How do you always find these?" he asked, poking fun at his friend.

When lunch was served, Josh leaned toward Joffre and half-jokingly said, "No MREs this time." Josh opted for Korean-style grilled beef, while Joffre chose teriyaki chicken. Each meal included a selection of stir-fried fresh mushrooms and seasonal vegetables, accompanied by wonton noodle soup. Not to be outdone by Josh, Joffre quipped, "No KFC?"

After breakfast service, the crew prepared for landing at Changchun Longjia International

Airport. Outside, fifteen hours ahead of Seattle time, the day was just beginning. As the 777 began its descent, Josh enjoyed a captivating view of the surrounding landscape. Ahead, he spotted the runway stretching out, its asphalt surface gleaming under the morning sun. The pilot skillfully guided the plane toward the tarmac, adjusting the flaps and spoilers. The gentle hum of the engines accompanied the gradual descent, and the wheels made smooth contact with the runway, slowing down the aircraft.

Outside, the airport came into view—a modern terminal building surrounded by neatly landscaped gardens. The air traffic control tower stood tall in the distance, overseeing the orderly ballet of arriving and departing flights. Once the plane reached the gate, ground crew members in fluorescent vests scurried about, ferrying suitcases from cargo holds to the terminal on baggage carts.

When the flight attendant opened the door, the scent of jet fuel mingled with the fresh air. Josh followed Joffre and Dawn down the gangway, her head scanning back and forth until she spotted what she was looking for: an expediter holding a large white poster board sign with the abbreviation "CVO" (Cascades Volcano Observatory) in large black letters.

Although his name tag displayed "Xiao Wei," the expediter insisted Dawn call him Shawn. "Shawn it is," Dawn smiled.

Shawn guided the team to the customs counter at the airport. As they followed behind Shawn and Dawn, he asked her for the team's customs declaration forms. "Nothing to declare," Dawn politely noted.

Shawn proceeded to Passport Control and stood by as each team member presented their travel documents to the customs officer. Dawn, as the first person in line from the team, spoke with the customs officer who peppered her with a list of questions: "What is your date of birth? Do you have anything to declare? Where have you flown from? Where are you staying? What is your occupation?"

Before she could respond, Shawn intervened. Speaking in Mandarin, he addressed the customs officer rapidly. Shawn's demeanor exuded authority and condescension. His voice, seasoned by years of experience, carried a weight that demanded attention. His words, though unknown to any of the team members, were deliberate, each syllable enunciated with precision. The younger officer stood rigid, eyes fixed on the man before him. Switching to English for the benefit of the team, the officer stammered, loud enough for the team members to hear, "Yes, sir, I understand."

After that, each team member needed only to present their passport to the shaken officer, who stamped their visas without hesitation. With nothing to declare, Shawn directed the team down the "Nothing to Declare Channel" (Green Channel Lane) and through the terminal to the waiting vans.

Landing at a foreign airport with their body's internal clock out of sync created a surreal experience. Josh felt a mix of excitement and fatigue—an eagerness to explore this new place tempered by the ache of sleep deprivation.

Outside the airport, a white minivan pulled alongside the curb. A gray-haired gentleman, his face marked by wrinkles and lines that conveyed years of experience and wisdom, approached Joffre. The gentleman wore a gray suit and matching pants. Joffre could only imagine what his team looked like in their ragtag assortment of jeans, t-shirts, and baseball caps.

Squinting through his glasses, the Chinese official spoke. "Mr. Wolfe, Joffre Wolfe."

"Yes," Joffre responded. "I'm Joffre Wolfe, Scientist-in-Charge of the Cascades Volcano Observatory." With a polite nod and accompanying smile, Dr. Wang shook Joffre's hand, maintaining eye contact throughout.

"Nice to meet you. I am Dr. Wang, Muchen Wang, Tianchi Volcano Observatory." Dr. Wang repeated the greeting with each team member, inquiring politely about their health during each exchange.

With the pleasantries complete, Dr. Wang directed the team to a waiting white minibus for the three-hour drive to the observatory.

The mix of unique urban views and the assortment of natural beauty kept the team glued to the windows. As they left Changchun, the road meandered through picturesque landscapes, including rolling hills, forests, and occasional glimpses of rural life. Charming villages, farmland, and roadside markets dotted the route.

Approaching the observatory, the majestic peaks of the Changbai Mountain Range came into view. The minibus' engine produced a deep clatter as it strained to climb ever upward through the dense forests that shrouded the volcanic mountains until, like a curtain unveiling before a grand stage, the dense forests gave way to reveal encircling peaks and sky.

For Josh, it was a serene and breathtaking sight that reminded him of the many volcanoes he had visited in his Northwest American home. As Josh's eyes surveyed the scene before him, the crystal-clear, emerald-green waters of Heavenly Lake, nestled within the volcanic caldera of the mountain, came into view, peering out over the caldera's crest to meet him.

As the minivan eased into the Tianchi Volcano Observatory's parking lot, Joffre's gaze fixed on the distant structure. Its gray concrete facade seemed to merge seamlessly with the volcanic ash-covered landscape, almost rendering it invisible against the desolate backdrop. In front of the building, the U.S. and Chinese flags fluttered side by side, a testament to the scientific cooperation that transcended borders.

Stepping out of the van, Josh felt the ground beneath his feet—pockmarked and ashen, strewn with jagged rocks and hardened lava flows. The air hung heavy, devoid of the usual sounds—the rustling leaves and distant bird calls replaced by an eerie silence, broken only by occasional gusts of wind that stirred the fine dust.

Sparse vegetation clung tenaciously to life—a few hardy shrubs with twisted branches, their gray-green leaves waxy and resilient. Their roots burrowed into the rocky soil, seeking sustenance where little existed. Above, the sky stretched pale and washed-out, devoid of clouds or signs of life. In this moon-like landscape, time seemed suspended—a canvas of solitude and mystery.

In the otherwise barren parking lot, a half dozen portable prefabricated container units stood. Dr. Wang proudly showcased the observatory's recent acquisition. Each of the six units comprised three sections: the top housed an office and small kitchenette, alongside a rooftop deck, while the lower level contained a bedroom and bath shower unit. An exterior steel stair led to the rooftop deck, allowing visitors access without passing through the living quarters. The pristine white units featured front-facing tinted glass walls.

Beyond the guest units, the government had provided a spacious separate kitchen and an open-air tented meeting space. Joffre expressed gratitude to his host for the generous accommodations.

"Does your staff stay onsite?" Joffre inquired.

"No," Dr. Wang replied. "Only one duty officer remains here." He explained officials hoped these accommodations would save Joffre's team time for further research. Joffre nodded, smiling politely in agreement. Dr. Wang then invited them for tea in the tent once they settled in.

"Of course," Joffre accepted, turning his attention to his road-weary team. "Alright, folks, get settled. We'll reconvene under the tent in an hour." Joffre concluded, ready to delve into the mysteries of Changbai Mountain's volcanic landscape.

Their hosts had added signs to each of the units, designating the name of the occupant. Josh thought it was a pleasant touch. He dumped his luggage and carry-on bag on the bed and looked at his watch. It was almost midnight back in Seattle. Knowing how early Emily had to get up for work, Josh sent off a quick text message to let her know he was well. He then turned his attention to unpacking. To his surprise, he discovered that Dawn had packed six MRE packages among his items. She really had thought of everything.

Josh took the time to sort out his belongings and tour the unit. No sign of wear or tear. The unit was pristine. Recently constructed, the unit had the distinctive aroma often associated with a new car. The smells, a result of the various materials used in the construction of the units, such as adhesives, plastics, and synthetic fabrics, created the scent. The smell of rich, earthy leather from the office chair contributed to the overall aroma. Josh was pleased to find that the glass wall included partitions he could open to let the fresh mountain air in.

Amidst the rugged expanse of Changbai Mountain, the American and Chinese volcanologists converged for the promised outdoor tea ceremony. The setting exuded serenity, a tranquil oasis within the volcanic wilderness.

Joffre, at the helm of the American team, settled on one side. Their attire—practical hiking gear—stood in stark contrast to the Chinese team's more formal garments. Dr. Wang, the gracious host, greeted everyone with a nod and a warm smile.

A rustic wooden table graced the center, adorned with delicate porcelain teapots and cups. The air carried the mingling scents of brewed tea and the earthy soil that cradled the mountain's secrets. With graceful precision, Dr. Wang poured the first cup, explaining each step—the rinsing of leaves, the precise water temperature, and the art of pouring.

Joffre listened intently. As they sipped the fragrant brew of the strong black tea, nods of approval passed between them. Across the table, the Chinese volcanologists engaged in animated conversation and laughter.

As the sun dipped behind the mountain peaks, stories flowed freely. The Americans recounted tales of Mount St. Helens and Yellowstone, while the Chinese wove legends of Changbai's fiery origins. Both sides marveled at nature's raw power—the same force that fueled their shared passion for volcanology.

In the fading light, they raised their cups in a toast—to discovery, unity, and the promise of collaboration. The tea warmed their hearts, binding them across cultures and continents. As darkness settled, they pledged to unravel Changbai's mysteries together—one cup of tea at a time.

CHAPTER 15

AT THE CALDERA'S EDGE

After the group meeting, Josh headed to his quarters and fell fast asleep. The unfamiliar ring of the room's telephone jolted him awake. It was Dawn, asking if he would join the team for breakfast. "Damn," Josh thought, realizing he hadn't set an alarm. His groggy voice emerged like a whisper wrapped in a soft fog, each syllable stumbling from the depths of slumber. Still half-immersed in a dream of home, he hoped Dawn wouldn't detect his lingering drowsiness. "Be right there," he managed to say.

Alone in his room, Josh rummaged through his carry bag, searching for his government-issued cellphone. Clearing his head, he realized that 6:45 am in Changbai corresponded to 3:45 pm the previous day in Seattle. Emily would still be at work. Probably for the better, he thought, knowing he was already late. Josh showered, dressed quickly, and met the team, who were already fast at work, preparing their MREs for breakfast.

Dawn found Josh and asked how he slept.

"A little more than I wanted to," he replied sheepishly, and thanked her for checking in on him.

Dawn explained to Josh how much Joffre valued team meetings.

"He wouldn't admit it to anyone, but he really loves them," she said. She detailed how Joffre, as a team leader, used the meetings to ensure that everyone agreed on and understood their roles and priorities, aligning them toward a common goal. Dawn appreciated how these meetings strengthened relationships and cohesion among team members, fostering camaraderie and trust through regular interactions.

"Yeah, I know it sounds corny," Dawn admitted, but she explained how Joffre felt these meetings provided a platform to share important information, updates, and insights. "Josh, I know you are new to the team, but trust me, we all encourage open discussions and want team members to voice any concerns and ask questions."

Almost as if on cue, Joffre rose to address the team. He thanked everyone for making the trip and expressed his excitement about the opportunity to work together in the field. As Dawn had predicted, Joffre emphasized that the visit's primary aim was to aid their Chinese counterparts, punctuating his statement with a firm "Period." He said, "If what you're doing isn't helping to enhance their understanding of the volcano, then stop. Reassess and reorient." Joffre asked if anyone had questions. There were none.

As the sun rose over the horizon, the American team, buzzing with anticipation, eagerly crossed the parking lot to the main three-story ash-colored building. Members from each team paired up with their respective distinguished counterparts and disappeared into the building to begin their collaboration. Josh convinced Joffre that he could best serve the team and his mission by floating between meetings as an observer. Joffre agreed and informed the other team members of Josh's unique role during that morning's breakfast meeting.

Cleared to proceed, Josh joined American seismologist Dr. Maria Chen in her meeting with her Chinese counterpart, Dr. Li Wei, a man. Reflecting on his colleague, the Chinese analyst at the Pentagon, Josh realized that the name Li could be both feminine and masculine. Together, the two seismologists pored over notes, seismic charts, and Dr. Wei's meticulous analysis of earthquake patterns and the insights he drew from the restless magma beneath the mountain.

The earliest eruption, known as the Millennium Eruption, occurred around 969 AD and was one of the largest explosive eruptions in the last 5,000 years. It released over eleven cubic miles of magma, or seventy-seven billion tons of debris—enough material to build over five hundred Great Walls of China. To put it in perspective, this was about twice the volume of the 1883 Krakatau eruption. The Millennium Eruption caused pumice and ash to fall as far away as northern Japan, over 600 miles to the east. The eruption left a large, bowl-shaped depression (caldera), now filled by Heavenly Lake.

Recent seismic activity was far less dramatic. The last recorded eruption was a minor explosion in April 1903. Dr. Wei noted that, in terms of volcanic activity, the volcano was dormant, except for a brief period from mid-2002 to mid-2005. During this time, earthquake swarms increased from an annual average of several dozen in 2004 to a peak of over seven hundred swarms in 2005, before returning to normal historical levels. However, Dr. Wei added, the volcano remained a concern because of its potential hazards. Lahars (mudflows) from the large lake within the three-mile-wide caldera posed a threat to the over 1.4 million nearby North Korean and Chinese people living near or on the slopes of the volcano. As the conversation continued, Josh explained he had to attend another meeting.

Josh found his friend Dan, the team's IT and remote pilot specialist, meeting with Dr. Wu Zhang, the Chinese team's data scientist. Dressed in a traditional Chinese robe, Dr. Zhang, like his teammates, spoke perfect English. Dr. Zhang shared with Dan a wealth of data from diverse sources, including satellite imagery, drone footage, and ground-based sensors.

With a flourish, Dr. Zhang demonstrated a 3D model of the volcanic system, revealing hidden magma chambers and conduits. China's advancements in using Computer-Aided Design (CAD) modeling methods impressed Dan, and he expressed his admiration for the model to Dr. Zhang. However, he added the important caveat that the lack of data constrained the model. Dan then promised that the array of drones he had brought along could help increase the data stream available to the team. Not wanting to insult his host, Dan refrained from mentioning that the

American drones were superior, choosing instead to emphasize the opportunity to collect more data.

But Dan knew better. American scientists, including him, had been at the forefront of using drones to monitor volcanoes and employed innovative techniques different from those used by Chinese scientists. They attached gas detectors to drones and flew them over volcanic vents. By measuring gas output, scientists could assess changes in volcanic activity, effectively allowing them to "smell" if a volcano's behavior was shifting. Gas samples collected directly from volcanic vents by drones helped volcanologists determine the composition and concentration of gases, such as sulfur dioxide, carbon dioxide, and hydrogen sulfide. Changes in these gas emissions could signal volcanic unrest or imminent eruptions.

Chinese scientists, like their American counterparts, used drones to capture high-resolution still and thermal images of volcanic terrain. These images helped monitor changes in topography, detect new cracks, and assess volcanic deformation. American scientists further used this drone data for 3D modeling. By combining detailed drone imagery with satellite data that provided a broader perspective, they developed an integrated approach to monitoring volcanic activity. This approach enabled the tracking of ash clouds, lava flows, and ground deformation over extensive volcanic areas, enhancing the understanding of volcanic processes. By comparing successive images, scientists could identify changes such as new cracks or fissures.

As the American team gathered for their lunch meeting, Joffre eagerly received reports from each member. He reminded them that collaboration and knowledge exchange between scientists worldwide were crucial for better understanding volcanic processes. "It benefits everyone involved," Joffre concluded.

For the next steps, Joffre urged his team to engage with their Chinese counterparts to understand the equipment they had deployed in the field. He emphasized the importance of working with Dan to integrate their equipment and enhance the data. He encouraged his team to explore opportunities to offer their equipment to the observatory.

To wrap up the meeting, Joffre used an old-fashioned chalkboard in the tent to jot down three critical questions:

1. "What equipment do they have?"
2. "How is their equipment connected?"
3. "What do they need?"

After the meeting, Josh excused himself from lunch to contact Emily at home. As he dialed her number, the phone rang with a distinct tone and cadence, noticeably different from the familiar sounds of U.S. carriers. After a few rings, Maya's cheerful voice greeted him.

"Mr. Josh, is that you?" Maya asked. She then informed him that Emily and the boys were out. Josh thanked her and resolved to reach Emily on her cell phone.

Josh eventually connected with Emily at the Lion Heart bookstore, a cozy Seattle classic with a robust children's section. Relief infused her voice as she asked, "Josh, are you safe?"

"Yes," Josh assured her. "Can I say hi to the boys?"

"Of course, let me find them," Emily replied, navigating the bookstore's maze of bookshelves and aisles. Finally, she triumphantly declared, "Go ahead, here's Johnny."

Jimmy's book selection at the store became the topic of conversation. Johnny revealed his brother had stumbled upon "The Wheedle on The Needle," a local Seattle legend ingrained in every child's upbringing. The story revolved around a creature called the Wheedle, who once lived peacefully in the forests of the Pacific Northwest. However, as the bustling city of Seattle expanded, the incessant noise and activity disrupted the Wheedle's serene home.

Seeking refuge, the Wheedle climbed atop the newly constructed Space Needle, hoping to find solace above the city's clamor. From his perch, he watched over the city, longing for the quiet he once knew. To keep the city quiet at night, the Wheedle placed a bright red blinking light on top of the Space Needle, which would blink whenever the city grew too noisy, reminding the people below to be quiet and respectful.

Despite already having a copy of the book at home, Josh understood Jimmy's desire for his own copy. He returned to the phone with Emily, expressing gratitude for her excellent care of the boys.

As he kissed the receiver, he promised to call back tomorrow.

CHAPTER 16

IN THE FIELD

After breakfast, the American team buzzed with excitement as their equipment arrived, accompanied by Ben and Victor, who had shepherded it from the airport. But it wasn't just the American gear that made its appearance. While the American team unpacked and unloaded their equipment, the Chinese team received a delivery of all-terrain two-man vehicles (ATVs).

Joffre and Dawn stood side by side, sipping coffee, their eyes fixed on the ATVs. Joffre recognized their potential for exploring the various monitoring sites scattered across Changbai Mountain. Using ATVs instead of trudging on foot would significantly cut down their ground time. Turning to his trusted operational specialist, Dawn, Joffre posed the obvious question: "Dawn, why didn't we think of this?"

Joffre and Dawn discussed the logistics of incorporating the ATVs into their operations. "These vehicles will be a game changer," Dawn said, her eyes gleaming with excitement. "We can cover more ground and get to the remote monitoring sites much faster."

Joffre nodded in agreement, already mapping out their new strategy. "We'll need to coordinate with the Chinese team and see how we can best use these."

Meanwhile, Josh approached Ben and Victor, who appeared sleep-deprived after their airport ordeal. Victor's dedication to his pioneering acoustic imaging equipment was clear; he had volunteered to stay behind with Ben to oversee the equipment's offloading and transport to Changbai. Victor also held a deep appreciation for his submersible vehicle, its sonar being the most sensitive military-grade equipment the team had brought along.

"Rough trip?" Josh teased, but Ben and Victor ignored the jest, their focus fixed on the cargo handlers using forklifts to unload their equipment from the flatbed trailer. Victor's eyes widened in alarm as he spotted a large gash along the crate containing his precious acoustic gear.

Victor quickly moved closer, examining the damage with a mixture of anxiety and frustration. “This can’t be happening,” he muttered under his breath, running his hand over the splintered wood.

Ben, equally concerned, joined him. “Let’s hope the contents are intact,” he said, trying to keep his voice steady.

Josh, sensing the tension, offered a reassuring pat on Victor’s shoulder. “We’ll get it sorted, Victor. Let’s check it out and see what needs to be done.”

With careful precision, they pried open the crate, revealing the sophisticated acoustic imaging equipment inside. Despite the external damage, the equipment appeared unharmed. Victor let out a sigh of relief, his shoulders relaxing slightly.

Crisis averted; Joffre introduced Victor to Dr. Wang. “Dr. Wang, allow me to introduce my esteemed colleague, Dr. Victor Müller, a pioneer in acoustic imaging.” Joffre prompted Victor to explain his equipment to Dr. Wang while Ben supervised the uncrating of the equipment.

Dr. Wang listened intently as Victor, now calmer, explained how the submersible vehicle with hydro acoustics could map Mount Changbai’s lake floor. “Single beam?” Dr. Wang inquired.

"No," Victor boasted, "multi-beam." He elaborated that his system employed multiple simultaneous beams, providing detailed coverage over a wider area—a crucial advantage for their scientific mission.

Victor's focus shifted back to the equipment laid out before him. His keen eyes scanned for any signs of damage, and there it was—the unit's orange radio head, bent free from its mounting bracket. The GPS component incorporated expensive innovative technology, ensuring unparalleled accuracy. Beyond GPS data, the sonar relied on the radio head to transmit survey data. This combination of pinpoint accuracy and robust performance made the radio head an ideal tool for Victor's surveying needs.

Noticing Victor's concern, Joffre attempted to console him. "Victor, the rest of the team is about to embark on their field survey," he said, his tone gentle yet firm. "Why don't you and Ben grab a meal and some rest? Afterward, we can test and troubleshoot the unit."

Victor hesitated for a moment; his eyes still fixed on the damaged equipment. But Joffre's words made sense; exhaustion wouldn't help them solve the problem. He nodded in agreement. "Alright, we'll take a break."

Joffre clapped him on the shoulder. “Good. We’ll need you at your best.”

Ben, who had been listening nearby, joined them. “Come on, Victor. Let’s get some food.”

As they walked towards the makeshift dining area, Victor couldn’t help but feel a mix of frustration and relief. The damage was significant, but not insurmountable. With some rest and a clear mind, he was confident they could repair it and proceed with their mission.

Meanwhile, Joffre and Dr. Wang continued discussing the logistics of their collaborative efforts. The arrival of the American equipment and the Chinese ATVs had sparked new possibilities for their research. Both teams were eager to share their expertise and learn from each other.

In the dining area, Ben and Victor found a spread of local delicacies prepared by the Chinese team. The aromatic dishes and the warm, inviting atmosphere provided a much-needed respite from the morning’s stress. As they ate, Ben tried to lighten the mood with stories from their travels, and slowly, Victor’s tense demeanor began to relax.

By the time they finished their meal, Victor felt more composed. “Let’s get some rest and then tackle that radio head,” he said, a determined look in his eyes.

"Sounds like a plan," Ben agreed, grateful for the brief respite. They made their way to their quarters, ready to recharge and face the challenges ahead.

Back at the equipment area, Joffre and Dr. Wang were completing plans for the day's fieldwork. The teams were eager to begin their exploration of Changbai Mountain, using the latest technology to uncover its secrets. As the sun climbed higher in the sky, casting a warm glow over the camp, there was a palpable sense of anticipation and collaboration in the air.

With the combined efforts of the American and Chinese scientists, they were ready to embark on a groundbreaking mission—one that promised to deepen their understanding of the volcanic landscape and forge stronger ties between their respective teams.

Meanwhile, the rest of Joffre's team focused on the survey plans. Collaborating with their Chinese counterparts, they aimed to visit and enhance the observatory's field sensors, with seismic sensors taking precedence. The observatory boasted eleven strategically placed seismograph stations around the volcano, which detected ground vibrations caused by magma movement, tremors, and earthquakes.

Changbai's permanent seismograph stations relied on cable transmissions and hard disk storage to transmit data to the observatory for analysis. The observatory deployed three hundred and sixty portable seismographs for monitoring seismic activity. These state-of-the-art short-period seismographs were compact, functional, and energy-efficient, intended for emergency observations rather than long-term use.

The plan involved upgrading the permanent seismographs with new, state-of-the-art electronic sensors. These upgraded sensors promised more precise ground motion measurements. Dan, the American team's data specialist, and his counterpart, Dr. Zhang, would integrate the station outputs into a new network for efficient seismic data processing and real-time monitoring. Working in pairs, the group aimed to complete the project in a day. Follow-on integration, testing, and calibration would extend over a few weeks, a task the Chinese team would handle after Joffre's departure.

Josh teamed up with Dr. Jiānglóng Liu, a seismologist who worked alongside Dr. Maria Chen. Together, they set off toward their first assigned seismograph station. The scientists had strategically spaced the eleven seismograph stations to ensure comprehensive monitoring of seismic activity across the region. They placed several stations near the summit, including one at the crater lake (Heavenly Lake), to monitor volcanic activity. Additional scientists distributed stations along the upper slopes to capture data from different elevations. They positioned a few stations around the mid-slopes to ensure coverage between the summit and the base, and finally, several stations sat at the base of the mountain to monitor seismic waves traveling through the broader area. This distribution allowed the scientists to triangulate the location of seismic events and provided a detailed picture of the seismic activity associated with Changbai Mountain.

Navigating rocky slopes and uneven terrain thrilled them, surrounded by the mountain's breathtaking natural beauty. Jiānglóng, responsible for collecting data from the hard disk storage units monthly, knew the trails well, and the pair swiftly reached the first site.

Jiānglóng and Josh collaborated to upgrade the station. He expertly guided Josh through the aging equipment, while Josh deftly installed the new electronics, mentoring Jiānglóng as they worked. As lunchtime approached, Josh suggested a break before tackling the next station.

To Jiānglóng's delight, Josh offered him an MRE package—an unfamiliar experience for Jiānglóng. Soon, the two men chatted, laughed, and unwrapped the contents like eager siblings on Christmas morning, their voices echoing across the mountain.

Before heading to the next site, Josh asked Jiānglóng if he didn't mind if he took a minute to call home before it was too late.

"Of course," Jiānglóng replied.

Stepping away, Josh retrieved his cellphone from his bag and dialed Emily's number. The hour was late, and the boys lay fast asleep in their beds. Their conversation shifted to the day's work—details Josh couldn't fully disclose because of the sensitive nature of his location. But that didn't stop him from weaving vivid tales of the outdoors, the exhilaration of that morning's ATV ride, and the wind tousling his hair.

Emily listened intently, her heart swelling with pride. Over the previous year, Josh had voluntarily confined himself within the sterile walls of a classroom, focusing on teaching equations and theories. Now, as he recounted the thrill of the ride, she glimpsed a different man—a man who belonged to the wild, untamed world beyond textbooks. His words were more than mere conversation; they unveiled his true self, like a butterfly emerging from its cocoon.

As they bid each other goodnight, Emily's voice held a promise: "When you return, let's take the boys for an ATV ride."

"Love it. Love you," Josh concluded. "Tell the boys I love them."

After lunch, the two scientists tidied up the site and hopped onto the ATV. Thirty minutes later, they reached the next station. Josh proposed reversing roles, having Jiānglóng install the new equipment. Although it would take longer, Josh wanted to ensure Jiānglóng grasped the installation process.

Josh, serving as an instructor, employed the fundamental "Tell-Show-Do" teaching strategy. He began by explaining the steps involved in installing the new equipment (tell), then demonstrated the process (show), and finally allowed Jiānglóng to apply what he had learned (do). Josh believed in this approach because it created an authentic and engaging learning experience that bridged theory and practice.

With the installation complete, Jiānglóng extended a traditional Chinese cup of tea to Josh. Graciously accepting, Josh settled quietly on the blanket his colleague had provided and observed Jiānglóng's deft movements as he prepared the tea.

At the heart of the tea set rested a clay teapot—an ancient vessel that absorbed tea flavors over time, enhancing subsequent brews. Josh's eyes lingered on the pair of small teacups, wondering if they were porcelain or ceramic. He refrained from interrupting Jiānglóng, who was setting up a small alcohol burner.

Within minutes, the water reached the desired temperature. Jiānglóng filled a stainless-steel strainer with loose oolong leaf tea and dipped it into the teapot for steeping. After a mere two or three minutes, he placed the teacups on an ornate mat adorned with mountain scenes and offered the first cup to Josh.

Josh allowed the tea to roll across his palate, savoring its delightful balance between green and black tea. The flavor was fragrant, smooth, and complex, with hints of blooming flowers and a subtle fruitiness. Beyond the taste, the joy lay in their connection with nature—the serene outdoor setting revitalizing both Josh and Jiānglóng.

As the sun dipped lower, casting long shadows, they made their way back to the observatory, hearts warmed by more than just tea.

CHAPTER 17

THE BEAST

As the American team convened for breakfast, Joffre outlined their ambitious plan for the day. Two teams would examine the observatory's ground deformation monitoring equipment, which tracked changes in the volcano and its surrounding land. Another pair would collect gas samples from five vents on the volcano's northern and western slopes. By analyzing the chemical composition and emission rates of volcanic gases, such as water vapor, carbon dioxide, and sulfur dioxide, volcanologists could gain valuable insights into the physical and chemical processes within the volcanic system. Meanwhile, Dan planned to launch a fleet of drones to enhance both the ground deformation and gas sample surveys. Last, Josh volunteered to assist Victor with setting up his sonar survey of Heavenly

Lake.

American seismologist Dr. Maria Chen and her Chinese counterpart Dr. Li Wei boarded an ATV and headed to the first ground deformation site. The scientists at Changbai employed various methods to monitor ground deformation, especially around volcanic areas, with GPS being among the most effective. Originally designed for navigation, GPS used satellite signals to calculate precise distances. By monitoring a network of GPS stations, they could track ground position changes with millimeter accuracy.

To protect it from the elements, they housed one unique set of survey equipment in a cave. This included a tiltmeter, a strain meter, and a tidal gravity meter. A tiltmeter measures the tilt or angular displacement of a surface, detecting even minor changes caused by the dynamic forces around a volcano. Dr. Chen and Dr. Wei planned to upgrade the tiltmeter by replacing its irregular data logger with one providing continuous wireless communication.

The strain meter in the cave monitored volcanic activity differently. It used a thin metallic strip arranged in a zigzag pattern on a non-conductive carrier to amplify small stresses for accurate measurement. When deformation occurred, the strain gauge detected minor changes in resistance, allowing it to calculate induced stresses. Traditionally, the strain meter stored its data on multimedia cards, which Changbai scientists retrieved and uploaded weekly to a computer. Today's plan was to upgrade this instrument to provide continuous wireless communication.

Their last task in the cave was troubleshooting the tidal gravity meter, which had stopped transmitting data. A tidal gravity meter measures variations in gravitational force caused by Earth's tides. The gravitational pull from the Moon and the Sun creates tidal forces, causing ocean water to rise and fall. Tidal gravity meters use sensitive accelerometers to detect tiny changes in gravity because of these tidal forces, including the subtle movement of magma within the mountain.

After completing their work in the cave, Dr. Chen and Dr. Wei planned to inspect a level line survey system used by Changbai scientists since 2002. Level lines, though not commonly used for measuring volcanic deformation, intrigued Dr. Chen, who was eager to observe Dr. Wei at work. A level line survey measures changes in elevation along a specific route using precise instruments like bubble levels.

These levels consisted of a frame with a glass tube filled with liquid, typically colored alcohol, and an air bubble. Traditionally used by carpenters, stonemasons, and surveyors for precise alignments, this instrument now aids in detecting ground deformation caused by volcanic activity.

In the heart of Changbai Mountain, Dr. Chen and Dr. Wei meticulously calibrated their scientific equipment within the dimly lit cave. As they worked, they communicated seamlessly, each bringing their expertise to the task. Their collaboration highlighted the importance of international teamwork in advancing scientific understanding and monitoring natural hazards. The upgrades they implemented would significantly enhance the observatory's ability to monitor Changbai's volcanic activity in real-time, providing crucial data for predicting potential eruptions and ensuring the safety of nearby communities.

Meanwhile, Dan—the team's IT specialist and seasoned remote pilot—collaborated with Dr. Wu Zhang, the Chinese team's astute data scientist. Their mission: to establish a makeshift airport in the observatory's parking lot, a launchpad for Dan's fleet of drones.

Dan had designed purpose-built landing pads with gray interlocking surfaces specifically engineered for drone operations. These pads provided stability during takeoff and landing, ensuring the safety of the airborne fleet. However, the true linchpin of their endeavor was the software—a marvel of modern engineering—that Dan had crafted. He designed this innovative solution for the unique landscape of Changbai Mountain, enabling the simultaneous deployment of multiple drones. Like a harmonious hive, the drones operated as a coordinated unit, each following predefined flight paths autonomously.

As the sun climbed higher, Dan started the first flight: six drones ascending in unison. Their cameras whirred to life, capturing images from various angles—craters, ridges, and ancient lava flows. The mountain revealed its secrets through their digital eyes. But Dan's quest didn't end there. Four additional drones awaited their turn. These specialized units carried gas analyzers, poised to sniff the air at scattered volcanic vents. Sulfur dioxide, a telltale sign of subterranean activity, would be their target.

As the symphony of drones soared, Dan and Dr. Zhang stood side by side, eyes fixed on the horizon. The distant hum of propellers blended with the mountain's murmurs. Together, they witnessed technology and nature dance—an orchestra of data gathering, a collective quest to unveil the volcano's hidden truths.

In the last mission of the day, Victor and Josh prepared Victor's massive, hand-built sonar system for transport to Heavenly Lake. The system included the primary sensor array, communication package, diesel generator, and fuel tanks. Their task was straightforward: move Victor's equipment to the lake and install it on a barge provided by the observatory, perched over a thousand feet below the lake's edge. Prior to their arrival, observatory specialists meticulously constructed the barge to Victor's specifications. It featured strategically mounted batteries that, once charged by the generator, would supply power to the array, communication gear, and two electric thrusters. These thrusters would propel the craft to its designated location at the lake's center and continuously adjust its position to keep the barge centered in the lake. To avoid disrupting sonar observations, the team relied on silent battery power during critical periods.

With care, Victor and Josh loaded the hefty diesel engine onto one trailer, followed by two fuel tanks on another. The sensor system and communication package would have to wait for a subsequent trip. As they descended the treacherous volcanic slopes of Changbai Mountain, adrenaline surged through their veins. Riding all-terrain vehicles (ATVs), they clung to the handlebars, navigating a narrow dirt path that hugged the precipitous edges of cliffs. The knobby tires of their ATVs gripped the loose volcanic soil, and Victor deftly balanced his weight to prevent the trailer from jackknifing. With foot brake and hand brake engaged, they maintained control, their hearts racing amidst the rugged grandeur of the mountain terrain.

As Josh descended, the harsh terrain seemed unyielding. The ATV's rear wheels occasionally skidded, but Josh deftly adjusted the throttle, seeking the delicate balance between traction and momentum. Too little throttle, and he risked stalling; too much, and disaster loomed. The trail narrowed further, and Victor, leading the way, navigated hairpin turns with precision, his trailer obediently following. Josh's knuckles whitened as he countered gravity's pull, the volcanic rock crunching beneath the tires. He willed the brakes to hold, finally reaching the lake's edge alongside Victor.

As they parked the ATVs and unhooked the trailers, Victor gazed out at the raw beauty of the lake, quietly hoping that the journey's reward would justify the risk.

Josh suggested a lunch break before they retraced their path up the slopes to collect the remaining equipment. Secretly, he hoped to use the time to call home and catch his sons before their bedtime routine.

Sitting by the tranquil lake, Josh retrieved his cell phone and dialed home. As expected, Emily was busy putting Johnny and Jimmy to bed, but she gladly paused their routine to let them speak with their dad. Josh's heart swelled as he heard their joyful screams of "Daddy!" For the first time since his departure, the boys were curious about his whereabouts. Josh hesitated for a moment, then decided there was no harm in sharing the truth: he was on a mountain, exploring a volcano.

"Cool!" the boys echoed in unison.

"Love you. Let me talk to your mom, please," Josh requested, beckoning to them. Anticipation bubbled within him as he prepared to update Emily on the team's remarkable progress.

"Honey, I think we could be back in a couple of days," Josh proudly informed his wife.

"Seattle?" Emily inquired.

"Yes, but first, I'll need to stop in D.C. to debrief Roger's team at the Pentagon, then it's on to Seattle," Josh pledged before ending the call.

Josh and Victor sat on the shore of Heavenly Lake, their MRE lunch spread out before them. The lake's natural beauty captivated them—the emerald-green waters created a serene, reflective surface that seemed to pause time itself, mirroring the encircling peaks and sky.

The buzz of one of Dan's circling drones interrupted their meditative moment. Victor and Dan refocused on their task. Working seamlessly together, they swiftly mounted the diesel engine and installed the fuel tanks onto the waiting barge. A quick trip back up the mountain retrieved the sensor system and communication package, completing the installation. As they prepared to power up the barge, allowing the electric thrusters to propel it toward its designated station at the lake's center, Josh raised his hand to signal a pause.

"Wait, Victor," Josh argued, "we should christen the barge."

"Like christening a ship when it's launched?" Victor asked.

"Yes, exactly. But what name should we give it?" Josh pondered.

After a brief reflection, Victor picked up an open water bottle and splashed it against the barge's front. "I christen you 'the Beast," Victor declared. With a flip of a switch on the barge's control panel, the thrusters came to life, guided by the onboard GPS as the barge began its crawl toward the lake's center.

Overjoyed with their successful mission, Victor and Josh mounted their ATVs and raced up the steep slope of the caldera. Amidst the rugged terrain, they embarked on an exhilarating race. Their ATVs roared, tires gripping the volcanic soil as they climbed higher. The sun painted the sky orange and gold, casting long shadows across the rocky landscape.

Victor, the daredevil, leaned into the curves, adrenaline surging. Josh followed closely, equally determined. The thrill intensified—the race wasn't just about speed; it was a dance with danger, a celebration of their shared passion for volcanoes.

Fate intervened abruptly. Victor's ATV collided with a loose rock, catapulting him into a tumble, his leg trapped beneath the machine. Pain surged through him, echoing across the barren landscape as he let out a primal scream. Josh, skidding to a halt, wore concern etched across his face. Without hesitation, he dismounted, hurrying to Victor's side. Together, they limped toward Josh's ATV. Victor leaned against him, and Josh revved the engine, tires biting into the volcanic soil. As they reached the caldera's rim, Victor's pain eased, and he surveyed the vast expanse—the dormant volcano and the crater lake shimmering far below. Josh's eyes met his, gratitude and camaraderie passing between them. They weren't mere colleagues; they were partners in this daring quest for knowledge.

Josh guided Victor to Dawn, the team's medical specialist, who was waiting for them. Besides scrapes and bruises, Dawn noticed Victor's swollen right knee. Victor, however, was more focused on his prized sonar system. He insisted Josh take him to the observatory to assess the equipment's condition.

Inside the observatory, Victor monitored the sonar equipment's communication signals, growing alarmed. The GPS signal wavered—something was amiss. Meanwhile, Dawn remained indifferent to Victor's sonar gear, urging him to seek medical attention for his knee. Victor stood firm.

"You don't understand," he asserted. "Without a clear GPS signal, the thrusters won't know when they've reached their designated location. They could propel the barge all the way to North Korea's side of the lake."

Josh intervened, proposing a compromise. If Victor allowed Dawn to take him to the hospital, Josh would return to the lake. Armed with the rigid-hull inflatable boat (RIB) anchored there, he'd attempt to fix the GPS signal.

"Just tell me what to do," Josh pleaded.

With that promise, Victor agreed to Dawn's demand. He instructed Josh to take the spare communication unit he'd planned to leave with the Chinese team and swap it out on the barge.

"It's straightforward," Victor assured him. "The unit unscrews easily. Unplug the three wires and replace the unit. Easy peasy."

"How will I find the barge?" Josh asked. "The lake is vast."

Victor lumbered over to his workbench, handing Josh a portable GPS monitor. "Go to these coordinates," Victor insisted, explaining that the monitor should pick up intermittent signals from the barge's GPS. "And if all else fails, look for the white navigation light on the barge."

CHAPTER 18

HEAVENLY LAKE

Josh, with the portable GPS monitor snug in his pocket, grabbed the spare communication unit and dashed towards the ATV. Time pressed against him—it was a race to reach the barge, effect repairs, and return to shore. The lake, elliptical and sprawling, stretched three miles from north to south and two miles from east to west. According to Victor's calculations, the barge rested near the lake's center, straddling the imaginary Chinese-Korean border that sliced through its heart.

The steep path to the water's edge lay before Josh, with Victor's abandoned blue ATV standing as a silent witness. As he reached the shore, he squinted across the jade expanse. The lake and sky blurred together, forming a seamless gradient of blue and green. There was no sign of the barge.

His destination awaited: the rigid inflatable boat (RIB). Its design was a marvel—a fiberglass hull rigid enough for stability and performance, crowned with inflatable tubes. These tubes, inflated to high pressure, granted buoyancy and absorbed impact. The boat was perfect for rough waters, though today the lake lay as tranquil as polished glass.

One quirk caught Josh's eye: electric outboard motors adorned the RIB, an unusual choice. His Chinese colleagues likely opted for silence, ensuring the engines' hum wouldn't disturb Victor's sonar equipment. Josh's pursuit wouldn't be a high-speed chase across the water; it would be a deliberate crawl at a turtle's pace.

Toward the lake's center, Josh ventured, eyes scanning the surface. Then, a distant thrum—a diesel engine's muffled rhythm. Victory. But why was the barge's generator on? Victor had charged the batteries. Puzzling, indeed.

Josh's RIB sliced through the water, its bow aimed at the distant diesel engine's thrum. The sun, a molten disc, cast blinding brilliance upon the lake's surface, obscuring his view. As the haze lifted, it revealed not the barge but two formidable patrol boats—each fifty feet of sleek menace. Their coxswains steered with precision, flanking Josh's vessel.

Olive-green-clad crewmembers stood sentinel on the patrol boats, machine guns slung over their shoulders. The weapons mirrored the ones mounted on the boats' bows. A blue and white flag fluttered defiantly at each stern, marking their allegiance.

Josh's mind raced as the patrol boats circled, forcing him to halt. Their crewmembers barked orders, a cacophony of urgency. The handheld machine guns, now leveled at Josh, spoke a universal language: Stop! He killed the electric engines and raised his hands in surrender.

Two crew members stepped onto Josh's RIB, embodying unyielding authority. Their eyes bore silent threats, devoid of empathy or remorse. Another crew member searched the vessel, eyes sharp as flint, dissecting every inch.

Silent cues orchestrated their actions: they forced Josh to his knees, bound his hands behind his back, secured his legs, and muffled his mouth with a cloth gag. They hoisted him into one of their patrol boats, events unfolding faster than comprehension allowed.

Back on the RIB, the two crew members continued their search. They retrieved the handheld GPS monitor and the sonar radio head, transferring them to their boat. Once back onboard their patrol boat, standing next to Josh, one crew member unslung his machine gun. He slid back the bolt, revealing the chamber—causing a metallic click that jolted Josh. The crew member loaded the magazine, savoring Josh's involuntary flinch. The well of the machine gun snapped shut, seemingly sealing Josh's fate in cold steel.

Josh's breath grew heavy, resignation settling over him like a shroud. He turned his thoughts inward, no longer grappling with the chaos unfolding around him, but focusing on his wife and sons. As he closed his eyes, the staccato bursts of machine-gun fire pierced the air. Relief washed over him when he reopened his eyes—the shots had targeted his boat, not him.

Chaos erupted. Gunfire tore into the rubbery skin of the vessel, leaving gaping holes. The inflatable tubes surrendered, and the boat shuddered, its buoyancy betrayed. Water surged, swallowing the vessel whole. Bubbles escaped from the vanishing hull, a desperate plea for survival. Then, silence—an eerie void where chaos once reigned. The boat slipped beneath the waves.

The crew's attention shifted to Josh. They shrouded him in darkness, a black cloth over his head, and flung him onto the boat's floor. His back pressed against the very equipment they'd removed. Josh fought for composure, each breath a struggle against the clinging hood.

The diesel engine roared, accelerating the boat toward an unknown destination. But these sensations sparked a realization: other senses remained. Determination surged within him. The equipment's sharp edges pressed against his back—it was the sonar communication array. Victor's words echoed: lithium backup batteries. The radio unit contained backup batteries.

With his hands bound behind him, Josh fumbled for the switch. His fingertips brushed the cover's smooth surface—a blend of rigidity and flexibility that shielded the delicate switch yet yielded to movement. Microscopic ridges provided grip, even when wet. And then, the moment of truth: he depressed the switch. A soft click, discernible only to his fingers. A minor victory—the unseen smile beneath his black hood defying his captors.

Back ashore, the American team assembled for their evening meeting and dinner. Joffre, the seasoned leader, scanned the group, noting three vacant seats. His thoughts raced: Dawn had accompanied Victor to the hospital for his injured leg, but where was Josh?

"Has anyone seen Josh?" Joffre inquired.

"Probably on the phone home," Ben suggested.

"Or asleep," Dan quipped.

"Dan, check on him," Joffre instructed.

Minutes later, Dan returned, shaking his head. Josh was nowhere to be found in his unit. Joffre's concern deepened. He reached for his radio, but Dan halted him, pointing out he had seen Josh's radio on the charger next to his bed, alongside his cellphone.

"Maybe Josh went to town with Dawn and Victor," Dan speculated.

Joffre switched to his cellphone, dialing Dawn. Her voice crackled through the line: "Victor's okay—just a sprained knee. We're almost back."

Ignoring her report, Joffre cut to the chase. "Is Josh with you?"

Dawn's reply caught him off guard: "No, Josh went to the barge to check a radio problem." She explained the deal Josh struck with Victor: the hospital visit for a promise to troubleshoot the comms.

"Is everything okay?" Dawn asked.

"I hope so," Joffre replied. "Get back soon," he urged.

Facing the concerned group, Joffre briefed them and issued resolute orders: "Dan and Ben, head down to the lake—find Josh. Maria and I will search the compound. Take radios, channel three."

As the team dispersed, Dawn and Victor returned. Joffre updated Dawn while Victor, crutches in hand, stood silently. Dawn volunteered to search the observatory, and Victor offered to join her.

"Channel three," Joffre directed. "Monitor it."

Thirty minutes later, Ben's voice crackled over the radio: "Found an overturned ATV and two trailers halfway to the lake."

"Josh?" Joffre demanded.

As Ben hesitated, Victor's radio call from the observatory sliced through the gathering dusk. "What color is the ATV?" Victor's demand hung in the air.

"Blue," Ben reported.

"It's not Josh's ATV," Victor clarified. "It's mine. Josh left it there after I flipped it. He carried me back on the red ATV he was using."

Joffre, unwilling to lose another team member to the encroaching darkness, issued orders. "Ben, Dan—return to base."

Moments later, Joffre's cellphone jolted him. Hope surged—was it Josh? But no, it was Victor.

"Joffre, I need you at the observatory. I found something," Victor urged.

"Where's your radio?" Joffre's weariness seeped into his voice.

"I have it, but you need to see this firsthand.

Didn't want to broadcast it," Victor explained.

Joffre hurried to the observatory, resisting the urge to sprint and alarm his team. Breathless, he faced Victor.

"What do you have?" Joffre implored.

Victor gestured to a display screen, revealing Heavenly Lake. "Look," he urged, tracing a track line from the lake's center southward.

"I wanted to verify if Josh installed the new radio unit," Victor explained. "You know, to see if he made it to the barge."

"And?" Joffre pressed.

Victor pointed again. "GPS data shows the GPS unit continued south at over twenty knots, then—after a pause—went overland."

"Overland?" Joffre's disbelief echoed. "You mean North Korea?"

Victor nodded.

CHAPTER 19

KCTV

At 6:00 a.m., the shrill ring of the phone shattered the tranquility of Josh's father-in-law's apartment. On the other end, Joffre's voice carried an urgent tone.

"Sir," Joffre began, only to be interrupted by Roger's stern inquiry, "Who is this?"

"I'm Joffre Wolfe, the Scientist-in-Charge at the Cascades Volcano Observatory," Joffre explained. "I apologize for disturbing you, but there's been an incident involving Josh." He then summarized the day's events.

Roger listened intently, while Meg, now awake, slipped away to the kitchen to brew coffee. Accustomed to such interruptions because of Roger's work at the Pentagon, she remained unaware of the call's gravity. Roger, however, hung on every word.

Once Meg was out of earshot, the conversation continued. "Do you think North Korea really has him?" Roger pressed.

"I don't know," Joffre replied.

"Let's keep this under wraps until I can make some calls," Roger requested, promising to call Joffre back within the hour.

Roger reached for the secure phone on his nightstand—an essential accessory given his position at the Pentagon. He dialed the National Military Command Center (NMCC), the nerve center for military operations, communication, and decision-making, staffed by a dedicated team of military and civilian personnel. If anyone had information about Josh's situation, they would know or soon find out.

Swiftly donning his clothes and grabbing a leftover bagel, Roger headed to the office. As he crossed the dimly lit south parking lot of the Pentagon, he mentally rehearsed his initial steps upon arrival. His military upbringing had ingrained in him the importance of promptly reporting developments to key officials. Timeliness allowed decision-makers to react swiftly, seizing opportunities and addressing threats as they emerged, even if adjustments were necessary based on new data.

Upon discovering that the senior watch officer had no updates, Roger reached for a phone. He dialed his boss, Colonel Walsh, who listened without interruption.

"Roger," Colonel Walsh's voice was steady, "you'll need to arrange a secure call with the Office of the Special Presidential Envoy for Hostage Affairs."

This specialized office collaborated with government and private sector entities to secure the release of U.S. national hostages and wrongful detainees held abroad. They also provided crucial support to affected families.

"I'll have the Department of State's NMCC watch officer set up the call," Roger assured him before ending the conversation.

His thoughts turned to his daughter, Josh's wife, asleep in Seattle. Roger didn't want her to hear about this from anyone else. Despite his usual policy of immediate reporting, he'd make an exception and wait until morning in Seattle to call her. That would give him three hours to unravel the mystery of what had happened to Josh.

An hour after speaking with Joffre, Roger called him back to update him on what he knew, which was nothing. "Hang tight, Joffre," Roger urged. "We're working on it."

Shortly after 8:00 a.m., the NMCC watch officer called Roger. The State Department watch officer had set up the call Roger requested, but instead of a telephone call, the Department of State official insisted on a video teleconference. They promised to send a Wash Fax directly to his office before the scheduled 9:00 a.m. meeting.

A Wash Fax—a specialized term used within Washington state agencies—referred to a fax machine employed for transmitting classified information between different government entities.

Roger stared at the fax machine, a silent sentinel on the table next to his desk, waiting to relay the secret agenda for his upcoming meetings. The machine bore the scars of countless paper jams and late-night urgencies.

In the meantime, Roger turned his attention to his computer, attempting to focus on the flood of waiting emails. It wasn't long before the mechanical whir of the fax machine coming to life commanded his attention. A grainy sheet of paper emerged, its pixelated dots unfolding before Roger's waiting eyes. The air faintly smelled of toner and paper. The delicate paper curled slightly at the edges, as if reluctant to leave the safety of the fax machine, finally sliding out and landing on the tray.

Roger snatched the still-warm paper and scanned the agenda from the Office of the Special Presidential Envoy for Hostage Affairs. The title was straightforward: "Possible Hostage Crisis in North Korea." However, the list of attendees raised his concerns. It included representatives from the National Security Council, senior officials from the Department of State specializing in China and the Korean Peninsula, and the Deputy National Intelligence Officer for North Korea from the Office of the Director of National Intelligence (ODNI). Each of these officials outranked Roger.

Recognizing the need for reinforcement, Roger took decisive action. To counter the influence of the Deputy National Intelligence Officer for Korea, he contacted the Deputy Defense Intelligence Officer for Korea. To balance the Department of State representation, he brought in analysts who had worked closely with Josh on the project. Finally, he asked his boss, Colonel Walsh, to join him.

Roger's team arrived early in the video teleconference room, allowing him to update them on the events leading to Josh's presumed kidnapping. As the meeting time approached, the video screens at the front of the room flickered to life, each displaying an image of a participant and an abbreviation of their sponsoring office in the lower left corner.

Roger reviewed the acronyms on the screens: State, NSC, and ODNI. Roger took the seat at the head of the table, flanked by Colonel Walsh on his left and the Deputy Intelligence Officer for Korea, Bill Stokes, on his right. The most senior official, in this case, Dr. Karen Harris representing the White House, would take the head seat. But today wasn't about seniority; it was about accountability, and Roger was in the hot seat.

At 9 a.m., Dr. Karen Harris, the director of the Office of the Special Presidential Envoy for Hostage Affairs, began the meeting. She expressed her gratitude for everyone's attendance, especially at such short notice, and then asked Roger to provide a synopsis of the current situation.

Roger cleared his throat and began outlining the project from its inception, starting with the White House's request for a U.S. team to respond to China's invitation to investigate Changbai Mountain. He then invited his analysts to summarize their findings and concluded with a recap of the events following the unexpected phone call from Joffre Wolfe.

Dr. Harris thanked Roger for his presentation and outlined the steps her office would take to address the current crisis. "Has anyone contacted the family yet?" she asked, though the question was rhetorical as she knew it was her office's responsibility to contact the families of detainees.

Roger spoke up. "Ma'am, if you don't mind, I would like to make the call."

"May I ask why?" she inquired.

Roger hesitated, then spoke. "Because she is my daughter."

"Who is your daughter?" Dr. Harris asked, shocked.

"Josh Cooper is my son-in-law. His wife, Emily, is my daughter," Roger replied.

At this moment, the Deputy National Security Officer, a brash young man named Kevin Hill, interrupted. "Did you just say that Josh Cooper is your son-in-law?" he demanded.

"Yes," Roger answered tersely.

"And why would you send your son-in-law on such a mission?" Hill demanded.

Roger explained that the joint staff needed expertise to assess China's request for a U.S. team to survey Changbai Mountain and that Josh had that expertise. "I knew I could trust him," Roger added.

Unconvinced, Hill continued his assault. "Who allowed you to plant your son-in-law as a spy on this survey mission?" he demanded.

"Your boss, the President," Colonel Walsh finally intervened. "Next time you attend a meeting, you might want to do your homework first."

"Okay, folks, let's move on," Dr. Harris commanded. "Captain Banks, please contact Josh's family and provide them with my office's contact information in case they need anything."

Dr. Harris then directed the Department of State Desk Officer for China to reach out to the U.S. Embassy in Beijing for any information, as well as the Swedish Embassy in Pyongyang, North Korea. Since the United States and North Korea do not have formal diplomatic relations, they rely on the Swedish Embassy for indirect communications. There was a touch-tone phone at the U.S.-led U.N. Command in the Korean border village of Panmunjom, which allowed for communication between the two countries, but the crisis hadn't reached a level high enough to warrant its use.

After the meeting, Roger returned to his office to call Emily. It was now 7 a.m. in Seattle. Maya answered the phone. "Hello, Mr. Roger." Roger found it endearing how Maya addressed everyone with their salutation, followed by their first name.

"Maya, is Emily there?" Roger asked.

"No, Mr. Roger, she is on her way to work. She is very excited. It is Ellen's first day at the clinic, and Emily wanted to be there to show her around," Maya reported.

"Maya, can you give me the number to the clinic, please?" Roger asked.

After what seemed like an eternity to Roger, Maya finally returned with the number. Roger thanked her and began dialing the clinic when Young Ho, his Korean analyst, interrupted him by pounding on the glass wall separating Roger's office from the sea of cubicles outside. Young was frantically pointing to one of the many television monitors in the J-2 spaces. On the screen was a report from Korean Central Television (KCTV), the state-run TV channel in North Korea.

Roger waved Young into his office. Young translated the KCTV report as Roger watched the images on the screen. North Korea had captured an American spy attempting to infiltrate their country across Heavenly Lake, known as Lake Cheonji. The screen shifted to show a display of equipment captured along with the alleged spy, including electronic devices and a large barge with what looked like a diesel engine mounted on it. The report concluded with a grainy image of an unnamed prisoner seated with his arms shackled to a wooden table.

"Give me the office," Roger demanded.

As Young rushed out, Roger dialed Emily's office number with urgency. He reached the receptionist on the third ring, but was too late. CNN had picked up the breaking news story and was reporting it as Roger's call came in. In the patient waiting area of the clinic, Emily and Ellen, Roger's two daughters, clung to each other as they stared at the image of Josh on the television screen mounted on the wall.

"Emily, it's your dad," the receptionist said as she handed her the phone.

"Daddy," Emily cried into the phone.

CHAPTER 20

CAMP SIXTEEN

Josh's world shrank to the suffocating embrace of the hood that enveloped him. Each jolt of the truck reverberated through his bones, a relentless reminder of his captivity. The captors' voices, foreign and incomprehensible, mingled with the acrid scent of their cigarettes. As the vehicle descended the rugged mountain road, Josh's anxiety intensified. The transition from hours of rocky terrain to smooth pavement signaled a shift—a destination, perhaps, or a new phase of his ordeal.

Finally, the truck came to a rest outside the iron gates of North Korea's Hwasong concentration camp (Camp 16). This sprawling labor camp held about 20,000 political prisoners, making it the largest in the country. Within its confines, Korean citizens faced a grim fate: life imprisonment with no hope of release. The regime classified most inmates as "anti-revolutionary and anti-party elements," detaining them on charges related to opposing the government. Tragically, many were family members of suspected wrongdoers, caught in a guilt-by-association punishment. The camp remained shrouded in secrecy, a place where hope was scarce, and freedom was a distant memory.

In the dead of night, under the harsh glare of prison lights, the guards dragged Josh from the truck and flung him to the ground. Two guards lifted him, still bound by his shoulders, dragging him toward an uncertain fate. Josh's senses sharpened—he heard the metallic clack of a lock against a chain-linked fence, the heavy thud of a wooden door, and the scrape of a chair across a stone floor. The guards placed him in a wooden chair, binding his wrists to cold metal shackles attached to a wooden table. Then, unceremoniously, they lifted the hood from Josh's head. The overhead light, suspended on a wire, seemed to explode in his eyes, momentarily stealing his thoughts.

As his vision cleared, Josh found himself face-to-face with his captor. The guard stood before him, clad in a ragged and stiff one-piece coverall adorned with a tricolor pattern. In one hand, he gripped a short black club—a stark reminder of the authority he wielded over Josh. As Josh's eyes adjusted to the dim surroundings, he discerned two other guards lurking in the shadows, vigilant sentinels.

Leaning over Josh, the interrogator began the questioning. The inquiries seemed innocuous: name, nationality, family background, education, and travel history. Josh, parched and drained, answered in a raspy voice. Having cooperated thus far, he pushed back. Summoning his strength, he demanded to know the reason for his detention.

"Silence!" The guard's scream reverberated, punctuated by the club slamming onto the table. The display of force lingered as the questioning resumed. Why had Josh entered North Korea?

Josh explained his mission—to study Changbai Mountain on behalf of the Chinese government.

"Lies," the guard erupted.

Each response from Josh seemed to stoke the guard's fury. The question echoed: Why had Josh violated North Korea's territory?

Josh tried again to explain, but the guard cut him off.

"Lies." The guard's voice hissed with hatred as the club descended, striking the back of Josh's left hand. Pain surged through Josh's hand, yet his shackled wrists prevented any escape. Another guard, unseen until now, pressed Josh back into his seat, enforcing compliance.

In that dank room, a grim routine unfolded—a ritual rehearsed countless times. The guards departed, extinguishing the light, leaving Josh alone in the suffocating darkness.

Josh sat in the dark, overwhelmed by disbelief. The sudden loss of freedom, familiar surroundings, and loved ones was too much to process. How had he ended up here? Was this real?

He didn't know how much time had passed before a different guard entered the room. After flicking the light back on, the guard unshackled Josh's left hand and wrapped a warm cloth around his wounded hand.

"Water?" the guard asked in flawless English.

"Please," Josh answered.

The guard handed him a cold bottle of water, and Josh gulped it down until it was empty.

They sat together in silence—no screaming, no clubs. Josh clung to these signs of improvement; a flicker of hope filled his heart. Maybe things would change.

Then the questioning resumed. Why was Josh spying against North Korea? Who were his contacts? How did he communicate with them? As the relentless questioning continued, Josh's thoughts turned to survival. How could he navigate this prison system? How could he avoid trouble? He knew he needed to adapt. What rules did he need to learn? Who could he trust? Having thought it through, Josh turned to his captor.

"I need something to eat, and I need to sleep," he implored. "I promise I will answer your questions in the morning."

To Josh's surprise, the guard left and returned with another, who carried two bottles of water, a stainless-steel bowl filled with rice mixed with various grains, a straw mat, a blanket, and a pail. The guard deposited the goods on the table and left Josh unchained, alone with the light on. His hunger pangs demanded immediate attention, and Josh examined the bowl of rice. It was a mix of white rice, black rice, barley, beans, red beans, millet, brown rice, oats, and chestnuts.

With no utensils, Josh ate the mixture with his fingers, gulping water in between bites. Once full, he spread the straw mat on the dirty floor, pulled the blanket over himself, and tried to sleep. The unfamiliar surroundings and the seriousness of his situation weighed heavily on him as he drifted into an uneasy slumber.

In the heart of Seattle, Emily clung to every word as her father meticulously recounted Josh's dire situation. The reality she now faced seemed insurmountable, a weight pressing down on her chest.

"Honey, go home. We can talk more later," her father urged, his voice laden with concern.

Home. The word snapped Emily back to the present. Home—the place where memories intertwined with love and responsibility. The boys. Oh my God, the boys. Panic surged within her.

Emily turned to her younger sister, Ellen. "I have to get home," she pleaded, desperation etching her features.

Ellen understood immediately. There was no way she'd let Emily drive home alone. Normally, both nurses leaving their shift would pose a challenge. Patient abandonment was a serious concern. Once a nurse accepted an assignment, completing it or ensuring a safe handoff was non-negotiable. But this morning was different. Ellen was only a trainee on the schedule, and Emily wasn't even supposed to be there—she'd come in to support her sister. The other nurses already scheduled could handle the shift.

"Don't worry, I'll drive you," Ellen said, taking her sister's hand. "We'll get through this together."

On the way home, Emily called Josh's parents, then his grandmother. Finally, she reached out to

Maya, explaining that she and Ellen were on their way to the house. Emily urged Maya to keep all the televisions off, promising to explain everything when they arrived.

As Ellen approached the house, a chaotic scene greeted them. News trucks lined the curb, satellite dishes pointed skyward, logos emblazoned on each one. Reporters huddled in clusters, clutching microphones and notebooks. Their faces glowed from the screens of laptops and smartphones. Neighbors peeked out from behind curtains, curiosity and concern etched on their faces. Flashing blue police lights marked each corner of the street, with officers maintaining order.

The state-run Korean Central Television in North Korea hadn't used Josh's name, but somehow, someone had leaked it. Perhaps a former student or, in this age of artificial intelligence, a facial recognition algorithm had swiftly identified him, providing the reporters with his home address.

Ellen drove past the frenzy of prying cameras and exploding flashbulbs circling to the back of the house. They entered through the mudroom, making their way upstairs. They surprised Maya in the kitchen, where she was huddled with the boys, seeking refuge from the chaos at the front door.

"Ms. Emily, Ms. Ellen. What's happening?" Maya's voice trembled.

Emily didn't answer. Instead, she kneeled, enfolding her two young sons in a cocoon of warmth and reassurance. No words were necessary. Their mother's arms, simultaneously strong and gentle, cradled them. She pressed her lips to their foreheads, a silent promise that everything would be okay. As they breathed together, the boys absorbed her calmness and love.

CHAPTER 21

EEOB

The imposing Eisenhower Executive Office Building (EEOB), next to the White House, buzzed with urgency. Today's meeting focused on the North Korea hostage crisis—a perilous situation requiring immediate action. Within these historic walls, the National Security Council (NSC) convened, providing a critical forum where the President and his top advisors deliberated on national security, military strategy, and foreign policy.

NSC attendees included Cabinet-level officials known as principals (e.g., Secretary of State, Secretary of Defense) or, as in today's case, deputy principals, who developed recommendations for their respective bosses. Today's attendees featured the senior adviser and chief spokesperson for the Vice President, the Deputy Secretary of State, the Deputy Secretary of

Defense, the President's Chief of Staff, the Assistant to the President for National Security Affairs, the Deputy Chairman of the Joint Chiefs of Staff, and the Deputy Director of National Intelligence, who provided crucial intelligence expertise.

Besides the deputy principals, other less senior officials, often referred to as "backbenchers," were present. These included the National Intelligence Officer for North Korea from the Office of the Director of National Intelligence (ODNI), the Deputy Defense Intelligence Officer for Korea, Roger, and his boss, Colonel Walsh.

As the meeting began, Damon Smith, the Vice President's chief spokesperson, turned to Mike Jackson, the Deputy Director of National Intelligence (DDNI). Jackson outlined the findings of the intelligence community, which had been working tirelessly for the past twenty-four hours to determine Josh's fate. Smith announced that the intelligence community had independently confirmed, based on satellite intercepts, the initial GPS information reported by Josh's colleagues. Jackson detailed they had tracked the GPS signal provided by the sonar array's communication system southward from Changbai Lake into North Korea and then eastward overland to one of three prisoner camps in the area, Camp Sixteen, next to North Korea's nuclear test facility.

"And the signal?" Damon asked.

"It went cold about four hours ago," Jackson replied, his voice steady, yet laden with the weight of uncertainty.

In the tense confines of the Eisenhower Executive Office Building, Damon Smith turned to Air Force General "Ace" Johnson, Deputy Chairman of the Joint Chiefs of Staff. His question hung heavy in the room: Was a rescue operation workable? General Johnson, known by his callsign "Ace," hadn't earned that moniker through aerial combat victories but from his uncanny prowess at late-night poker games.

Ace contemplated his response. Rescuing a hostage from the remote reaches of North Korea would be a labyrinthine endeavor—a high-stakes gamble. "Joint Special Operations Command (JSOC) is already running preliminary plans," Ace informed the group. However, the challenges loomed large. A sea-borne rescue operation across the narrow Sea of Japan into North Korea meant traversing hundreds of miles. The maximum range depended on vessel types, fuel capacity, and logistical support. North Korea's vigilant, well-equipped military posed formidable obstacles.

Damon shifted his attention to Paula Shultz, the Deputy Secretary of State. "Paula," he implored, "what are our political options?" hoping diplomatic negotiations might secure Josh's release.

Ms. Shultz's response was sobering. Hostage diplomacy with North Korea is intricate. The regime, like Iran and Venezuela, wielded hostages as strategic pawns in negotiations with Washington. The hitch? There were no ongoing or expected talks with North Korea.

"And China?" Damon pressed.

Her eyes flickered. "I thought you might ask." China, with historical ties and economic sway, held the key. Diplomatic pressure from Beijing could nudge North Korea toward goodwill gestures or de-escalation. As North Korea's largest trading partner, China's economic clout could tip the scales, potentially securing Josh's freedom.

In the hushed chambers of the Eisenhower Executive Office Building, Damon Smith cut to the core. "What about the ongoing negotiations with China over a state visit?" he inquired.

Paula Shultz appreciated the directness. The prospect of a presidential visit loomed large on President Steve Paul's agenda. Its implications were twofold: political and strategic.

Politically, a presidential visit would signal diplomatic engagement—a commitment to dialogue. The media frenzy surrounding such an event would bolster the president's image, portraying him as a capable leader adept at navigating complex international relations.

Strategically, the visit held transformative potential. Echoes of Nixon's 1972 China visit reverberated—a seismic shift in the Cold War landscape. Improved U.S.-China relations could weaken the growing Russian influence in the region. Discussions on trade, investment, and economic cooperation could fortify bilateral ties. And, crucially, security concerns—like North Korea's nuclear program—could find resolution.

In the room's shadowed recesses, Josh's father-in-law sat silently. As the council wavered, hesitant to jeopardize the prized upcoming meeting between the two countries, Roger erupted. His demand echoed through the room: "We must pressure China to secure Josh's release—even if it means threatening to cancel or postpone the meeting."

"I'm sorry. Who are you?" Damon asked.

"I'm Captain Roger Banks," he responded, his voice steady. "China must act. D.C. sent Josh to China at Beijing's request. China is responsible for his safety."

"Thank you for your concern," Damon offered, trying to soothe Roger.

But Damon's attempt fell short. Roger's urgency persisted. "He knows things that endanger his life," Roger insisted. "We must extract him now." As Colonel Walsh escorted Roger toward the exit, the room remained charged with tension.

After Roger's abrupt exit, Damon turned toward the conference table, his expression a mix of bewilderment and urgency. "Can someone explain what that was all about?" he demanded, looking to the Deputy Secretary of Defense, the Deputy Chairman of the Joint Chiefs of Staff, or the Deputy Director of National Intelligence.

Dr. Karen Harris, the unassuming director of the Office of the Special Presidential Envoy for Hostage Affairs, broke the silence. With a calm demeanor, she recounted her initial video teleconference with Roger and the revelation that Josh was Roger's son-in-law. The news that Josh Cooper, the missing hostage, was Captain Banks's son-in-law and held a dual role—as a volcano expert and a Defense Intelligence Agency operative—sent shockwaves through the room.

"Wait," Damon interjected, his voice edged with disbelief. "Josh worked with the DIA in the Pentagon before joining the U.S. Geological

Survey team in China?"

Ace, the Deputy Chairman of the Joint Chiefs of Staff, nodded. "Common practice," he confirmed. "The J-2 frequently consults with external experts."

Damon's next question hung heavy. "Sensitive information? Did Josh have access?"

Ace's response was chilling. "Full clearance. TS/SCI."

Damon's exclamation echoed through the room. "Jesus," he muttered. "His father-in-law was right. Josh is in danger. We need to get him out—now."

CHAPTER 22

SKAGIT VALLEY

In the heart of Seattle, Emily and her family were besieged by a relentless swarm of media personnel outside their Montlake Park home. The news of Josh's precarious situation had drawn the press to their doorstep. Emily, along with Josh's mother, Sarah, and stepfather, Frank, were now united in their resolve to escape the suffocating attention.

Arrayed neatly beside the house were their vehicles: Maya's robust Suburban, Ellen's sleek SUV, and Frank and Sarah's unassuming sedan. The driveway, stretching discreetly to the street behind the property, promised a path to freedom. With Maya's Suburban strategically hidden from view, it was designated to transport Emily and the boys. Ellen and Sarah planned to follow closely in the SUV. Meanwhile, Frank, positioned nearest to the media horde, was ready to act as a decoy, drawing the press away with his movements.

As dusk settled, the family's plan swung into motion. They congregated around Frank's sedan, ostentatiously opening and slamming doors to create a spectacle that captured the media's attention. With the press distracted, they swiftly moved to their respective vehicles. Their ruse functioned flawlessly on the street; the throng of reporters, drawn by the commotion, surged toward Frank's sedan. Frank, with expert timing, sped from the driveway, leading the media on a wild chase. Even the police, stationed at nearby street corners, were swept up in the ensuing parade. The scene quickly vacated, leaving the dark streets eerily quiet.

Maya and Ellen, seizing the moment, guided their vehicles onto a parallel street, slipping through the night toward their sanctuary. In the backseat of Maya's Suburban, the boys, wrapped up in the excitement, giggled under Emily's playful guise of an elaborate car-based game of hide-and-seek. Their destination lay ahead: Irene's ranch, Josh's grandmother's home, located sixty miles north of Seattle, a haven from the chaos.

Nana Irene, as the boys called her, presided over a sprawling six-hundred-acre property in the lush Skagit Valley. Her home served a dual purpose: a cozy haven and a working farm. Here, organic, grass-fed beef roamed the pastures alongside contented pigs, and chickens scratched the earth, laying eggs in nest boxes—a bounty of over one hundred thousand annually. Josh's grandparents had gained the ranch at a bargain during a real estate downturn triggered by a controversial plan to build nuclear power plants by the Puget Sound Power and Light Company. When the county abandoned the plan, the ranch's value surged, but for Irene and her late husband, it was never about profit. They believed in humane animal treatment, sustainability, and organic practices—a legacy Irene continued, even after losing her husband.

After an hour and a half behind the wheel, Maya and Ellen turned their vehicles onto the dusty dirt road, passing through the open gate that led to the ranch. For Maya, this place held memories woven into its very fabric—memories from when she lived there with Josh's grandparents before Josh's grandfather insisted she move in with Josh. Now, it felt like a poignant homecoming. Irene stood on the wraparound porch, her presence a comforting beacon for the weary travelers. Emily cradled a drowsy-eyed Jimmy in her arms, while Maya gently guided a groggy Johnny onto the porch.

"Nana!" Johnny exclaimed, rubbing his eyes and smiling.

"Welcome home," Irene said softly, embracing them. Her warm smile and the familiar scent of the ranch offered a sense of safety and belonging. For Emily and the boys, Nana Irene's ranch was a sanctuary—a place where the tumult of the outside world could not reach them.

In the confines of Camp Sixteen, Josh's captors simmered with mounting frustration. Their attempts to extract valuable information from him had hit a dead end. As the first light of dawn crept across the horizon, the guards—clad in drab uniforms—swung open the heavy cell door. Josh's pulse raced, uncertainty gnawing at his insides. Approaching with buckets of icy water, the guards doused him. The shock was immediate—the frigid liquid seeped into Josh's bones, leaving him shivering uncontrollably. The guards displayed a chilling indifference. Josh's teeth chattered, his entire body trembling. Satisfied with their cruel work, they departed, leaving him sprawled on the cold, unforgiving floor.

Wrapping the scratchy wool blanket around himself, Josh found solace in its dryness—it had miraculously escaped the deluge of icy water. How many more mornings would he wake to biting cold or other cruelties? Yet, deep within, a spark of defiance flickered. He would endure. Even in the bleakest circumstances, he would fight to survive. Memories of sunlight, warmth, and freedom fueled his determination.

When the cell door creaked open once more, Josh huddled in the corner. The guard laid out fresh, coarse clothing and a meager meal on the wooden table. Then, with a perfunctory gesture, the guard opened the slotted windows, revealing the mid-morning sun. As swiftly as he had arrived, the guard vanished. Convinced he wouldn't return; Josh approached the table. Soaked and chilled, he changed into the baggy drawstring pants and loose pullover shirt left for him. Dressed, he devoured the stale bread and watery porridge. These provisions symbolized the guard's control, yet Josh's survival hung in the balance.

Peering out of the slotted window, the stark reality of the prison camp unfolded. Tall walls, crowned with menacing barbed wire, encircled the compound. Guard towers punctuated the perimeter, each manned by armed sentinels whose rifles remained ever ready. Beyond the walls, the landscape was desolate—a harsh tableau of sparse grass and struggling shrubs. The prison buildings, monotonous and gray, blended into the bleakness. Gaunt faces, hollow eyes, and broken spirits filled the yard, painting a cruel scene of suffering and despair.

In the dim confines of the prison cell, Josh's heart raced as two guards approached. Their footsteps echoed off the cold stone walls, prompting him to retreat to a corner. One guard tossed a pair of worn leather slippers at his feet, gruffly pointing toward the door. Josh complied, slipping the slippers on, his dread mounting. He feared what awaited him beyond the door's threshold.

Outside, the sun bore down, casting harsh shadows on the cracked earth of the courtyard. Hundreds of prisoners stood in rigid formation, their faces etched with fear and resignation. They understood that resistance was futile, that defiance would only invite more suffering. The air hung heavy with tension, pressing down on every soul present.

The guards shackled three prisoners to wooden posts at the center of the courtyard. Their arms stretched painfully overhead, wrists bound by heavy iron cuffs. Raw marks crisscrossed their backs—a testament to previous beatings. Their bodies trembled from a mixture of dread and exhaustion. The guards, clad in stark black uniforms, moved with chilling efficiency. Their faces revealed no compassion; dark sunglasses shielded their eyes, reflecting the suffering they inflicted. The leader of the guards stepped forward, a cruel smile playing at the corners of his lips as he surveyed the gathered prisoners. His voice, sharp and commanding, echoed off the prison walls.

With a nod, the guards began their grisly work. Leather met flesh with sickening thuds, each blow reverberating through the courtyard. The prisoner closest to the onlookers arched his back in agony, a guttural scream escaping his throat. Blood mingled with grime, forming rivulets of crimson that traced down his skin.

The beatings continued, escalating in brutality. The prisoners' screams merged into a haunting symphony, echoing in the ears of those forced to witness the violence. Tears streamed down their cheeks, intermingling with sweat and blood. The guards showed no mercy, their blows precise and unyielding, turning the prisoners' backs into canvases of pain.

For Josh and the other captives watching, it was a harrowing spectacle. His wide eyes remained fixed on the scene, unable to look away. Helplessness engulfed him; any attempt to intervene would only invite further brutality upon himself.

As the beatings drew to a close, the courtyard fell silent, save for the ragged breathing of the beaten prisoners and the hushed satisfaction of the guards. The leader stepped forward once more, surveying the broken bodies with twisted pleasure. Addressing the assembled prisoners in Korean, his voice dripped with menace. Though Josh didn't understand the words, the message was obvious: "Remember this day. Remember the consequences of defiance."

The guards dispersed, leaving the three prisoners hanging limply from their posts—battered, bloodied, their cries of pain lingering like ghosts. The formation of prisoners dissolved, their hearts heavy knowing that this fate awaited anyone who dared step out of line. Two guards escorted a shaken Josh back to his cell, where he braced himself for yet another round of interrogation.

In the dim light of the prison cell, the guards returned, flanking a stranger whom Josh had never encountered. Clearly not one of the usual enforcers, this man stood out in his formal attire. A guard placed a pitcher of ice water on the table, alongside two glasses, and in flawless English, the stranger invited Josh to drink.

For hours, the stranger probed Josh about his work on Changbai Mountain. His questions were precise, delving into the monitoring instruments already deployed on the volcano and those the American team had installed or upgraded. The stranger's depth of knowledge hinted at a profound understanding of volcanism. As the interview segment drew to a close, he posed a critical query: What was the likelihood of a volcanic eruption? Josh explained that the monitoring equipment had led the team to conclude that, despite recent activity, the volcano remained dormant.

The gentleman rose, thanked Josh, and then delivered an unexpected twist: a few more questions awaited, but he would conduct them in the prison yard. Josh hesitated, his mind replaying the morning's brutal events. "You are safe," the interviewer assured him. With little choice, Josh followed the guard and the gentleman into the yard. To his relief, they bypassed the site of the earlier torture, heading instead to a secluded corner. There, an array of electric equipment lay sprawled on large blue plastic tarps. It was the gear confiscated from Josh's boat on Heavenly Lake, along with items pilfered from Victor's barge.

Seated cross-legged on the tarps across from Josh, the interviewer resumed his questioning, probing Josh about the collected equipment. Josh recounted how the sonar array—submerged in the crater lake—held the promise of revealing the volcano's hidden features. Echo soundings would construct a bathymetric map, measuring water depth across the lake and unveiling the submerged topography. Beyond that, the array would serve as a vigilant sentinel, monitoring potential volcanic activity. It would detect underwater seismic events linked to volcanic processes—subtle tremors that hinted at magma movement or shifts in pressure within the volcano.

His interrogator leaned forward, curiosity replacing the usual sternness. "And the magma chamber?" he inquired, his tone more akin to that of an intrigued colleague than a jailer.

Josh hesitated, realizing he hadn't fully considered that critical aspect. After a moment's reflection, he admitted that the sonar array's signals lacked the power to penetrate the depths required to reach the magma chamber—buried three to five miles beneath the lake. However, it remained sensitive enough to detect subtle shifts in the lake floor's shape, a telltale sign of magma activity.

As the interview concluded, the gentleman rose and extended a hand to assist Josh to his feet. The guard escorted him back to his cell, where a remarkable transformation awaited. The grimy mat and worn gray blanket had vanished, replaced by a bamboo bed adorned with crisp cotton sheets and a cozy flannel blanket. On the table, bottles of water and a bowl of apples beckoned. A wooden dish held eggs, a modest portion of fish, fermented kimchi, cucumber, and eggplant. Soup and rice completed the spread, accompanied by a pitcher of soju, a traditional Korean alcoholic beverage.

Josh turned to his interviewer, bowing, disbelief etched on his features. The official returned the gesture and inquired if there was anything Josh needed.

"I'd like to speak with my family," Josh requested, his voice tentative. "To let them know I'm safe."

"Soon," the official pledged. "Perhaps in the morning." He also promised to arrange for the camp doctor to examine Josh's injured hand.

As Josh savored the meal, his mind echoed with longing—for home, for familiar faces, for the comforting routines of daily life.

CHAPTER 23

RETURN TO HEAVENLY LAKE

As dawn painted the sky over the sprawling ranch, Grandma Nana and Maya busied themselves in the spacious kitchen, orchestrating a breakfast symphony for Nana's granddaughters and grandsons. Upstairs, Emily kept company with Josh's stepfather, Frank—a man who had recently eluded relentless paparazzi after escaping from the Montlake Park house. His arrival, cloaked in midnight shadows, had brought both relief and intrigue.

The ranch, a living canvas of rustic beauty, thrived as a working farm. Here, organic, grass-fed cattle roamed sun-drenched pastures alongside contented pigs and free-range chickens. The promise of a hearty morning meal hung in the air, woven into the very essence of the place. At its heart stood Nana's homemade bread—an aromatic masterpiece that filled the kitchen with warmth and comfort.

Seated around the sturdy wooden table, the boys wielded butter knives with precision, slathering slices of Nana's bread with jam made from sun-ripened berries. Meanwhile, an old percolator on the stove bubbled and gurgled, coaxing the essence of coffee beans into existence. The rich aroma permeated every nook and cranny of the house, offering solace and rejuvenation.

Nana and Maya operated as a well-practiced duo. Nana, her hands deft from years of tending to the land, cracked farm-fresh eggs into a cast-iron skillet. The eggs sizzled and scrambled, seasoned with a pinch of salt and pepper—their comforting fragrance filling the kitchen. Nearby, Maya stirred a mound of thick-cut bacon, its smoky dance enticing everyone in the house. The clink of a milk pitcher against ceramic mugs signaled that the meal was ready—a symphony of flavors and memories, orchestrated by love and tradition.

In the sun-drenched morning, Johnny and Jimmy burst forth from breakfast, their young limbs energized by the meal and brimming with anticipation. The farm sprawled before them—an uncharted territory of wonder and adventure.

"Don't chase the chickens." Emily's voice trailed after them as she stepped into the yard. Her eyes crinkled with fondness; this place held memories etched into her very being.

Emily's mind rewound to her inaugural visit—the day Josh's grandmother had handed her a bag of Red Delicious apples. The horses, sturdy and patient, awaited their treats. Among them stood Rusty, the stalwart stallion Josh had ridden in his teenage years.

Rusty, with his chestnut coat and eyes like ancient amber, had been more than a horse. He'd been a confidant, a silent listener to Josh's adolescent secrets. And now, as Emily recalled, Rusty would nudge his head out of the stall, lips puckered in a silent plea for apples. His circular motion—a dance of anticipation—had been endearing.

Unconsciously, Emily guided Johnny and Jimmy away from the chickens, her heart attuned to the rhythm of the ranch, toward the horse stable. In that moment, Emily knew the farm held not just horses and chickens, but a tapestry of stories waiting to be woven anew.

As the sun climbed over the ranch, casting long shadows across the weathered wooden stables, Emily and her two sons—Johnny and Jimmy—hurried toward the familiar structure. Their footsteps echoed in the crisp morning air, anticipation fueling their every stride.

But Emily's attention shifted as she caught sight of her younger sister, Ellen, running towards the stables, waving urgently. "Emily, the phone!" Ellen called out, her voice carrying across the yard. She waited, breathless, until Emily reached her side, chest heaving from the sprint.

"Emily," Ellen gasped, gathering herself. "It's Josh. He's on the phone, at the house. I've got the boys—go!" Her eyes pleaded with Emily to move faster.

Emily's heart raced as she sprinted toward the house. Inside, Maya, her eyes wide with excitement, thrust the phone into Emily's trembling hands. "Josh, Josh, is that you?" Emily's voice cracked, the connection crackling like a fragile lifeline.

In a dimly lit room at the camp commandant's quarters, Josh clung to the receiver. His fingers trembled, bridging the gap between captivity and freedom. The guard, an unyielding figure by the door, watched him with eyes like shards of ice.

"Emily," Josh whispered, his voice fragile yet resolute. "It's me."

Emily's breath hitched on the other end. "Josh? Oh my God, Josh!" The static danced across the line, mirroring her disbelief. "Are you—?"

"I'm coming home," Josh interrupted, the words catching in his throat. "They're releasing me. I—I can't believe it."

Emily's joy collided with doubt.

Josh closed his eyes, picturing her face—the sons he'd left behind. "Tell the boys I love them," he murmured. "Tell them I'll be there soon."

The crackling intensified, as if the wires strained to bridge continents. Josh's heart raced. But then, silence. The call dropped, leaving Josh gripping the receiver, knuckles white. Was this real or a cruel trick orchestrated by his captors?

He pressed the phone to his chest, willing it to ring again. The guards, unmoved by the emotional display, pointed Josh toward the door.

Emily clung to hope, waiting for another call. But as minutes stretched into eternity, she resigned herself to the unknown. Tears streamed down her cheeks as she turned to her family, gathered on the porch. "It was Josh," she announced. "He's coming home."

Driven by determination, Emily rummaged through her purse. Her father had given her a number—the lifeline to Dr. Karen Harris, director of the Office of the Special Presidential Envoy for Hostage Affairs. It was Saturday, and Emily hoped someone would answer.

"Dr. Harris," the voice on the other end greeted. "How may I help you?"

"Dr. Harris," Emily's voice trembled, "it's Emily Cooper. I just received a call from Josh. He said he's coming home."

Dr. Harris listened, gathering the scant details Emily offered. She assured Emily that she would investigate and get back to her. After the call ended, Emily dialed her father. If anyone could uncover the truth, it would be him.

Freed from the grip of the phone, Emily sank into a chair, her emotions swirling like leaves caught in a tempest. The news of Josh's release tugged her heart in opposing directions. Joy and relief surged through her veins, yet the weight of captivity still clung to her. Could it be over? The anxiety that had gnawed at her for so long now clawed its way to the surface. It was an emotional rollercoaster, each feeling crashing against the other.

Meanwhile, in the heart of D.C., Dr. Harris and Roger navigated a labyrinth of diplomatic channels and intelligence networks. Their mission was to uncover any trace of the truth behind Emily's report about Josh's impending release. Despite the Saturday sun casting long shadows, Roger sprinted to his office. His uniform hung ready, a symbol of duty and determination. Meg, watching him, beamed with pride. “If anyone can find answers,” she declared, “it’s you.” Her words echoed across the apartment, brimming with unwavering confidence.

Roger’s path led him to the National Military Command Center. Conversations with the senior watch officer yielded fragments of information. He pivoted to the Department of State officer on duty, hoping for official updates. The intelligence agencies—silent sentinels on the watch floor—scanned the world for signs. Human informants shared secrets, intercepted communications crackled, and satellite imagery revealed hidden truths. Yet, Roger knew that even their clandestine methods often traced back to unclassified media. News outlets held keys to negotiations and shifting tides.

And then, the linchpin: Dr. Harris. She moved in shadows, aware of secret negotiations between the U.S., China, and North Korea. Sweden, the silent intermediary, wove threads of communication. Dr. Harris held the answers—the confirmation that would bridge continents and reunite hearts. Soon, Emily would hear the good news, and her world would shift on its axis.

In the dusky embrace of the secluded valley, Josh stepped through the rusted iron gates, their reluctant groans echoing his newfound freedom.

The air tasted of possibility, yet memories clung to his consciousness like gossamer threads. The prison walls, once his confining world, now dissolved into shadows.

Before him sprawled a cracked asphalt parking lot, its surface etched by years of neglect. Gnarled trees stood guard, their twisted branches reaching skyward—a silent plea for release. And there, at the edge of desolation, rested the military truck that had ferried him here—a relic from a bygone era, its green paint faded and chipped.

Josh scrutinized the truck. Worn tires, a scarred metal frame—how many others had endured this unforgiving cargo hold, blindfolded and disoriented? But now, a sleek black SUV beckoned nearby—an obsidian gem against the muted landscape. Its modern lines promised escape.

The driver, an enigma behind the wheel, awaited. Suspicion warred with hope. Was this a trap, a final deception? The SUV's engine hummed, urging Josh to decide. They left the prison behind, crossing a silver river that wound through the valley. Ahead lay mist-shrouded mountains—a path to uncertainty.

Together, they ascended—a prisoner and a guide—toward an unknown horizon. Behind them, the prison blurred into memory; ahead, the mountains held secrets. Josh found the courage to ask about his destination. The driver jabbed at the faded map and, with his tobacco-stained finger, pointed at Heavenly Lake—a destination etched in smoke-stained lines.

CHAPTER 24

FRIENDSHIP BRIDGE

After a grueling four-hour drive westward, the SUV eased to a halt at the Sino-Korean Friendship Bridge. Also known as the China–North Korea Friendship Bridge, it spanned the Yalu River, stitching together China and North Korea. Constructed by the Imperial Japanese Army between April 1937 and May 1943 during its occupation of Korea, the bridge now served as one of the few ways to enter or leave North Korea. Today, it was Josh's gateway to freedom.

North Korean border guards awaited them, their expressions etched in stone. Rifles rested against their shoulders; fingers poised near triggers. Josh's driver handed over the paperwork. The guards scrutinized it, eyes sharp for any hint of subterfuge. Their stern faces betrayed nothing, but their vigilance spoke volumes.

They appeared satisfied, though their expressions betrayed nothing, as they inspected the SUV with its doors open and trunk exposed. They scanned every nook and probed every crevice. Josh's heartbeat echoed in the confined space. Tension filled the air, and for a moment, Josh felt himself transported back to the prison he had just escaped. The bridge symbolized not only freedom but the weight of survival. As the guards moved on, he exhaled, knowing that each second brought him closer to a world beyond prison walls.

As the search proceeded, the guards communicated in hushed tones—a clandestine symphony of caution. Radios crackled, their static-laden voices relaying information to unseen superiors. Suspicion hung in the air like a taut wire; any misstep could ignite the fuse.

Finally, the guards stepped back, their scrutiny complete. They exchanged nods with the driver, a silent pact of relief. The gate lifted, granting passage toward the Chinese border. Josh and the driver exhaled in unison, their shared tension dissipating like fog under the morning sun.

On the far side of the bridge, the SUV jerked to an abrupt halt, its tires gripping the asphalt. The driver emerged; urgency etched on his face. He swung open Josh's door, gesturing toward a white van parked near the Chinese border guard station. Josh hesitated, indecision gnawing at him—freedom or trap?

Then, like a guiding light in the fog, he glimpsed Joffre in the van's passenger seat. Determination surged within Josh. The only obstacles between him and freedom were two vigilant Chinese border guards. Their eyes bore into him, assessing his resolve. One guard clutched a photograph—a secret shared between them. With a nod, he signaled to his companion, who lifted the hinged white-and-red-striped pole—the gateway to a new chapter.

Josh stepped forward, heart pounding, and crossed the threshold. The bridge behind him blurred—a fragile thread connecting past and present. Ahead lay Joffre, waiting in the van's shelter. And as the gate closed behind him, Josh knew that freedom was no longer a distant dream, but a tangible reality.

Inside the van, Joffre made his way back to Josh, his embrace a lifeline forged through trials. For Josh, it was sweet relief—the warmth of camaraderie after the icy grip of captivity. Joffre transcended mere colleague or friend; he was a steadfast presence, a surrogate father in this tumultuous journey.

Beyond Emily and his boys, Josh couldn't imagine anyone he'd rather be with. Joffre's eyes traced the contours of Josh's face, seeking answers. Physically, Josh appeared well, but there was a shadow—an intangible weight—that clung to him. Joffre sensed it, like a dimmed star in the night sky.

"Josh," Joffre began, his voice low, "we're about a hundred miles east of Changbai Mountain." He gestured toward the winding road that followed the Yalu River. "The actual distance by road will be longer, but we're on the right path."

Josh nodded, gratitude and determination intertwining. The van rumbled forward, carrying them toward safety. And as the miles slipped away, Joffre's presence—a guiding star in the wilderness—reminded Josh that he was no longer alone.

"Here," Joffre offered, handing Josh a cellphone. "Call Emily before we lose reception in the mountains."

Josh accepted the phone, its weight a lifeline connecting him to the world beyond the rugged terrain. He dialed Emily's number, each digit echoing with anticipation. When she answered, her voice carried relief—an invisible bridge spanning the distance between them. He apologized for losing the connection earlier and warned her it could happen again. Emily had already learned from Dr. Harris about the plan for Joffre to meet Josh at the border and drive him back to the observatory, yet she listened silently, allowing Josh to recount the details, including the news that once arriving at the observatory, Josh and the rest of the team would evacuate the station and return to Vancouver, Washington.

In the background, the sweet symphony of his sons clamored for their turn to speak with Josh.

"Dad, are you done working?" Johnny's voice, innocent and eager, tugged at his heart.

"Yes," Josh replied, picturing their faces.

"How many more sleep days?" Jimmy's curiosity danced through the phone.

"Two, maybe three," Josh estimated. "It all depends on how fast the plane flies."

"Daddy, get a fast one," Johnny chimed in, his imagination soaring.

"Faster than a P-40 Warhawk," Jimmy added, their dreams painted in the hues of adventure and reunion. Josh held the phone tighter, knowing that with each passing moment, he was one step closer to safety and one step further from danger.

With the call ended, Joffre updated Josh on the research at the mountain.

"Are you done?" Josh asked.

"We finished days ago," Joffre admitted. "We didn't want to leave without you. Plus, we couldn't have left if we wanted to. The State Department insisted that we stay put to avoid jeopardizing the ongoing negotiations over your release."

The conversation shifted to the work completed on the mountain. Despite the existing Chinese equipment and the upgrades the American team had painstakingly installed, the mountain remained silent—a dormant giant refusing to reveal its secrets.

"Couldn't find a pulse," Joffre summarized, frustration tugging at his features.

"Frankly, I am not sure why the Chinese government spent the money to bring us all the way here," Joffre confessed. "We didn't tell them anything more than they already knew."

"Maybe they needed us to check their work or enhance their monitoring capabilities for the future," Josh suggested.

The conversation reached a stalemate, and the two men rode along in companionable silence. Then, as if scripted by fate, Joffre reached into the backseat and produced three MREs—their survival rations. One for their Chinese driver, one for him, and one for Josh.

Josh stared at the meal package resting on the seat. Then laughter bubbled up from deep within him. Joffre joined in, their shared amusement a balm for their weary souls.

"That's got to be about the best damn thing I've seen in a week," Josh admitted, wiping tears from his eyes.

Soon, steam from the prepared meals fogged the van's windows, cocooning them in warmth. It wasn't too much longer before the van began its familiar climb up the slopes of Changbai Mountain, heading toward the observatory. Climbing out of the van, Josh's colleagues greeted him. First among them was Victor, his face etched with concern. A soft cast encased Victor's right knee, serving as a visible reminder of their shared ordeal. He approached Josh, moving as if Josh were a wounded animal—fragile.

Victor felt the heavy burden of guilt, believing he should have been taken captive instead of Josh. His voice, barely above a whisper, carried the weight of remorse. "I'm sorry," Victor said, his eyes searching Josh's face for forgiveness. "It should have been me." "Nonsense," Josh declared, his voice unwavering. He made it loud enough for all to hear. "It could have been any of us. We're a team."

Dawn, the team's medical specialist, stepped forward next, her eyes reflecting a blend of relief and concern. Ever since she learned about Josh's captivity, she scoured websites, seeking information on the medical needs of released hostages. She understood that the conditions captives experienced could cause significant health issues.

With practiced concern for a patient's privacy, Dawn pulled Josh aside. But for this moment, she suspended her medical worries. Instead, she enveloped Josh in her arms, offering him a pause from the chaos of the past days—a moment to recharge.

Josh, raised more by women than men, appreciated the unique gentleness that a woman brought to a hug. Dawn's embrace was like a warm cocoon, soft and reassuring. Stress, anxiety, and loneliness fell away as her caring energy surrounded him. He could have lingered there forever, finding solace in her presence.

But Dawn had medical matters to attend to. Breaking away from the hug, she half-seriously, half-jokingly declared, "You know I'll need to give you a brief medical exam later."

One by one, Josh's colleagues and their Chinese counterparts found their way to him, their eyes reflecting relief and joy at his safe return. The shared ordeal had forged bonds that transcended borders. To celebrate both the occasion and the impending departure of their new American friends, the Chinese scientists presented a generous assortment of Baijiu—a potent liquor crafted from whole grains: sorghum, peas, rice, barley, wheat, or millet.

The Baijiu was fragrant, colorless, and clear, yet it carried the weight of resilience. Its alcohol content, ranging from 40% to 60%, mirrored the strength of their camaraderie. Under the team tent, the liquor flowed alongside stories—the joyous accumulation of days spent together.

As the night wore on, the crowd thinned. Dawn, ever watchful, approached Josh. His eyes were blurry, his steps unsteady from the Baijiu's hold. She offered to guide him to his makeshift bed inside the portable prefabricated container that had been his refuge on the mountain.

"I can't," Josh stubbornly declared.

"Can't what?" Dawn asked, her voice gentle.

Josh shook his head. "Not tonight. I can't sleep in that box."

Dawn understood. She disappeared and returned with a pile of pilfered blankets. Together, they stepped beyond the tent's confines, away from the walls and ceilings. The vast sky stretched above them, adorned with stars—the same stars that had witnessed Josh's struggles and resilience.

"Then tonight," Dawn whispered, "we sleep under the stars."

CHAPTER 25

WELCOME TO AMERICA

The team's return journey from Changbai Mountain to Vancouver, Washington, mirrored their initial expedition, but with a clandestine twist: they unanimously decided to alter their destination. Instead of landing in Vancouver, they would touch down in Seattle. They planned this secret change to bring Josh a step closer to the homecoming he richly deserved.

Joffre orchestrated the details flawlessly. He contacted Emily to inform her of the revised itinerary and arranged for Josh's BMW to be returned from Vancouver to his house. He ensured a comfortable van awaited the rest of the team at the airport to ferry them back to Vancouver. Every detail reflected their camaraderie and thoughtful planning, ensuring Josh's homecoming was seamless and heartfelt.

On a moonless night, the China Air jet began its descent towards Seattle-Tacoma International Airport, hidden within the vast, dark expanse of the Pacific Northwest. The runway lights sparkled like distant stars, guiding the aircraft home. As the plane descended, the team skillfully distracted Josh, preventing him from recognizing the city lights of Seattle and Tacoma stretched out below. Their glow painted a shimmering canvas against the inky backdrop, a silent testament to the grand deception underway.

The pilot and crew, fully aware of the plan, avoided any mention of the true destination. With Joffre's team being the only passengers on this chartered flight, it made the ruse easier to maintain. The pilot skillfully aligned the aircraft with the runway, adjusting flaps and throttles to bring the jet to a gentle landing. The sensation of soft deceleration marked the journey's end.

Through the velvet night, the ground crew moved with practiced precision. The tug vehicle, a robust machine adorned with yellow caution stripes, slid up to the plane's nose gear. Its operator, dressed in fluorescent safety gear, communicated with a symphony of hand signals and radio chatter. The tug's engine roared to life, gently nudging the massive plane forward, aligning it perfectly with the waiting jet bridge.

The seamless coordination and quiet efficiency of the ground crew underscored the careful planning that had gone into this special homecoming.

Hydraulic arms extended, smoothly connecting the plane to the terminal. A soft thud reverberated through the fuselage, signaling the journey's conclusion. Joffre unbuckled his seatbelt with a sense of urgency, eager to deliver Josh to his waiting family. The team gathered their few belongings, a mixture of excitement and anticipation hanging in the air.

Finally, the cabin door opened, revealing the gangway leading to the terminal. The air was thick with expectation. Josh, still unsuspecting, stepped onto the bridge. Inside, his teammates marveled at how Josh had yet to recognize the terminal as Seattle's, not Vancouver's. The ruse had held perfectly.

The gangway seemed to stretch endlessly, each step echoing with the quiet thrill of the impending revelation. Josh remained unaware of the switch in destinations. The team's careful planning and heartfelt intentions had paid off. The moment of truth was imminent, and the air buzzed with the shared excitement of what was about to unfold.

Following the signs to passport control, the team queued behind fellow travelers from distant lands, each awaiting their turn. The immigration officer scrutinized Josh's passport, and with a welcoming smile, said, "Welcome back to America, Mr. Cooper." Josh paused for a moment, savoring the words that confirmed his true location. The realization dawned on him, but he quickly composed himself, moving forward like the rest of the team.

With nothing to declare, they moved swiftly toward the whirring conveyor belts, picked up their luggage, and approached the glass doors marking the entrance to the bustling terminal. However, before they could pass further, a Transportation Security Administration officer in a distinctive blue uniform greeted them and directed them to a side exit. This detour led them into a spacious, empty room, reminiscent of a conference hall. From behind a blue partition, Josh's family emerged, his sons proudly carrying the same "Welcome Home" banner they had made to mark his return from Washington, D.C.

The scene ahead unfolded in a rush of emotion. Josh's family eagerly awaited his arrival at the forefront of the crowd. Their faces lit up with joy and relief, reflecting the love and longing that fueled this elaborate surprise. The team's efforts culminated in this perfect moment of reunion, where the bonds of family intertwined to create a cherished memory.

Josh stood in pleasant disbelief, his heart swelling with emotion. Emily rushed forward to embrace him, followed closely by Johnny and Jimmy, who, in their excitement, had abandoned the banner to the care of Maya. Josh's parents, Sarah and Frank, captured the heartwarming reunion in a flurry of photographs. Emily's family, including her sister Ellen and her parents Meg and Roger, who had flown in for the occasion, added to the joyful atmosphere. Josh would soon learn that Roger had carried an ulterior motive all the way from Washington, D.C.

Adding to the surprise, Dr. Karen Harris, the director of the Office of the Special Presidential Envoy for Hostage Affairs, had also flown in from Washington, D.C. The moment gained added importance because of her presence. After the heartfelt parade of hugs and warm welcomes, Dr. Harris gently called Emily and Josh aside. She informed them that a sea of reporters awaited them in the terminal, eager to capture the story of Josh's return and the extraordinary efforts that had made it possible.

The room buzzed with a mix of excitement and relief as the gravity of the moment sank in. Josh, surrounded by his loved ones and supported by the unwavering efforts of his team, felt a profound sense of gratitude and joy. This reunion, meticulously planned and executed, was more than just a welcome home—it was a testament to the resilience of the human spirit and the power of love and determination.

"Josh, I don't expect you to make a statement," Dr. Harris began, her voice calm and reassuring. "However, I will make one, and I would deeply appreciate it if you, Emily, and your sons could stand by my side as I read the prepared remarks."

She continued, "Josh, we owe a debt of gratitude to those who assisted in your release. By thanking them today, we not only show our appreciation for their efforts, but also help to spark future cooperation." Josh and Emily exchanged a glance and agreed, gathering Johnny and Jimmy close.

Outside in the terminal, the atmosphere was electric. Cameras flashed incessantly, and the bright lights of news cameras illuminated the scene. Josh, with Johnny at his side, and Emily, holding Jimmy's hand, flanked Dr. Harris as she spoke.

"Good afternoon," Dr. Harris began, her voice carrying a mix of relief and joy. "I am profoundly grateful and overjoyed to announce the safe return of Dr. Josh Cooper, who North Korea has released from custody. This momentous occasion marks the end of a challenging ordeal for Dr. Cooper and his family, and we are relieved to welcome him back home."

The terminal seemed to hold its breath as Dr. Harris continued. "This successful resolution would not have been possible without the unwavering support and collaboration of our international partners. I would like to extend my deepest gratitude to the government of China for their critical diplomatic efforts and mediation, which played an essential role in facilitating Dr. Cooper's release."

She paused, allowing her words to sink in before continuing. "I would like to express our sincere appreciation to the Swedish government, whose consistent and dedicated commitment to delivering consular services and acting as a protecting power helped ensure Dr. Cooper's well-being and safe return."

"Our heartfelt thanks also go out to the teams at the Office of the Special Presidential Envoy for Hostage Affairs and other U.S. government agencies, whose relentless work and dedication have made this reunion possible."

Dr. Harris's voice grew more resolute as she neared the end of her statement. "Dr. Cooper's release is a testament to what we can achieve when nations and communities come together with a shared commitment to humanitarian principles and justice. We will continue our tireless efforts to bring all Americans held hostage or wrongfully detained abroad back to their families. Thank you."

As Dr. Harris concluded, the terminal erupted in applause and the flash of cameras intensified, capturing the emotional moment. Josh, Emily, and their sons stood together, a united front of resilience and hope, the relief and joy of their reunion clear in their smiles. This moment, filled with gratitude and shared triumph, would etch itself into the memories of not only those present, but also countless others inspired by their story.

After the press statement, the airport's bustling energy carried everyone toward the exit. There, bathed in the soft glow of overhead lights, stood a waiting passenger van to carry the team, minus Josh, back to Vancouver.

Gathered in a tight-knit circle, their faces etched with both weariness and camaraderie, the group of colleagues who had shared so much together exchanged heartfelt farewells. The air hummed with the distant rumble of jet engines, a reminder of the distance that would soon separate them. Each hug held a promise—to stay in touch and to reminisce. Joffre clasped Josh's hand and squeezed it, promising to stay in touch.

With a last wave, Josh and his family moved across the arrival area to short-term parking. Emily's mother and father said their goodbyes and climbed into Ellen's car to make the short drive to Ellen's flat, where they would spend the night until the planned breakfast reunion at Montlake Park in the morning.

Holding hands in grateful relief, Emily guided Josh, Maya, and the boys to her car. Emily started the short drive home. Everyone rode in silence. Even the boys seemed to sense the somberness of the moment. Before long, the two boys posed the familiar question that every child asks when a parent returns after an extended absence: "Daddy, did you bring us anything?"

Josh's heart warmed at the innocence of the question. How could he tell his hopeful sons that he had returned empty-handed?

It was then that Josh felt Emily tugging at his arm. He looked over to see her motioning at the package resting on the floorboard. Inside, Josh discovered two gifts, wrapped in airplane-themed wrapping paper. Josh smiled at Emily and handed the gifts over the seat to Maya to give to his sons.

"Can we open them now?" Jimmy pleaded.

"Daddy, can we?" Johnny echoed.

"Of course," Josh relented.

In the cozy confines of the car's back seat, Johnny and his little brother squirmed with excitement. Josh sat in the passenger seat, eyes twinkling. The anticipation hung thick in the air as he handed each boy the small package.

"Go ahead, open them," their father encouraged, his voice a mix of tenderness and joy. Johnny tore into the wrapping paper with practiced precision. His brother, wide-eyed and eager, followed suit. And there they were—two blow-up aircraft, designed after Alaska Airlines airliners, complete with the iconic lion's face emblazoned on the tail.

Johnny's fingers traced the image of the plane, while his brother hugged his own tightly. The lion's face seemed to wink at them, promising adventure and skies yet unexplored. Josh reached over the seat, ruffling each boy's hair.

CHAPTER 26

DÉJÀ VU

A mixture of emotions overwhelmed Josh on his first night back home. The familiar creak of his bedroom door, the soft glow of a bedside lamp, and the scent of his own pillow, once distant memories, now cradled him. He lay there staring at the ceiling, feeling the weight of his ordeal lift, like a heavy backpack finally removed. Emily lay beside him, her warmth a comforting anchor. He reached for her hand, tracing the lines of her palm, reassured by her presence. The room felt smaller, cozier. Josh listened to the night sounds—the distant hum of traffic, the rustle of trees outside—and they were like a lullaby, soothing his frayed nerves. Josh closed his eyes, and for the first time in a while, he was not afraid. He was home. Safe. And that was all that mattered.

Night turned into morning, and soon laughter filled the house, emanating from downstairs. The boys enjoyed their morning cartoon ritual, their laughter echoing through the house in a delightful symphony of shared joy. Josh and Emily showered, dressed, and joined the boys downstairs. Maya busied herself preparing breakfast. The house would be full this morning, with Emily's mother, father, and sister planning to join them. Josh's mother and father wouldn't be far behind.

In the kitchen, Maya—the culinary maestro—orchestrated a symphony of sizzling pans and fragrant spices. The sun peeked through the window, casting a warm glow on the kitchen's marbled surfaces. Maya's apron, adorned with a rainbow of colored handprints, a gift from the boys, told the shared story of love and nourishment.

Maya's secret breakfast weapon? Hotcake art! She whisked together a batch of her tried-and-true pancake batter. The batter was velvety and promising—a canvas for her morning masterpiece. She grinned, knowing that her hotcakes would soon transform into beloved characters. Today's selection was a parade of dinosaur molds she knew would delight the boys.

Maya surveyed her arsenal: a ladle for generous dollops of batter, a spatula for precision flips. With the eggs and bacon already prepared, Maya turned her attention to the pancake batter. She poured batter onto the sizzling griddle. Tyrannosauruses (T-Rex), brontosaurs, and triceratops soon emerged. The boys would giggle when they saw these edible heroes. Maya's heart swelled; cooking was her love language.

The kitchen smelled of warmth, love, and anticipation. Emily and Ellen helped Maya carry the plates to the deck where everyone else had already gathered, their stomachs growling like dinosaurs in anticipation. The boys' eyes widened—their breakfast had come alive! Laughter filled the deck as they devoured their edible art. Maya watched, her heart full. Breakfast wasn't just about sustenance; it was a canvas for love, creativity, and shared moments. And on that sun-kissed deck, Maya had delivered another meal of joy.

As breakfast drew to a close, the morning sun cast a golden hue over the table. Roger leaned in closer to Emily, his voice barely above a whisper as he requested a private conversation. The gentle murmur of their family faded into the background as Emily nodded and guided him to a secluded corner of the lush garden. There, surrounded by blooming flowers and the soft rustle of leaves, she listened intently to Roger's plea.

"Emily," Roger began, his tone urgent yet measured, "I need to take Josh back to Washington, D.C." His eyes searched hers, hoping to convey the gravity of the situation. "Josh needs both physical and psychological evaluations to assess any impact from his captivity."

"Being a former hostage can have lasting effects," Roger emphasized, his voice tinged with a mix of concern and determination. He hoped to appeal to Emily's empathy, knowing her dual roles as a devoted wife and a skilled nurse would resonate deeply with his appeal.

Emily understood the necessity of a thorough examination to assess Josh's overall health, identify any hidden injuries, and address pressing medical needs. The threat of infectious diseases from his prison exposure loomed large in her mind.

Despite Josh showing no overt signs of mental distress, Emily knew that diagnosing PTSD, with its insidious symptoms like flashbacks and anxiety, was beyond her expertise. The weight of the decision pressed heavily on her heart as she grappled with the thought of letting Josh go again.

As the morning breeze gently stirred the leaves, Emily felt the magnitude of the moment. Her duty to protect Josh's well-being clashed with the emotional turmoil of possibly sending him away. The decision was complex and fraught with emotions, but Emily knew she had to weigh them all.

"Daddy, why can't he complete his assessment here?" Emily asked, her voice tinged with a blend of curiosity and concern.

"Emily," Roger replied gently, "the people best qualified to diagnose Josh's physical and psychological state and provide any needed treatment are in Washington, D.C." He paused, searching for the right words.

"And?" Emily prompted, sensing there was more Roger hadn't yet revealed. "And what?"

Roger hesitated; his hidden agenda now laid bare. He took a deep breath and confessed, "Emily, if the assessments clear Josh medically, I need him to complete his work at the Pentagon."

"Daddy," Emily protested, her voice carefully controlled so as not to carry across the yard, "Josh needs to return to Washington, D.C. to complete the work," Roger reiterated. "It's crucial. If he doesn't finish it, everything he's been through will have been in vain. He'll regret it for the rest of his life."

"But Dad, what if it's too difficult for him?" Emily asked, her worry for Josh's well-being clear.

"Emily, sometimes the most important things are also the hardest," Roger pleaded, his eyes earnest. "Josh can do it. We just need to believe in him."

Emily felt the weight of her father's words. She understood the importance of the mission and the psychological closure it might offer Josh. With a heavy heart but a clear sense of duty, she concluded the conversation by agreeing to talk to Josh, hoping that he, too, would understand the necessity of returning to Washington, D.C.

Emily returned to the deck, her eyes captivated by the morning sun's hues dancing over the horizon. She found Josh leaning against the railing, lost in thought, and gently touched his arm. "Josh, can we take a walk?" she asked, her voice soft yet insistent.

Two parks bordered their house—the charming West Montlake Park and the sprawling East Montlake Park. The choice was simple for them; they turned west, hand in hand, setting off along the Lake Washington Ship Canal trail. The canal, a shimmering ribbon of water, united Portage Bay to the west with Union Bay to the east.

As they walked, their arms swinging in unison, Emily broke the silence that had enveloped them since they left the house. She recounted her conversation with her father. They stopped intermittently alongside the historical colonnade lampposts that lined the trail, reflecting on the weight of her words.

Josh's hesitation to return to the Pentagon was a complex tapestry of emotions—personal trauma, professional anxiety, and unresolved psychological scars. He opened up to Emily, sharing that his captivity had been far more harrowing than he had ever let on. The thought of revisiting those memories through a medical assessment filled him with dread, fearing it would unleash a flood of painful memories and flashbacks.

Emily squeezed his hand, her voice steady and supportive. "The professionals in Washington, D.C., know how to handle this. If you don't face these memories now, they might become even harder to deal with later."

Josh looked down, his brow furrowed with concern. "What if I'm not ready to get back to work?" he asked.

"Then don't," Emily replied simply. "Complete the medical assessment and come back home."

Josh sighed, his thoughts a whirlpool of doubt. Returning to the high-stress environment of the Pentagon felt overwhelming. He knew he was the only one with the security clearance to debrief the team's findings, a responsibility that weighed heavily on him. The pressure to deliver results, compounded by the urgency of the upcoming presidential trip to China, was almost too much to bear.

"Emily," he confessed, "I feel like going to Washington, D.C., in the first place had been a mistake. During my captivity, I promised myself I'd put our family first."

Emily laughed gently, shaking her head. "Josh, that's ridiculous. I love you as my husband, and your sons adore you as their father. But you are so much more."

She spoke of his dedication to his research and his role as a professor, integral parts of his identity. His findings were not just important; they had the potential to make a significant impact. Emily reminded him of his sense of duty and service, a core part of who he was, and how his insights could be crucial for national security and policy.

"Completing your work and debriefing your findings could give you a sense of closure," she echoed her father's words. "It could turn this painful chapter into something meaningful."

Josh listened, her words resonating deeply within him. Abandoning his work would be a betrayal of his principles and the promises he had made to himself. Emily's belief in his abilities and the importance of his contributions rekindled his determination.

"Déjà vu," Josh finally declared, a resolute look in his eyes. "It looks like I'm going back to Washington, D.C."

Resolved, the couple continued their walk, the path now lit by their newfound determination. They reached the yacht club at the trail's end, then turned back toward Montlake Bridge. As they arrived at the bridge, Emily reached over and kissed Josh on the cheek.

"Josh, I love you," she said, the words carrying the weight of all their shared experiences. It was a meaningful echo of a kiss they had shared on this same bridge on their first date, a symbol of their enduring bond.

And with that, they walked on, ready to face whatever came next, together.

CHAPTER 27

FIT FOR DUTY

The flight from Vancouver to Washington, D.C., with Emily's mother and father, unfolded like a muted symphony—unremarkable yet laden with Josh's unspoken burdens. As the plane glided through the sky, Josh's gaze wandered beyond the clouds, retracing the contours of his past. He dared not share with his in-laws the haunting nightmares that reverberated in his mind. Instead, he feigned casual conversation, masking the turmoil within.

Upon arrival, the trio descended into the bustling hive of the Metrorail Blue Line. The train's rhythmic hum seemed to mirror Josh's heartbeat, a metronome of uncertainty. They stepped onto the platform at Pentagon City, their footsteps a hesitant cadence. The short walk to his in-laws' apartment felt like crossing a fragile bridge—one that connected the familiar present to the shadowed past.

Inside the apartment, the air held memories—the scent of Emily's mother's cooking, the creak of the floorboards underfoot. The furniture stood as silent witnesses, their upholstery worn by countless conversations, laughter, and quiet contemplation. Josh sank into the armchair, its embrace a balm for his restless soul. The familiarity of the space enveloped him, whispering that he was no longer a captive but a survivor.

Morning light filtered through the curtains, casting gentle stripes across the room. Josh emerged from a fitful sleep, his mind still navigating the labyrinth of memories. Roger stood by the window, transformed. Gone was the military uniform, replaced by a suit and tie—a symbol of civilian life. Roger's eyes held a blend of concern and resolve as he ushered Josh to the waiting car. The engine purred, carrying them to the medical appointment—a voyage toward healing.

At the clinic, Josh's pulse quickened. Nurses, their smiles kind but clinical, guided him through the process. They measured his weight and Body Mass Index, numbers that might hold secrets of deprivation. Blood flowed into vials, a river of answers. The nurses explained their mission: to unveil the hidden scars, to detect the remnants of North Korea's grip. Under the microscope, they later checked for hepatitis, tuberculosis, and parasites—all ghosts of confinement.

As Josh sat in the sterile room, he wondered if healing was possible. Perhaps the physical evaluation was merely a preamble—a bridge to cross, one step closer to reclaiming his life. Roger's presence, unwavering and paternal, anchored him. Together, they faced the unknown, seeking solace in the familiar and hope in the resilience of the human spirit.

The sterile clinic walls absorbed Josh's unease as he sat on the edge of a vinyl-covered examination table. The nurses, their voices gentle yet matter-of-fact, unraveled the intricacies of parasite infections. Josh's stomach churned at the mere mention of tapeworms, hookworms, and flukes—their clandestine entry into the body, their insidious routes: ingestion, skin contact, and the unsettling proximity of egg-laying near the anus. He interrupted, half-jokingly, "If I didn't ask, I didn't want to know." The nurses exchanged knowing glances, their eyes harboring compassion for a survivor who had glimpsed hell.

Next came the physical therapists—a duo of strength assessors. Their hands pressed against Josh's muscles, gauging resilience and vulnerability. Prolonged immobility during captivity had left its mark—muscles weakened, their fibers disclosing tales of confinement. Satisfied, they led Josh to the dentist, who inspected his teeth with clinical precision. No cavities, no fractures—only the shadow of resilience.

Then came the moment Josh dreaded—the psychiatrist's office. The room lacked the clichéd couch, and Josh quipped about it, masking anxiety with humor. The doctor, a small-framed man with eyes that held more stories than his journal, dismissed the jest and instead asked Josh to tell him about his time in captivity. Josh spilled his ordeal—the cold cells, the hidden secrets, the gnawing hunger for freedom. The doctor's pen scratched across the paper, capturing fragments of trauma.

Questions followed, probing Josh's emotional landscape. The doctor's voice softened, coaxing out nightmares—their jagged edges, their nocturnal grip. Josh recounted his first night back at the observatory, the walls pressing in, the open sky beckoning. Claustrophobia, the doctor assured, was a familiar companion for those who had danced with confinement.

"Any other trauma?" the doctor asked, peering into Josh's eyes.

"Define trauma," Josh countered.

"Nightmares, flashbacks, hyper-vigilance, or detachment from reality," the doctor replied.

"Nightmares," Josh confessed, their tendrils still clinging.

"Tell me," the doctor encouraged, and Josh wove dreams into words—their darkness, their unraveling.

"They'll pass," the doctor promised, closing the session. "Consider therapy—a compass for your recovery." His hand rested on Josh's shoulder, a silent reassurance. "You're just fine," he murmured, "a precaution against the shadows."

Josh stood, the doctor's words echoing in his mind like distant chimes. His assessment was complete—charts, measurements, and hushed consultations. Roger delivered the verdict: "Fit for duty, pending any negative findings." The military's language—clinical, precise—masked the truth. Josh's scars, both visible and hidden, were now part of his dossier.

"Where next?" Josh asked, his gaze shifting from the sterile walls to Roger.

Roger cleared his throat, the sound scraping against the silence. "Josh," he began, "there's something we need to discuss. It's about your return to work."

Josh's silence hung like a shroud. "What's going on?"

Roger hesitated, then stepped into the breach. "A polygraph," he said, "it's no longer routine. Given your recent ordeal, they want to ensure—"

"—that I'm not compromised," Josh finished, his voice faltering. "I understand."

Roger's gaze softened. "It's not doubt, son," he said. "It's vigilance."

"Why didn't you tell me about this sooner?" Josh protested.

"Because you would've over thought it, and you would've been a wreck for the exam," Roger explained.

Roger leaned closer, his voice a quiet anchor. "We'll get through this, Josh. Together."

Father-in-law and son-in-law rode in silence, the car's engine a muted hum. The "non-disclosed building" loomed ahead—an enigma wrapped in concrete and secrecy. People whispered about it in national security circles—a place where shadows danced, and secrets slumbered. Roger, usually resplendent in military uniform, wore civilian attire today. The building demanded discretion; its very existence thrived on anonymity.

Inside, the air tasted of caution. Roger handed Josh over to the polygrapher—a sentinel of truth, despite the term he despised: “lie detector.” The polygrapher knew better—the instrument didn’t detect lies; it traced autonomic symphonies—the crescendo of heartbeats, the staccato of breath, the skin’s electric signals. Josh settled into the chair, his pulse a clandestine Morse code. The questions would come—structured, unyielding. Deception, if it lingered, would reveal itself in the tremor of skin, the flutter of truth. The polygrapher, guardian of secrets, leaned forward. “Ready?” he asked. Josh nodded, and the dance began—the rhythm of survival, the cadence of redemption.

Unbeknownst to Josh, the initial phase of his examination had unfolded weeks earlier when he meticulously completed the Standard Form (SF-86) Questionnaire for National Security Positions. The examiner, a sentinel of scrutiny, now wielded that information like a compass, navigating the labyrinth of Josh’s life. His examination was a symphony of inquiries—an intricate dance of words and pulse.

The examiners divided the questions into four groups: relevant questions, irrelevant questions, control questions, and finally concealed information (guilty knowledge) questions.

Relevant questions probed the bedrock of Josh’s existence—the very ground he had laid bare on the SF-86. Employment history, credit trails, driving routes—they dissected his past, seeking anomalies. Josh, the boy scout, answered with unwavering honesty. The examiner, perhaps weary from unraveling countless narratives, yawned discreetly.

Questions related to Josh's mental health were the only ones that seemed to concern both him and the examiner. It took several more questions for Josh to explain his reaction adequately to the queries about his mental capacity. Once he explained his recent psychological screening, the examiner seemed satisfied that this was the reason behind the elevated physiological arousal factors that inferred potential deception.

These physiological arousal factors included an increased respiratory rate measured by bands placed around Josh's chest and abdomen to track his breathing patterns, increased blood pressure and heart rate from the blood pressure cuff attached to his arm, and changes in his skin conductivity detected by electrodes on his fingertips due to increased sweating associated with lying.

The examiner intermingled irrelevant questions alongside the probing relevant questions. These were cosmic dust—scattered, inconsequential. Josh's favorite color, the last book he read—the mundane mingled with the momentous. His responses, like stardust, drifted into the ether. Irrelevant questions helped the examiner establish a physiological baseline by giving the subject a rest period to reduce their overall nervousness, which, once elevated, might mask other responses.

Concealed information questions were trickier. Unlike relevant and control questions, which ask if you've committed a crime or lied on your application, concealed information questions concealed information questions allow the examiner to detect evidence about incidents only guilty people have. In Josh's case, specific questions related to North Korea's security services.

After nearly two hours of intense scrutiny, the polygraph examination concluded. Josh emerged from the sterile room, his pulse still racing. In the lobby, he spotted Roger waiting patiently. Roger's eyes twinkled with curiosity.

"How'd you fare, Josh?" Roger asked, a playful grin tugging at his lips.

Josh chuckled, relieved to be out of the hot seat. "Well enough, I suppose."

Roger nodded. "The evaluators will take their time. We'll hear something by day's end."

CHAPTER 28

WELCOME BACK

Cleared by the polygraphers' to return to the Pentagon, Josh, with Roger at his side back in uniform, stepped through the imposing entrance, their footsteps reverberating against the marble-clad corridor. Navigating the labyrinthine halls, they reached the J-2 Directorate for Intelligence—Josh's clandestine hive of analysis, secrets, and muted urgency. His heart raced; these halls were familiar, but the weight of responsibility felt newly heavy on his shoulders.

There they were—the old team. Li, the unassuming China analyst whose eyes held centuries of history; her team lead, Major Rick Stevenson, a man who'd seen too much and slept too little; and Chris Wyatt, the brilliant but perpetually disheveled data whiz. They stood like sentinels, their camaraderie forged in late-night sessions and shared cups of lukewarm coffee.

But today held surprises. Young Ho, the enigmatic Korean specialist, had joined their ranks. His eyes held secrets—perhaps the very ones that danced across satellite images and intercepted communications. And then, the anomaly: Thomas Miller, the reclusive counter-proliferation guru, stood among them. His perpetual scowl softened, replaced by a nod of acknowledgment. Even the most introverted among them recognized the gravity of this moment.

As if scripted by fate, Colonel Walsh, the grizzled commander of the J-2, materialized. His silver-streaked hair framed a face etched with decades of service. He extended a hand to Josh, palm calloused from both desk work and fieldwork. But it wasn't a mere handshake; it was a transfer of legacy, a silent pact. In Josh's palm, the cool metal of a challenge coin materialized—a POW/MIA coin, black as midnight, etched with the silhouette of a soldier's bowed head.

"Josh," Colonel Walsh's voice held the weight of battles fought and lives lost, "this is not official. Unfortunately, the military recognizes only military combatants held as POWs or still missing. But we here—your colleagues, your friends, your family—know better. We honor your courage, your sacrifice. Welcome home."

Josh blinked back unexpected tears, the coin a talisman against the shadows that clung to his memories. He followed the team into the dimly lit room, where the aroma of brewed coffee mingled with the sweetness of glazed donuts. Around the table, they sat—a mosaic of expertise, scars, and unwavering purpose. Here, in the heart of intelligence, they forged bonds stronger than steel.

Afterward, back at his former desk, Josh felt the familiar groan of the swivel chair as he settled into its contours. The J-2 Directorate for Intelligence welcomed him back like a long-lost prodigal.

Li, the unflappable China analyst, leaned against the cubicle divider. "Josh," she said, "meet Cindy Mark." Cindy, the team's newest acquisition from the National Security Agency (NSA), stood beside Li.

"Apologies for bugging you on your first day back," Cindy said, her tone a blend of efficiency and curiosity. "We've got a question."

Josh knew the NSA's game—their work with signals intelligence (SIGINT). They wove patterns from the ether, unraveling covert messages and encrypted murmurs. What had they picked up about Changbai Mountain during his absence? "That's what I'm here for," Josh replied. "What's the mystery?"

Cindy leaned in, her voice low. "The term 'Tonga.' It keeps surfacing in our traffic. We're not sure what it refers to."

Josh's mind raced. Tonga—a code name? A clandestine operation? Or perhaps a linguistic quirk? "Can I review the raw data?" he asked. "Context matters."

"Of course," Cindy agreed, already summoning files. As she worked, Josh's fingers danced across his keyboard. He dug into the digital trenches, hunting for answers.

And there it was: Tonga. Not a spy's alias or a geopolitical maneuver. No, it was geological—the Hunga Tonga-Hunga Ha'apai submarine volcano near the Kingdom of Tonga in the South Pacific. In January 2022, it had erupted with primal fury, birthing a volcanic plume that soared over thirty-five miles—the highest ever recorded.

But why did the Chinese care? Josh wondered. What else had he missed during his absence?

"Li," Josh said, "what else happened while I was away?"

Her eyes flickered toward the corner. "Talk to Young Ho and Thomas Miller," she advised. And with that, the intelligence web tightened around Josh once more, threads of mystery and duty pulling him deeper.

Josh gathered the two analysts, leading them into the dimly lit conference room—the kind where secrets murmured, and shadows clung. Miller, the grizzled veteran with eyes that had seen too much, leaned against the scratched table. Young Ho, the enigmatic Korean specialist, stood by the door, his gaze fixed on the distant horizon.

"Josh," Miller began, his voice a low rumble, "we think they're building another bomb."

Josh's mind raced. "Another atomic bomb?" he asked, his voice echoing off the sterile walls.

Miller appreciated the question. Josh wasn't just worried about mushroom clouds; he was concerned about thresholds—the seismic tipping point that might awaken the slumbering giant beneath Changbai Mountain.

Uncertain of Josh's knowledge, Miller launched into a tutorial. "Atomic bombs rely on nuclear fission," he explained. "Heavy atomic nuclei—uranium, plutonium—split into fragments, releasing energy. Hiroshima, Nagasaki—those were atomic bombs."

"But hydrogen bombs," Miller continued, "the thermonuclear beasts—they dance with nuclear fusion. Like stars, they fuse light atoms. A thousand times more destructive, perhaps. But they're elusive. Harder to make. Need tritium, a rare hydrogen isotope. Not your run-of-the-mill enriched uranium."

Josh nodded, absorbing the gravity. "But why not go full hydrogen?"

Miller grinned. "They lack the ride. No giant aircraft or intercontinental missiles to carry that beast."

Josh's mind raced back to conversations with Li—the bottom line up front. "So, what are they building?"

"A better atomic bomb," Miller said. "Boosted. Small amounts of hydrogen isotopes trigger fusion, amplifying the atomic punch."

"And the test site?" Josh pressed. "Collapsed, right?"

Young Ho stepped forward, his voice like distant thunder. "Not collapsed. Not decommissioned. They've been digging, working day and night."

"Using prisoners from the camp that you were in. Did you realize that the test site was only miles away from the camp?"

"No," Josh answered, tragically aware of the irony of the proximity of the two locations.

Like a flash, it dawned on Josh. Tonga!

The cryptic term lingered in Josh's mind: Tonga. It wasn't just a word; it was a breadcrumb, a trail leading somewhere dark and dangerous.

"I've got to go," Josh exclaimed, bolting from the room. The cubicles blurred as he sprinted, heart pounding. Cindy—NSA analyst, keeper of secrets—was his lifeline now.

He found her at her desk, eyes glued to the screen. "The raw traffic," Josh gasped. "You found it?"

Cindy nodded, her fingers dancing across the keyboard. "Anything about 'Heavenly Lake'?"

"No." Josh leaned in, his breath warm against her ear. "Try Cheonji."

Josh scribbled the name on a notepad, urgency fueling his pen strokes. Cindy's terminal hummed, algorithms sifting through the digital debris. And there it was—the correlation. Tonga and Cheonji, the Chinese name for Heavenly Lake—entwined like myth and reality.

"I'll print it for you," Cindy offered, her eyes searching his. "But Josh, why help the Chinese government after what they did to you?"

Josh froze. "What do you mean, did to me?"

Cindy's eyes widened, realizing her mistake. "I thought you knew..."

"Knew what?" Josh demanded, his voice sharp.

Cindy took a deep breath. "Josh, the Chinese government used you. They had North Korea capture you to extract secrets about Changbai

Mountain."

Josh's mind raced, piecing together the fragments of his captivity. "Why risk it all?"

Cindy's gaze held sorrow. "They needed answers, and you were the pawn they sacrificed."

Josh's world spun. "Did they just capture me by chance?" he asked, sadness clouding his eyes.

"Yes," Cindy whispered.

The truth hit Josh like a tidal wave—raw and unyielding. The Chinese had played puppeteer, and he had been the bait dangled in the shadows. All to extract secrets, all for answers. And now, standing at the precipice of revelation, Josh felt the weight of betrayal and duty collide within him.

CHAPTER 29

TONGA

Josh's heart raced as he burst into his father-in-law's office, the door swinging shut behind him. Roger, engrossed in paperwork, looked up with a mix of surprise and curiosity. He had never seen Josh so animated before.

"Tonga!" Josh blurted out, his voice echoing off the walls. "Roger, I know what the Chinese are up to!"

Roger leaned back in his chair, eyebrows raised. "Alright, Josh," he said, "calm down and tell me what you're talking about."

Taking a deep breath, Josh launched into a rapid-fire summary. He recounted his recent conversations with Cindy Mark and her question about the term Tonga that had surfaced in the communications traffic she was monitoring.

Josh's eyes sparkled with excitement as he described the Tonga eruption—a colossal event that dwarfed even the most dramatic Hollywood disaster scenes.

"Scientists have never seen an eruption on this scale," Josh explained, diving into the remarkable sequence of events that caused the eruption. He detailed how this type of explosion, known as a phreatomagmatic eruption, resulted from the interaction of water and magma, creating immense amounts of steam that expanded over a thousand times, leading to a massive explosion.

"That's the bang. Five hundred times more powerful than Hiroshima," Josh added for emphasis.

"But it can only happen in a Goldilocks zone," Josh continued.

"A Goldilocks zone?" Roger asked.

"Right," Josh said, explaining that if the water-magma reaction had occurred in deeper waters, the water pressure would have likely contained the explosion, and if it had been any shallower, there wouldn't have been enough water to create such a massive explosion.

Turning back to the eruption, Josh described how a column of billowing clouds of debris shot up over twenty-five miles into the atmosphere, and how a mushroom cloud of ash spread out to encompass an area twice the size of South Carolina.

"The shockwave was so powerful that it circled the Earth three times and sent ripples into space," Josh paused to let Roger absorb the information.

Roger, growing impatient, asked, "What does this have to do with China?"

Josh grinned. "Everything," he revealed. "Changbai Mountain is China's version of Tonga."

Roger didn't understand what he was driving at. Josh had seen that look of bewilderment on many students' faces as they grappled with confusion during a lecture. Their faces often revealed subtle yet telling signs—furrowed brows, a slight squint, or a thoughtful tilt of the head. Perhaps they scratched their temple or pursed their lips, lost in the labyrinth of unfamiliar concepts. In his classroom, these expressions were visible cues for him, as the astute professor, to intervene and guide the student, in this case, Roger, toward clarity.

"Please give me a chance to explain," Josh requested.

Thinking back to the presentation he had worked on before leaving for China, Josh gathered his thoughts.

"Remember, we said that we thought China was concerned that North Korea's nuclear testing could cause the mountain to erupt?" Josh began.

"Yes," Roger nodded.

"Well, that was only half of the problem. What we should have said was that China was concerned that North Korea's testing of a boosted nuclear device would cause Heavenly Lake to implode into Changbai's volcanic caldera, causing a Tonga-like eruption."

And there it was, the look on Roger's face that Josh was looking for—not unlike that on a student's face when they finally grasp a complex concept. Their face undergoes a subtle metamorphosis. Furrowed brows relax, like a wound spring releasing its tension. Eyes widen, pupils dilating as if absorbing a newfound light. A spark ignites—a synaptic firework—behind those eyes, illuminating the previously murky corridors of understanding. Lips part, perhaps forming an involuntary "aha" or a silent "eureka." It's as if the mental fog dissipates, revealing clarity like sunlight piercing through storm clouds.

At that moment, the student transcends confusion, bridging the gap between ignorance and enlightenment. Their face becomes a canvas where comprehension paints its masterpiece: a blend of relief, wonder, and intellectual triumph.

"Are you telling me," Roger asked, leaning forward, "that China's volcano could erupt even more violently than you previously explained?"

"Yes," Josh agreed, satisfied. "Much worse."

"But," Roger interrupted, "you said that this type of volcano could only happen underwater."

"I did," Josh acknowledged. "But the Mount Changbai volcano is underwater. It's beneath Heavenly Lake, which holds over two hundred trillion gallons of water."

"And," Roger, who had been paying close attention, added, "you said that the Tonga eruption occurred five hundred feet below the surface of the ocean, right?"

"Yes," Josh confirmed.

Continuing, Roger said, "And let me guess, the bottom of Heavenly Lake is five hundred feet deep?"

"Four hundred and ten feet," Josh corrected, adjusting his father-in-law's estimate.

"Goldilocks zone?" Roger concluded.

"Yes," Josh affirmed.

Roger's skepticism melted into curiosity. "Tell me more," he urged, leaning in.

The conversation continued. Roger asked Josh what a Changbai eruption would look like. Josh rose and, with the practiced hand of a professor, drew on the whiteboard mounted on the wall of Roger's office. He sketched a rough diagram of Changbai Mountain, labeling the vertical axis with the mountain's height—nine thousand feet. Next, he drew a dotted line representing Heavenly Lake and marked its height at seven thousand feet, then another dotted line below the lake to show the lake's bottom, four hundred and ten feet below the surface.

To Roger's surprise, Josh then drew a similar diagram for Tonga, labeling the top of the volcano five hundred feet below the surface of the Pacific Ocean, and the bottom of the caldera two thousand three hundred feet below the rim. What was Josh driving at? Roger wondered.

"It's all about mass," Josh explained. "How much material is available for an eruption to eject?" Referring to his drawing, he noted that the difference between the top of Tonga's caldera and its base was two thousand three hundred feet. In comparison, the difference between the top of Changbai's caldera and the bottom of Heavenly Lake was seven thousand five hundred feet, plus an additional two thousand feet above the crater, a distance four times that of Tonga.

"Tonga ejected about one and a half million cubic feet of debris. We could expect Changbai to erupt at least four times that amount, or about six million cubic feet of debris. That's on a scale with the 1883 Krakatoa eruption."

"And the consequences?" Roger asked.

Josh, still at the whiteboard, began listing the potential outcomes. Ashfall would blanket vast regions, disrupting ecosystems, agriculture, and infrastructure. Ash and mudslides (lahars) would bury the one hundred thousand North Koreans living near or on the slopes of the volcano. The ejected ash would reflect sunlight, causing global cooling effects, potentially leading to crop failures and famine.

"No emails, no phone calls," Roger ordered.

After Josh left his office, Roger stepped next door to speak with his boss, Colonel Walsh.

"Colonel, do you have a second?" Roger asked, knowing his boss needed to hear this news.

Roger conveyed an abbreviated version of Josh's report to a stunned Colonel Walsh.

"Christ, Roger, do you believe him?" Colonel Walsh asked.

"Absolutely," Roger replied.

"Well then, this is the biggest intelligence story since the disclosure of nuclear weapons on the island of Cuba during the Cuban missile crisis," Walsh declared. He added that if Josh was right, Roger could soon be called Admiral Rogers.

"Let me make some calls," Walsh told Roger.

"Meanwhile, let's keep this under our hats," he insisted.

As Josh returned to brief the crisis response team, he realized he hadn't spoken to his father-in-law about his captivity or China's role in it. But he understood it didn't matter. This was about events much larger and more important than himself.

CHAPTER 30

CRISIS ACTION RESPONSE TEAM

Josh found the crisis response team huddled around a table strewn with maps, satellite images, and hastily scribbled notes. The atmosphere was tense, charged with a mix of anxiety and determination. As Josh leaned in, his eyes gleamed with a newfound purpose, ready to weave together the threads of the urgent conversation he had just had with his father-in-law. Inadvertently, Josh had emerged as the leader of the team, his presence commanding attention and respect. The team members looked up at him, their faces a blend of hope and anticipation, eager for his guidance on how to proceed in the critical hours ahead.

"Josh, how do you think we should proceed?" Li, the team's expert on China, inquired, her voice steady but edged with urgency.

"From the beginning," Josh replied, his tone resolute. He then outlined the plan, taking shape in his mind. "We need to start by addressing the fundamental question that China has posed: Is Changbai Mountain dangerous? The simple answer is no. The volcano is currently dormant."

Team members exchanged glances, silently agreeing. Josh continued, "However, we emphasize it will remain dormant unless North Korea resumes nuclear testing. That would change everything."

Josh's gaze swept across the room, ensuring each team member grasped the gravity of the situation. "Next, we need to detail the potential impact on China and the region if an eruption were to occur. Captain Banks specifically asked for a comprehensive analysis of this scenario."

The room fell silent, the weight of Josh's words settling over the team. Each member understood the critical importance of their next steps, their faith in Josh's leadership unshaken.

"One more thing," Josh added, his voice firm. "Captain Banks wanted me to emphasize that this is a top priority. This requires an all-team effort. He wants all the bells and whistles, no holding back."

The weight of his words hung in the air as Josh continued, "Resources are not an issue. We have the full backing to deploy whatever we need to get this done right."

The team members nodded, their determination solidifying. With Josh at the helm and the full support of Captain Banks, they were ready to tackle the monumental task ahead.

Josh knew the stakes were high as he delved deep into the potential effects of a Mount Changbai eruption on China and the surrounding region. He was determined to prepare a comprehensive analysis that would leave no stone unturned.

He first addressed the catastrophic threat posed by pyroclastic flows. These fast-moving currents of scorching gas and volcanic matter, capable of reaching speeds over sixty miles per hour and temperatures exceeding eight hundred degrees Fahrenheit, would devastate everything in their path for up to twenty miles. Tens of thousands of people living near Changbai Mountain would face almost certain death from asphyxiation, burial under volcanic debris, and the sheer impact force.

With concern etched on his face, Josh delved into the grim details with his team. He worked closely with his colleagues from the National Geospatial-Intelligence Agency (NGA) to prepare detailed, high-resolution maps showing potential flow paths. These maps were crucial for illustrating the severe impact on nearby communities and infrastructure. The team used satellite imagery, topographical data, and historical eruption patterns to identify the most vulnerable areas.

NGA's advanced mapping technology allowed them to create predictive models showing the likely trajectories of these deadly flows. The maps highlighted residential zones, critical infrastructure, and evacuation routes, providing a comprehensive view of the potential disaster.

"Imagine this," Josh said, his voice steady but somber. "A pyroclastic flow moving faster than a speeding car, hotter than a raging inferno, consuming everything in its path. Houses, schools, hospitals—nothing would stand a chance."

Josh and his team worked tirelessly, double-checking data and refining their models. They knew the accuracy of their maps could mean the difference between life and death for thousands. They meticulously analyzed each detail, from the slope of the terrain to the density of the vegetation, ensuring that their predictions were as precise as possible.

As the maps took shape, they revealed a stark reality: entire towns lay directly in the path of destruction. Despite the dire nature of these predictions, Josh knew pyroclastic flows were only the beginning of their concerns.

Josh continued with unwavering resolve as he addressed the next formidable threat: lahars. These volcanic mudflows, triggered by the eruption, posed a significant danger to life and property in the surrounding communities. Drawing on his extensive knowledge and experience, Josh meticulously calculated the potential reach of these devastating lahars, determining that they could travel as far as 240 miles from the eruption site.

Consulting detailed population data, Josh reached a sobering conclusion. The powerful volcanic mudflows, carrying over 15 million tons of debris, could affect 750,000 people in China and an additional 650,000 people in North Korea. The enormity of the threat was staggering. Thick layers of mud and debris could bury entire communities, altering their lives irrevocably.

Josh shared his findings with the team. "Picture a wall of mud and volcanic material hurtling down mountainsides, engulfing everything in its path," he said, his tone serious. "Homes, roads, farmland—all swallowed up in a matter of minutes."

He and his team pored over geological surveys and historical data from previous eruptions, seeking patterns and clues to better understand the potential behavior of these lahars. They examined past events, comparing similar volcanic activities to predict the outcomes.

With the aid of sophisticated simulation software, Josh created dynamic models showing the predicted paths of the lahars. These models incorporated various factors, such as the terrain's slope, rainfall patterns, and the composition of the volcanic material. The results were alarming: vast areas of land, both in China and North Korea, lay in the direct path of these destructive flows.

The models painted a dire picture: lahars would swallow entire villages, submerge bridges and roads, and bury fertile farmland under tons of volcanic debris. Josh's calculations also highlighted the risk to critical infrastructure. The eruption could destroy roads, bridges, and communication networks, complicating rescue and relief efforts. Farmlands, crucial for local food supplies, faced devastation, leading to potential food shortages and economic turmoil.

The next threat radiating from any eruption would be ash, with its insidious impact on air quality, water supplies, and infrastructure. Reviewing historical data from other eruptions,

Josh determined that in the hours following a Changbai eruption, two billion tons of ash could reach as far as a thousand miles to China's east coast, blanketing an area of over eighty thousand square miles in feet of ash—equivalent to the entire state of Kansas. While the immediate fallout would affect the region, the ash cloud wouldn't stop there. Within about two weeks, some of the ash particles would drift around the globe, carried by atmospheric currents. An eruption of this magnitude would inject massive amounts of ash and sulfur dioxide into the stratosphere, causing global cooling that would affect weather patterns, agriculture, and global food supplies.

"The ashfall poses a significant threat to life and property in the surrounding region," Josh explained to his team. "People will face respiratory issues, infrastructure damage, and disruptions to daily life. This event would be a stark reminder of nature's power, leaving an indelible mark on both local and global scales."

Josh took a deep breath before continuing. The team set to work, each member driven by a shared sense of urgency and purpose. They combed through data, consulted experts, and ran simulations. Josh coordinated their efforts, ensuring they meticulously analyzed every detail and considered every potential consequence.

They analyzed air quality models, predicting severe respiratory health impacts for millions. They studied water contamination scenarios, forecasting dire shortages and the need for emergency clean water supplies. Infrastructure models showed widespread damage to buildings, roads, and power lines, causing prolonged outages and hampering rescue operations.

Besides the immediate effects, the team examined long-term global affects. Atmospheric scientists predicted a significant drop in temperatures because of the ash and sulfur dioxide reflecting sunlight away from Earth, leading to unpredictable weather patterns. Agricultural experts warned of potential crop failures and food shortages, exacerbating the already critical situation.

Two days later, they presented their exhaustive findings to Captain Banks, who reviewed their work, nodding in approval.

"Outstanding job, everyone," he said, his voice filled with pride. "This analysis is exactly what we need."

Josh looked around at his team, proud of what they had accomplished together. Their collective effort had produced a crucial tool for tackling the impending disaster.

"What's next, boss?" Josh asked, turning to Captain Banks.

"The White House," Captain Banks announced, nearly knocking Josh off his feet with the gravity of the statement.

Josh's heart raced. This was the moment they had been preparing for—their work was about to guide national policy. It was a monumental responsibility, but Josh felt a surge of pride and determination. They were ready.

CHAPTER 31

PDB

The President's Daily Briefing (PDB) is a highly classified document that provides a curated summary of the most urgent intelligence issues and developments requiring the President's immediate attention. This essential briefing forms the foundation of the President's daily decision-making on national security and foreign policy matters. As the primary recipient, the President relies on this vital intelligence to make informed and strategic decisions that protect and advance the nation's interests.

Besides the President, the Vice President frequently attends the President's Daily Briefings. This ensures that the Vice President remains well-informed and can provide valuable input on key issues, maintaining continuity in government leadership and preparedness.

The National Security Advisor played a pivotal role in these sessions, orchestrating the presentation of information and offering expert advice on national security matters. This advisor ensured that President Steve Paul received a coherent and comprehensive view of the security landscape, enabling swift and effective responses to emerging threats.

The Director of National Intelligence (DNI), who oversaw the entire intelligence community, was a crucial attendee. The DNI ensured that the intelligence presented was accurate, timely, and comprehensive, providing the President with essential information needed to address the dynamic challenges facing the nation.

Depending on the specific issues slated for discussion, other senior officials were invited to attend the President's Daily Briefing. On that day, the roster of attendees included the White House Chief of Staff, whose role was to oversee and coordinate any follow-up actions arising from the intelligence presented. This ensured that the administration's response was swift, cohesive, and effective.

Typically, the President's Daily Briefing featured multiple briefers from various intelligence agencies, each providing specialized insights and updates. However, today was different. The sole briefer present was Dr. Josh Cooper, whose expertise and focused presentation underscored the gravity of the day's topics, ensuring that the President received a thorough and nuanced understanding of the critical issues at hand.

President Paul welcomed Dr. Cooper with a nod of approval, inviting him to begin his briefing. Seated comfortably on a couch directly opposite the President, Josh started his prepared presentation. Over the next twenty minutes, the room fell into a hushed silence, each attendee riveted by the gravity of the information being delivered.

Using a series of flip charts mounted on a stand positioned between himself and the President, Josh methodically detailed his team's initial research into China's recent invitation for a U.S. team to visit Mount Changbai. The charts provided a visual accompaniment to his precise explanations, enhancing the impact of his words.

Josh summarized the comprehensive work conducted on the mountain, elaborating on the sophisticated equipment the Chinese had deployed prior to the U.S. team's arrival and describing the additional measures taken by the U.S. team to enhance this equipment. His concluding assertion was clear: Mount Changbai did not present an immediate threat unless North Korea resumed nuclear testing.

Choosing to bypass the harrowing details of his capture, Josh swiftly transitioned to discussing the NSA's interception of Chinese communications regarding Lake Cheonji and its correlation with the Tonga eruption. He then presented recent intelligence suggesting that North Korea intended to resume nuclear testing with a new and significantly more powerful boosted bomb.

Josh explained his assessment that such testing might trigger a Tonga-like eruption of Changbai's dormant volcano. After a brief pause to invite questions and receiving none, he moved on to the final segment of his presentation.

Josh painted a stark picture of the potential consequences of a volcanic eruption: devastating pyroclastic flows, destructive lahars, widespread ash fall, significant climate impact, catastrophic loss of life and livelihoods, severe economic disruption, and extensive health issues. His comprehensive briefing left the room in contemplative silence, the weight of the scenarios hanging heavily in the air.

With no questions forthcoming, President Paul rose from his seat, offering a sincere and appreciative nod toward Dr. Cooper. "Thank you,

Dr. Cooper, and thanks to your team for this thorough and crucial presentation," he said, his tone reflecting the gravity of the situation and the value of the insights provided.

After acknowledging the President's gratitude, Josh collected his materials, and a Secret Service agent escorted him out of the Oval Office. This marked a clear transition: the meeting was now shifting from an intelligence briefing to a high-stakes policy discussion. The departure of Dr. Cooper signaled to the remaining attendees it was time to pivot from absorbing information to planning a strategic response, underlining the critical importance of the decisions that would follow. The room, now steeped in the weight of the presented intelligence, prepared to delve into the complex layers of policy-making essential to national security.

President Paul turned to his team and, as was his habit, asked for their impressions of the briefing. The Secretary of Defense was the first to speak. Retired Admiral Evelyn Stone, the first woman ever appointed to the office and a holdover from the previous administration, was renowned for her no-nonsense approach and unwavering stance on national security. As a former senior military officer in the Pacific, she had gained firsthand experience with the strategic challenges presented by China—a nation she acknowledged as a formidable peer competitor to the United States.

"Fuck them," Stone declared, her blunt response shocking everyone in the room except President Paul, who remained stoic and composed.

"Evelyn, please explain," the President requested calmly.

The Secretary of Defense elaborated, her voice steady. She argued that a potential eruption could be a strategic opportunity, setting China and North Korea back fifty years.

"Mr. President, I don't mean to be harsh, but, as you know, China's defense spending continues to escalate while our defense budget lags behind other federal expenditures," she continued. "In this new cold war, they are threatening to do to us what we did to the Soviet Union—outspend us into oblivion."

Then, the President directed his attention to the Deputy Secretary of State, Paula Schultz, who had assumed the responsibilities of the Secretary of State, currently engaged in another demanding round of peace negotiations in the Middle East.

"Paula, what's your take on this?" The President's voice, though steady, carried an edge of urgency that cut through the room's oppressive silence.

Paula, a seasoned diplomat with decades of intricate experience in international relations, felt the air in the room thick with tension, a tangible anticipation that seemed to amplify the soft rustle of paper and the faint hum of the air conditioning. Seated at the polished mahogany table, she could almost feel the weight of the historical and geopolitical stakes bearing down on her.

A natural caution marked Paula's demeanor, a trait honed over years navigating the treacherous waters of global diplomacy. Her eyes swept over the assembled advisors and generals, their faces reflecting a mixture of expectation and restrained impatience. President Paul, his sharp eyes fixed on her, leaned forward, signaling that he was ready for her insights.

Yet Paula recognized her own vulnerability. Her boss, the Secretary of State, exhibited decisive leadership and nearly unshakable confidence in the realm of national security. She felt a pang of longing for his assured presence, a reassurance she could rely on in moments of high stakes.

Her gaze fell to the briefing documents laid out before her. The intelligence reports on Changbai Mountain were stark and alarming. The possibility that North Korea might resume nuclear testing was alarming enough, but the notion that such testing could cause the dormant volcano to erupt was an unexpected development. Such a catastrophe could wreak havoc on the region, putting millions of lives at risk and destabilizing the fragile balance of international relations.

Paula's heart quickened. She could almost hear her boss's voice, urging her to weigh each word with precision and foresight. As she fought to gather her thoughts, she couldn't help but wonder how he would have navigated this moment, balancing the delicate threads of diplomacy and strategy.

The President's gaze was unwavering, a silent demand for her to break through her hesitation. "Deputy Schultz," he said, his tone brooking no delay, "what are your thoughts?"

Paula inhaled, her fingers unconsciously tracing the edge of the folder in front of her. "Mr. President," she began, her voice resolute yet measured, "this situation is indeed a multifaceted challenge, primarily involving the intricate and often contentious relationship between China and North Korea." She launched into a comprehensive analysis, detailing the historical entanglements, economic dependencies, political alliances, and security concerns that framed the relationship between the two countries.

As she spoke, she could sense the President's growing impatience. His eyes, sharp and discerning, flicked with irritation as her detailed exposition dragged on—a history lesson he was already well-versed in.

"Paula," the President interrupted, his tone cutting through her lengthy discourse, "I'm aware of the historical context. Let's cut to the chase. Do you believe China holds any real leverage over North Korea in this situation?"

Realizing her initial approach had missed the mark, Paula quickly recalibrated. "Sir, while China wields significant economic influence over North Korea, it does not have absolute control. North Korea's leadership is notoriously unpredictable, often acting on its own volition. However, China can use its economic leverage to steer North Korea's behavior when the situation demands it." Her response was firm, reflecting a blend of caution and strategic insight.

"Thank you, Paula," the President said, his gaze shifting to his White House Chief of Staff. He had considered calling on Wesley Scott first for his blunt yet insightful commentary, but he knew that Scott's unfiltered observations would have overshadowed the nuanced perspectives of others in the room.

President Paul took a moment to absorb the insights shared. The room buzzed with tension, the stakes high, as each voice contributed a vital piece to the puzzle. With Paula's analysis fresh in his mind, he knew he needed Wesley's perspective to balance the strategic and domestic dimensions of the situation.

In the heart of Baltimore, where sirens wailed and streetlights flickered, two young men forged a bond that would shape their destinies. Steve Paul and Wesley Scott, childhood friends, shared more than just a beat on the city's police force. They built their camaraderie in the crucible of danger, late-night stakeouts, and the relentless pursuit of justice.

They were inseparable, patrolling the same streets, their footsteps echoing off the worn pavement. Steve, with his calm demeanor and analytical mind, was the yin to Wesley's yang—a tempest of passion and quick decisions. Together, they cracked cases, navigated Baltimore's gritty underbelly, and earned the respect of their peers.

But as the years passed, disillusionment set in. The politicians, safe in their ivory towers, seemed indifferent to the sacrifices of the police force. Fueled by frustration, Steve took matters into his own hands. He ran for local office, determined to change the system from within. His campaign speeches echoed through the alleys where he once chased down criminals.

Steve's ascent was meteoric. From the governor's mansion in Annapolis, he implemented reforms, spearheaded community policing, and restored faith in law enforcement. Wesley, ever loyal, stood by his side. When Steve announced his bid for the presidency, Wesley didn't hesitate. He left behind the historic halls of the governor's mansion and followed Steve to Washington, D.C.

The Oval Office was a crucible of decisions—some measured, others urgent. Steve remained the steady hand, weighing options with the precision of a surgeon. Wesley, fiery and impulsive, challenged him. Their debates were legendary—sometimes erupting into shouting matches—but always leading to better solutions. Steve knew that Wesley's passion was the spark that fueled progress.

From national security threats to economic crises, Steve and Wesley faced it all. When tensions escalated, Steve's calm diplomacy met Wesley's fierce resolve, creating a formidable team. The President trusted Wesley; he knew that behind the bluster was a man who'd take a bullet for him.

In the quiet moments when the weight of the world pressed down, Steve and Wesley reminisced about their beat cop days. They'd share a bottle of whiskey, laugh about close calls, and toast to their unbreakable bond. The White House walls held secrets—their secrets. Steve confided in Wesley about sleepless nights and the burden of leadership. Wesley revealed vulnerabilities hidden beneath his gruff exterior.

Now, the President needed Wesley's candor. He turned to his White House Chief of Staff, knowing that Scott's keen insights would cut through the complexity and provide the clarity needed for the road ahead.

"Wesley, what do you think we should do?"

Wesley quickly responded. "Anything you want, Mr. President. Sir, China is in a real pickle, and I believe we have a genuine opportunity. What do you want, Mr. President?" Scott asked.

President Paul weighed his friend's words. He was right; this was an opportunity, but how did the President want to take advantage of it?

In the hallowed Oval Office, President Steve Paul sat, his gaze fixed on the portrait of George Washington. The weight of the presidency rested on his shoulders, but he was already thinking beyond the first term. His vision extended to a legacy that would transcend his time in office—a legacy etched in the annals of history.

The question haunted him: What would define his presidency? People remembered the great leaders of the past for their decisive actions during times of crisis. Abraham Lincoln's resolve during the American Civil War and Franklin Roosevelt's leadership in World War II created indelible legacies. But there was another path—one less traveled. Peace.

President Paul had studied the Nobel Peace Prize laureates. Theodore Roosevelt's mediation in the Russo-Japanese War had earned him the accolade. Woodrow Wilson's vision for a League of Nations had left an imprint. Steve wanted to join their ranks—to be remembered not for battles won, but for conflicts averted.

The room hummed with anticipation. The President's eyes swept across the faces—some stern, others hopeful.

"I want peace," the President declared. "I want peace, peace on the Korean Peninsula," he said, his voice steady.

The seventy-fifth anniversary of the armistice that brought an end to the bloody conflict but left North and South Korea separated by a Demilitarized Zone (DMZ), one of the most heavily armed places on Earth, was fast approaching, and the President sensed an opportunity.

The Chief of Staff, Wesley Scott, leaned toward the staff, his gravelly voice cutting through the tension. "Okay, folks, let's make this happen. We leave in three days."

"Paula," Wesley's gaze bore into her, "we need the framework for an agreement between the U.S. and China for a peace proposal for the Korean Peninsula."

"We leave in three days," Wesley announced, the clock ticking, each second a heartbeat.

"Who'll brief the Chinese?" Wesley asked, his voice low.

"Cooper starts," he decided. "Lay the groundwork. Then the Secretary follows—the framework, the solution."

The room exhaled.

The President rose to his feet and turned to his staff, ending the meeting with these words, his face resolute. "Peace," he whispered, "is the greatest war we wage."

CHAPTER 32

THE FRAMEWORK

Deputy Secretary of State Paula Schultz rushed back to her office at the Department of State, located in the building often referred to as "Foggy Bottom." This nickname refers to the once marshy region of Washington, D.C., where the building stands. For some, it also symbolized the perceived ambiguity and indecisiveness that sometimes characterized the decision-making within its stately, white-clad limestone walls.

However, indecision was not the tone Paula carried into the building that day. Upon her arrival, she called the Secretary of State on a secure line to brief him on the outcome of the day's intelligence briefing. Her recent performance at the White House had been a setback, and she was in no mood to seek forgiveness or permission. Her only duty was to inform him he needed to be back in Washington, D.C., in time to fly to China with the President on Friday morning. She concluded the call by promising to handle everything.

"If needed, I'll brief you on developments on the way to China," Paula assured him. As the call ended, she contemplated she would either lose her job or inherit her boss's.

After lunch, Paula gathered all the key players in the large, secure conference room on the third floor of the State Department. She stood at the head of the expansive conference table, her expression grave yet determined. Around her sat senior advisors, each waiting to understand the reason for this urgent, short-notice meeting.

Paula cleared her throat, commanding the attention of her team. "Ladies and gentlemen, today we embark on an endeavor of immense importance. The President has tasked us with developing a comprehensive peace proposal to bring lasting stability to the Korean Peninsula."

She outlined the President's vision of a framework agreement between the U.S. and China, which would serve as the foundation for an eventual peace proposal. She acknowledged the complexity of obtaining such an agreement, emphasizing the many political, security, and diplomatic considerations involved.

Paula concluded her initial remarks emphatically, in rather undiplomatic terms, declaring that failure was not an option. "I don't care why you think this might not work. I only care about how you will make this work."

Her announcement that they had less than forty-eight hours to complete the framework sent the room into a flurry of activity and concern. Raising her hands to calm her advisors, she suggested breaking into teams, each addressing their own key issue. The group settled down and, working with Paula, divided the issues into work groups, agreeing to reconvene the following morning to discuss their findings.

Across town at the Pentagon, Josh reviewed that morning's briefing with his team, acutely aware of the weight his words carried with the President. As he recapped the briefing, Josh meticulously highlighted how each team member's contributions had shaped the final presentation. For the analysts seated before him, their input in this critical briefing could very well be a defining moment in their careers.

Turning to Cindy Mark from the NSA, Josh said, "Your insights on Chinese SIGINT were pivotal. The clarity and depth of your analysis particularly impressed the President."

To Thomas Miller, the team's seasoned non-proliferation analyst, and Young Ho, the team's Korean expert, he remarked, "Your data on the Korean nuclear program and the leadership's intention to resume testing provided the solid foundation we needed to argue the threat that this testing presented to Changbai Mountain. It was the cornerstone of our argument."

Finally, turning to Li Liu, his trusted civilian China analyst and intelligence mentor, Josh told her, "I could have done none of this without you."

The analysts nodded and murmured appreciatively in response to each acknowledgment, absorbing the significance of their contributions. For many of them, this moment would lead to a promotion and an acceleration of their careers.

For Josh, however, the situation was different. He didn't need a promotion; he already had another career waiting for him back in Seattle. What mattered most to him was the broader impact his contributions might have.

The next morning at the State Department, Paula's team reassembled to discuss each group's findings. Paula had instructed her team to be bold, insisting on no half measures. She was eager to hear what they had developed.

The first group to present covered denuclearization, a major sticking point in negotiations. South Korea and its allies, including the U.S., demanded denuclearization, while North Korea viewed its growing nuclear arsenal as essential for its regime's survival. The group's proposal was indeed bold.

Dr. Thompson, the group's leader and a leading expert in nuclear disarmament, adjusted her glasses and spoke. "North Korea views its nuclear arsenal as essential for its survival. We must offer robust security guarantees." She recommended two mutual security pacts: one between China and North Korea and an updated one between South Korea and the U.S. She proposed a formal non-aggression pact among all parties, which would include suspending all nuclear testing and removing all nuclear weapons from the Korean Peninsula.

She continued, "After removing all nuclear weapons, the U.S. will gradually reduce and eventually withdraw its military forces from South Korea, while North Korean and South Korean forces will slowly pull back from the DMZ."

Maria Rivera, the Secretary's top economic advisor, kicked off the second group's presentation. "We can propose a comprehensive economic package that includes infrastructure development, humanitarian aid, and integration into regional trade initiatives. These incentives would be conditional on North Korea's commitment to peace and gradual denuclearization."

"How much economic aid?" the Deputy Secretary of State pressed. She had been considering this point herself over the past few hours.

"Ma'am, I don't know. We haven't gotten that far in our thinking yet," Maria admitted.

"Maria, if you don't mind, I have given it some thought, and with your permission, I would like to share my conclusions," Deputy Secretary Schultz suggested.

"Please do," Maria agreed.

Her declaration of a "one trillion dollars" investment stunned the room into silence. As the murmurs subsided, she delved into her analysis, explaining that this staggering sum was necessary to lift North Korea out of poverty and modernize its economy, a task that would span multiple decades. She arrived at this figure by drawing parallels to monumental historical efforts, such as the Marshall Plan of 1948, which helped rebuild Europe after World War II, and the cost of German reunification following the fall of the

Berlin Wall in 1989. These comparisons underscored the immense scale and potential challenges of such an undertaking, offering a sobering context for the discussion.

She noted that the estimated cost of German unification ranged from $1.7 trillion to $2.3 trillion in today's dollars. Once completed, the process significantly improved the living standards in the former East Germany but also imposed a long-term financial burden on the German economy.

Turning to North Korea, she pointed out that its economy, relative to South Korea's, was significantly underdeveloped, with widespread poverty, a lack of infrastructure, and limited access to basic services. To close this gap, she reported that while precise estimates vary, some experts suggest that lifting North Korea out of poverty and modernizing its economy could require a multi-decade effort, with costs potentially ranging from $500 billion to over $1 trillion.

"Our focus for the funds will be on extensively rebuilding infrastructure, including transportation, energy, and telecommunications. We will also prioritize humanitarian aid, such as immediate food and medical help, and improvements in housing and sanitation, alongside economic development through long-term investments in education, industry, and technological advancement."

Maria Rivera acknowledged the proposal with a nod of approval. "These incentives would be conditional on North Korea's commitment to peace and gradual denuclearization," Maria reiterated.

"Of course," the Deputy Secretary confirmed.

Ambassador Lee, a regional expert, asked about the role of the other regional stakeholders, Japan and Russia.

Deputy Secretary Paula Schultz speculated that the President would have no trouble securing Tokyo's support. Regarding Russia, she noted that the President had clearly stated, "We didn't invite Russia."

As the discussion continued, the framework of the peace proposal took shape. It was a delicate balancing act, requiring careful consideration of political, security, economic, and humanitarian factors. Paula felt a sense of cautious optimism. The path to peace was fraught with challenges, but with a unified and strategic approach, it was within reach.

The meeting stretched into the night, but by the end, the team had crafted a comprehensive proposal that addressed the key issues. Paula looked around the room at her team, feeling a surge of pride.

"Ladies and gentlemen," she said, her voice firm, "we have a plan. Let's make history."

As they left the conference room, the first light of dawn was breaking over the capital. For the first time in years, there was a glimmer of hope for lasting peace on the Korean Peninsula.

CHAPTER 33

ANDREWS AIR FORCE BASE

Josh, with the unwavering support of his team and countless others, immersed himself in the detailed preparations for his upcoming trip to China. His responsibilities extended beyond the usual briefings and logistical arrangements; his father-in-law arranged a session with the program manager of the Defense Intelligence Agency's "Dress for Success" initiative. This program, typically reserved for military officers transitioning to overseas assignments as attaches, helps these career officers adapt from the uniforms they have long been accustomed to into the civilian attire required for their new roles.

The program manager's advice was straightforward yet impactful: conservative attire was key. She recommended darker suits with subtle pinstripes to convey authority, complemented by suspenders for a touch of elegance. With his new wardrobe ready and his bags packed, Josh looked the part of a confident leader ready for an important mission.

Both Josh and Roger planned to spend a quiet evening at home before Roger would drive Josh to Andrews Air Force Base, the home of Air Force One, in the morning. Josh intended to call Emily, who was still unaware of his imminent departure, to let her know that his work in Washington, D.C., was nearing completion and that he would be home by Sunday or Monday at the latest.

Before he could dial her number, his phone rang. Emily's voice, trembling with fear, came through the line. "Josh, you need to come home. It's Jimmy... our little Jimmy. He fell into the Montlake Cut."

Josh's heart raced with anxiety. "What happened? Is Jimmy okay?"

Emily, her voice breaking with emotion, recounted the incident. The boys had been at the park with Maya, playing with the inflatable planes Josh had given them—models of Alaska Airlines planes. But a sudden gust of wind had carried Jimmy's plane into the waterway, and when he reached for it, he fell in. Maya couldn't swim, and Johnny, drawing from his YMCA swimming lessons, had bravely encouraged

Jimmy to float. "Somehow, it worked," Emily explained, "but it was terrifying. I felt so helpless."

Josh's voice was tight with concern. "Is Jimmy okay? Where are you now?"

Emily replied, her voice strained, "We're at the hospital. Jimmy inhaled water, and the doctors want to keep him overnight for observation. They're worried about pneumonia."

Josh could hear the weight of fear in Emily's words. "Josh, I can't bear this weight alone anymore. I need you here with us."

Silence filled the call as Josh grappled with his emotions. He knew he needed to be on that plane in the morning; so much depended on this mission. Yet, his family needed him, too. Under his breath, he cursed the burden of secrets. "Damn secrets," he muttered.

Before he could respond, Emily had to go; the doctors were waiting to talk to her.

Before the line went silent, Josh promised, "We will get through this together. I love you."

Josh sat in stunned silence after hanging up the phone, his mind racing with worry for his son and guilt for being so far away. Roger, observing Josh's troubled expression, knew something was wrong.

"Josh," Roger began gently, "I couldn't help but overhear part of your conversation with Emily. How's Jimmy?"

Josh looked up, his eyes filled with concern. "He's at the hospital. He fell into the Montlake Cut. The doctors are keeping him overnight for observation. They're worried about pneumonia."

Roger walked over, placing a reassuring hand on Josh's shoulder. "I know this is hard, but Emily is not alone. Maya is with her, Ellen is there too, and I'm sure your parents are on their way to the hospital. They're all there to support her and ensure Jimmy gets the best care possible."

Josh sighed, some tension easing from his shoulders. "I just feel so helpless being here. I should be with them."

Roger nodded understandingly. "I know, Josh. But right now, you need to take care of yourself, too. You've been working nonstop, preparing for this trip. You're exhausted. Getting some rest is important, not just for you, but for Emily and the kids too. You need to be at your best for tomorrow."

Josh hesitated, the weight of his responsibilities pressing down on him. "But what if something happens? What if they need me?"

Roger squeezed Josh's shoulder gently. "I'll keep an ear out for any news. I promise I'll wake you if there's any update. Emily's strong, and she's surrounded by people who love her. Right now, the best thing you can do is get some rest."

Josh nodded, feeling a bit of the burden lifting. "Thank you. I don't know what I'd do without you all."

Roger smiled warmly. "We're family, Josh. We'll get through this together. Now, go get some sleep. We'll handle things here and keep you informed."

Hours passed, and sleep came fitfully to Josh. He tossed and turned, his mind a whirl of worry and fatigue. The bedside clock ticked away the minutes, and the darkened room seemed to press in on him. A soft knock on the door roused him from his restless slumber. Blinking against the dim light, he saw his mother-in-law, Meg, standing in the doorway, her face illuminated by the hallway light.

"Meg?" Josh mumbled, still half-asleep.

Meg approached the bed, her expression a mixture of relief and quiet joy. "Josh, I have good news. The crisis has passed. The doctors have cleared Jimmy, and everyone is back home safe."

Josh struggled to sit up, the fog of sleep still clouding his mind. "Emily called?" he asked, his voice thick with grogginess.

"No, Josh," Meg replied gently. "It was Maya. Emily is sleeping, and we didn't want to wake you. Maya said everything is okay now."

Josh let out a long breath he hadn't realized he was holding, the tension in his body easing. "Thank God," he whispered, his eyes moist with relief.

Meg sat on the edge of the bed, her hand resting on his. "Roger and I stayed up to make sure everything was fine. We wanted you to get some rest. You've been through so much today."

"Thanks," Josh said, his voice filled with gratitude. He felt a profound sense of relief knowing that Jimmy was safe and that Emily had managed to get some much-needed rest.

Meg offered him a plate of dinner she had brought up, the comforting aroma of home-cooked food filling the room. "Are you hungry? You should try to eat something."

Josh shook his head. "No, I'm just too tired. I think I'll just go back to bed."

She nodded, understanding. "Alright, honey. You get some more rest. We'll see you in the morning."

As she left the room, closing the door behind her, Josh lay back down, feeling a weight lifted from his shoulders. The crisis was over, and his family was safe. He closed his eyes, finally allowing himself to drift into a deeper, more peaceful sleep, comforted by the knowledge that his loved ones were there for each other, no matter what.

As dawn painted the sky, Josh rose early, his stomach growling with hunger. Skipping dinner had left him famished. Meg, his mother-in-law, sensed his need for sustenance and took charge of the kitchen. She prepared an extra robust classic English breakfast, a hearty spread fit for a hungry traveler. She adorned the table with an array of comforting dishes: eggs scrambled to perfection, their golden hue promising warmth and nourishment; bacon, crispy and fragrant, its savory aroma filling the room; baked beans, a generous portion, rich and tangy; grilled tomatoes, juicy and slightly charred; and toast, thick slices toasted to that ideal balance of crunch and softness.

Meg's culinary gesture was more than a meal; it was a way to kick off the day with love and care. As Josh sat down to eat, he felt the warmth of family bonds and the anticipation of what lay ahead.

"Ready to go?" Roger, his father-in-law, broke the morning silence. The early hour seemed ambitious for their drive across the Potomac River to Andrews Air Force Base. Traffic on the 14th

Street Bridge, connecting Arlington, Virginia, and Washington, D.C., was notorious for its congestion.

Roger, ever the thoughtful host, had a surprise in store. He pulled his treasured black Lincoln Continental out of storage—a car that held memories and significance beyond its sleek lines. Roger had purchased this remarkable vehicle in 2002, just before Lincoln discontinued production. The decision was part of Ford's strategic shift toward trucks and SUVs, but for Roger, the Continental was more than a casualty of market trends. It was his "baby," a blend of craftsmanship, performance, and elegance that defied time.

Josh settled into the passenger seat, the leather cool against his skin. The forty-minute drive to Andrews Air Force Base—now renamed Joint Base Andrews—unfolded with Roger as the guide. He explained the base's transformation, the result of Base Realignment and Closure (BRAC) proceedings. Joint Base Andrews, a shared hub for the Air Force and Navy, played a critical role in air transportation, special missions, and dignitary travel, including hosting Air Force One.

At the base gate, Roger presented his military identification. The airman saluted and directed them toward the terminal—the very heart of departure and arrival for the presidential aircraft. But strict security protocols awaited them. Two checkpoints passed smoothly, but at the third, an unyielding Secret Service agent stood guard. His earpiece snaked across his neck, and dark sunglasses shielded his eyes.

"Sorry, Captain," the agent said, scrutinizing his clipboard. "You don't have clearance beyond this point."

Josh thanked his father-in-law for his unwavering support and promised not to disappoint him.

Roger, still in the driver's seat, looked at Josh. His face lit up, eyes crinkling at the corners—a silent proclamation of pride. His nod affirmed both Josh's accomplishments and the trust placed in him. No grand speeches were necessary.

Finally, Roger spoke: "Go get them, tiger." With that, Josh stepped out, ready to face the extraordinary day ahead.

CHAPTER 34

AIR FORCE ONE

The sequence of events leading to President Paul's arrival and departure from Andrews Air Force Base aboard Air Force One began early that morning. In the pre-dawn hours, the White House was already buzzing with activity. The Marine Helicopter Squadron One (HMX-1) team diligently prepared the VH-92A helicopter, which had recently replaced the older VH-3D and VH-60N models. This state-of-the-art aircraft underwent a thorough security sweep and pre-flight inspection to ensure everything was in perfect order for the President's flight.

President Paul, accompanied by Secret Service agents, made his way from the Oval Office to the South Lawn. The familiar sight of Marines standing at attention and saluting him as he approached Marine One was a reminder of the disciplined precision of the operation. The President paused to wave to onlookers and media, who were still unaware of the purpose of his travel.

With President Paul securely on board, Marine One's engines roared to life. The helicopter lifted gracefully off the South Lawn, cutting through the crisp morning air as it headed toward Andrews Air Force Base. The short flight, accompanied by a fleet of support helicopters, provided President Paul a moment to review last-minute details and mentally prepare for what lay ahead.

As Marine One descended onto the tarmac at Andrews Air Force Base, military personnel, high-ranking officials, and a contingent of Secret Service agents orchestrated the scene with efficiency. They strategically positioned themselves to ensure the President's safety and a smooth transition to Air Force One. The helicopter's landing was flawless, a testament to the skill and professionalism of the HMX-1 pilots.

Upon disembarking Marine One, military officers greeted President Paul with salutes and engaged in brief, respectful exchanges. President Paul walked with purposeful strides toward Air Force One, the iconic Boeing 747 that symbolized American prestige. As he ascended the stairs, he turned once more to wave before stepping into the aircraft.

Inside, the attentive Air Force One crew stood ready to ensure his comfort and security. He expected to be escorted to his luxurious private office on the new Air Force One, a state-of-the-art replacement for the aging 747-200 aircraft, embarking on its inaugural overseas flight. But that day, events deviated sharply from the meticulously orchestrated script.

Wesley Scott, the President's White House Chief of Staff, met him at the door, his face flushed with anger and frustration, his fist clenched. Usually composed, Scott appeared visibly agitated—an unusual and unsettling sight.

"What's the problem, Wesley?" President Paul asked, noting the tension etched on his Chief of Staff's face.

"Dr. Cooper, Mr. President," Scott replied, his voice tight with irritation. "He's in the passenger lounge and refuses to board the aircraft." Scott's brows furrowed, his eyes drawn together in a vertical crease, reflecting his frustration.

With a clenched jaw and nostrils flaring, Scott pointed toward the terminal. "I was just about to get him," he said, his voice laced with impatience.

"Wesley, I don't think that would be a good idea," the President interjected calmly. "Why not let me talk to him?"

Scott paused, taken aback by the President's suggestion. He opened his mouth to protest, but the steady determination in President Paul's eyes made him reconsider. With a curt nod, Scott stepped aside, allowing the President to take the lead.

President Paul walked toward the passenger lounge, his mind racing. Josh was key to the success of the upcoming summit. President Paul knew he had to resolve whatever was troubling Josh, which was why he intervened personally.

As he entered the passenger lounge, he saw Josh standing by the window, staring out at the tarmac. His shoulders were tense, and his posture rigid, conveying the weight of his turmoil.

"Josh," the President called out gently. Josh turned his head, surprised to see the President standing before him.

"Mr. President," Dr. Cooper began, but President Paul raised a hand to stop him.

"Let's talk," the President said, his voice calm and reassuring. "Tell me what's on your mind."

Josh hesitated, then exhaled deeply. "I can't do it anymore, Mr. President. I just can't. I want to go home." After a moment's pause, he began to unburden himself, sharing his initial reservations about leaving his position as a professor and his decision to abandon his family to run off to the

Pentagon and then to China, only to be kidnapped and tortured. He concluded his confessional by recounting the near-death of his son just hours ago.

President Paul listened intently, nodding as Josh spoke. After a moment, he said, "I understand. You have been through a lot. But we need your expertise and insights. We're all relying on you to help guide these discussions."

Josh looked at the President, the tension easing from his face as he felt understood.

"Josh, I'll make you a deal. If you complete this mission with me, then I promise that once it is over, I will ensure you fly straight home," President Paul offered. To sweeten the deal, he promised to call Emily once Air Force One was airborne.

Josh considered the President's words, the weight of responsibility balanced by the reassurance of support. "I'll board the plane," he said finally.

"Agreed," President Paul replied with a reassured smile. "Let's get this summit started on the right foot."

As they made their way back to Air Force One, the President felt a renewed sense of determination. Although the carefully orchestrated script had fallen apart, Dr. Cooper's presence ensured they were ready to face the challenges ahead.

Air Force One embarked on its historic mission to China, engines roaring to life as the massive Boeing lifted gracefully into the sky. Its wings sliced through the morning air, the sunlight glinting off its polished surface. As the aircraft climbed higher, the landscape below unfurled like a tapestry—a patchwork of fields, cities, and rivers stretching to the horizon.

Equipped with advanced communication systems, Air Force One ensured constant and reliable connectivity for the President and staff. True to his word, President Paul escorted Josh to his private onboard office to call Emily. Josh's pulse quickened with anticipation and anxiety. He had never imagined that his work would lead to such a moment of direct connection to both the President and his family.

He dialed Emily's number, his fingers dancing across the sleek touchscreen of the Airborne Executive Phone (AEP). The phone felt substantial in his hand, a conduit to the world beyond the aircraft's metal skin. When the call connected, Emily's voice crackled through the line. Her shock was immediate as Josh stammered, "Emily, it's Josh. I'm... I'm onboard Air Force One with the President."

Silence hung in the air, broken only by the distant hum of engines. Emily's disbelief was palpable, but then President Paul leaned over, his presence reassuring. He gestured for Josh to hand him the phone.

"Ms. Cooper," President Paul's voice was steady and authoritative. "This is President Paul. I'm here with Josh."

Emily's heart raced as she recognized the timbre of his voice—the weight of responsibility it carried. "Mr. President," she managed, her mind racing with disbelief and amazement.

"I know you and your family have been through a lot lately," President Paul began. "How is Jimmy?"

"Fine, Mr. President. Thank you for asking," Emily replied, gratitude welling up. The President's concern touched her deeply.

"As I was saying," President Paul continued, "Josh's work with us has been crucial. We're almost there—so close. If you don't mind, I need to borrow him for just a few more days. Please."

Emily hesitated, torn between duty and family, sensing the gravity of the situation. "Of course, Mr. President," she agreed, her voice steady. "Thank you."

"Thank you, Ms. Cooper," President Paul said warmly. "I should have him home by Sunday,

Monday at the latest."

As the call ended, Josh felt a profound sense of relief mixed with the weight of his responsibilities. The conversation had reminded him of the importance of his mission and the strength of his family's support.

After the call, President Paul introduced Josh to the salt-and-pepper-haired Secretary of State, Henry Caldwell.

Secretary Caldwell took Josh's hand and shook it firmly. Josh appraised the Secretary, noting the tailored suit that exuded authority yet conveyed an effortless grace—a confidence born of decades of experience. Caldwell began his journey, like Josh, in the halls of academia, where he earned degrees in international relations and law, sharpening his analytical mind and deepening his understanding of global dynamics. He started his career with stints at the United Nations, where he cut his teeth on multilateral negotiations. As he brokered peace agreements in war-torn regions, his reputation grew, earning him both accolades and adversaries.

When a crisis erupted, Caldwell didn't hesitate. His decision-making process was swift, rooted in a profound understanding of history, geopolitics, and human nature. Whether mediating border disputes or countering terrorist threats, he acted with clarity and resolve. His motto: "Inaction is a luxury we cannot afford."

Caldwell's confidence bordered on unyielding. He never second-guessed himself; he trusted his instincts. When intelligence briefings arrived, he absorbed them with intense focus, then stepped forward, ready to chart a course. His team admired his resolve, even in the face of complex, high-stakes negotiations.

As he neared retirement, like the President, his legacy weighed heavily on his mind. He wanted his portrait, soon to hang in the State Department, to serve as a reminder to future secretaries that leadership demands courage, conviction, and the ability to navigate the labyrinth of global affairs. And for now, that included working seamlessly with Dr. Cooper. The two men, each at opposite ends of their journeys, headed off to the onboard Air Force One conference room to rehearse their presentations, their minds already turning to the challenges that lay ahead.

The hours flew by in a blur of empty coffee pots and cleared meal trays. Conversations ebbed and flowed, punctuated by the occasional clatter of silverware and the hum of the aircraft's engines. Josh and Secretary Caldwell worked with unwavering focus as they pored over documents and refined strategies. Despite the long hours, there was a tangible energy in the air, a sense of purpose driving each action. The steady rhythm of work, interspersed with brief moments of camaraderie and laughter, made the time pass swiftly.

After the dinner service, President Paul interrupted Josh and Secretary Caldwell.

"Okay, guys, enough for now. We need to set up the conference room for the poker game," the President urged with a grin.

"Poker game?" Josh asked, intrigued.

"Josh, are you interested?" President Paul invited with a knowing smile.

"Yes, sir," Josh replied enthusiastically, unaware of the President's unique purpose for the game.

President Paul had an unconventional yet effective method for gauging the character of those around him: poker games. Long before he ascended to the presidency, Paul had been an avid poker player. He believed that the game, with its intricate balance of skill, strategy, and psychology, offered unparalleled insights into a person's true nature.

In poker, Paul found a microcosm of human behavior. The game demanded not just an understanding of the odds, but an ability to read people, to sense when they were bluffing or when they held a powerful hand. Over countless games, Paul honed his ability to observe the subtle cues—nervous tics, changes in breathing, the way someone held their cards—that revealed far more than words ever could.

As President, Paul often invited key advisors, diplomats, and even political rivals to informal poker nights at the White House. These sessions were more than just a way to unwind; they were a strategic tool. Around the poker table, the usual formalities of politics fell away. People revealed themselves in ways they never would in a boardroom or during a press conference.

Through these games, Paul could gauge a person's patience and risk tolerance. He observed those who played conservatively, folding at the first sign of trouble, and those who took bold, calculated risks. He noted who bluffed frequently and who only did so when they had no other choice. These insights proved invaluable, offering him a nuanced understanding of how someone might behave in a high-stakes negotiation or during a crisis.

Paul's opponents often underestimated him, mistaking his affable demeanor and love of the game for frivolity. But those who had played with him learned to respect his sharp mind and keen instincts. His poker games became a legendary aspect of his presidency, a unique method for cutting through the facades people often wore and seeing them for who they truly were.

Through countless hands played, and many pots won and lost, President Paul gained a profound understanding of human nature—an understanding that served him well in the Oval Office, where the stakes were always high and the need for keen insight was never greater.

As Air Force One soared through the stratosphere on its historic mission to China, the tension inside the cabin was anything but sky-high. In the Air Force One conference room turned private lounge, President Paul, Secretary of State Henry Caldwell, White House Chief of Staff Wesley Scott, and Josh Cooper sat around the conference room table. The dimmed lights cast an intimate glow, and the rhythmic hum of the engines provided a steady background to their game.

For hours, the pot ebbed and flowed between the four men. Chips exchanged hands, and the stack in the center grew and shrank with each round. Bursts of laughter and moments of intense concentration punctuated the camaraderie around the table.

Josh, new to this high-stakes political poker circle, held his own remarkably well. As the night wore on, he noticed the fatigue setting in on the faces of the more seasoned players. This was his chance. In the next hand, after drawing just one card, Josh's expression remained inscrutable.

"Your move, Josh," President Paul said, his eyes twinkling with curiosity.

Without hesitating, Josh pushed his entire stack of chips into the center of the table. "All in," he announced, his voice steady and confident.

The atmosphere in the cabin shifted as the three senior leaders exchanged glances. The President studied Josh's face, searching for any telltale sign of a bluff. Caldwell, with his decades of negotiation experience, looked for the same. Scott, ever the strategist, weighed the odds carefully.

One by one, each man folded, placing their cards facedown with a mixture of respect and frustration.

Scott chuckled as he pushed his cards away. "You're a bold one, Josh. I'll give you that."

With a triumphant grin, Josh raked in the chips. But Scott, unable to resist his curiosity despite the breach of poker protocol, leaned forward and flipped over Josh's discarded cards. A collective gasp filled the room as they revealed a pair of mismatched low cards, nowhere near a straight. "Well, I'll be damned," President Paul exclaimed, a broad smile spreading across his face. "Wesley, make sure that Josh gets paid."

The men laughed, the tension dissolving into mutual admiration. Josh's daring move had earned their respect, showing he could hold his own not just in the academic halls but in the unpredictable arena of real-world strategy and negotiation.

CHAPTER 35

THE SUMMIT

After fifteen grueling hours aloft, Air Force One descended gracefully onto the tarmac at Baishan Changbaishan Airport—the gateway to Changbai Mountain. The air crackled with anticipation as President Paul stepped onto the runway, his gaze drawn to the distant, majestic peaks.

Nine miles separated the airport from the mountain, a mere whisper in the landscape's vastness. As the crow flies, it was a fleeting distance; by ground, a ninety-minute journey through winding roads and lush forests.

Today, however, the Presidential limousine would remain idle. The Secret Service had orchestrated the delivery of Marine One in the cavernous belly of a C-17 Globemaster. Soon, the helicopter blades, sharp and resolute, would slice through the crisp mountain air, ferrying the

President and his staff to meetings that would shape the world's destiny.

After the short flight, President Paul and his staff stood on the precipice, gazing out across the serene expanse of Heavenly Lake. The setting was nothing short of breathtaking. He wondered whose idea it had been to convene the summit amidst the rugged grandeur of Changbai Mountain. Though he didn't know, he silently applauded their brilliance. It was a backdrop befitting the message he and his team aimed to deliver—a message of unity, diplomacy, and shared purpose.

With resolve etched into his features, President Paul stepped forward to meet his Chinese counterpart, President Li Wei. The summit awaited, and the fate of nations hung in the balance.

President Li Wei's path to office had diverged significantly from tradition. Educated in the West, he embodied a unique blend of Eastern wisdom and Western pragmatism, seamlessly integrating Confucian principles with a modern approach. While he deeply valued harmony, consensus, and filial piety—a virtue rooted in Confucian, Chinese Buddhist, and Daoist ethics encompassing love, respect, and care for one's parents, elders, and ancestors—he was unafraid to challenge convention. An openness to diverse perspectives characterized his leadership style, surrounding himself with seasoned bureaucrats unafraid to challenge his thinking.

President Li Wei's governance prioritized pragmatic action over legacy-building. His tenure had brought tangible improvements to the Chinese people, including healthcare reform, environmental stewardship, economic revitalization, and an overhaul of China's education system.

Accompanying President Li Wei were his key advisors: Foreign Minister Li Wei Xiang, the equivalent of the U.S. Secretary of State; Ding Xuexiang, the Director of the General Office of the Communist Party of China, equivalent to the White House Chief of Staff; and Dr. Mei Ling Chen, the President of the Council of Advisors on Science and Technology, equivalent to the U.S. Science Advisor to the President.

As the summit began, both leaders stood flanked by their most trusted advisors. In the serene setting of Changbai Mountain, they prepared to engage in discussions that could alter the course of history, guided by a shared vision of cooperation and mutual benefit. The stakes were high, but both leaders were determined to seize the moment, bridge their differences, and forge a path forward.

Josh looked out in stunned disbelief over the transformed parking lot that had been his home atop Changbai Mountain only weeks ago. Gone were the Connex box housing units and the bustling team area. In their place, the Chinese government had constructed an outdoor meeting space that seamlessly blended cultural symbolism, functionality, and natural beauty.

Nestled alongside Heavenly Lake was a traditional Chinese courtyard that embodied the essence of Chinese culture. It included a massive pavilion with intricately carved wooden beams and painted eaves, offering shelter from the elements. At the heart of the pavilion stood a round table, crafted from polished rosewood. On one side sat American officials, their chairs adorned with stars and stripes, while on the opposite side were Chinese officials, their seats embellished with embroidered dragons and phoenixes.

Before discussions began, the Chinese delegation hosted a traditional tea ceremony using priceless ancient porcelain teapots filled with fragrant oolong tea. The delicate aroma wafted through the air, mingling with the crisp mountain breeze, creating an atmosphere of tranquility and reflection.

President Li Wei rose, clay teacup in hand, and toasted the American delegation. "We drink from a shared cup to emphasize our unity despite differences," he began, his voice resonating with sincerity and warmth. "May our diplomacy, like the tea leaves we now enjoy, unfurl to reveal layers of possibilities. Each sip of conversation moves us a step closer to mutual understanding, fostering the growth of our diplomatic relations."

The words echoed across the pavilion, carrying with them a message of hope and collaboration. The ceremony set the tone for the summit, highlighting the importance of patience and respect as both nations worked toward common goals.

As President Paul raised his cup in response, Josh felt a renewed sense of purpose. The summit was more than just a meeting of minds; it was a testament to the power of dialogue and the potential for progress when two great nations came together in the spirit of peace.

After the ceremonies concluded, the meeting began with an air of formality. Josh was the first to present, stepping forward with the same confidence he displayed in the Oval Office. He carefully laid out the research he and his colleagues conducted, emphasizing that the Chinese government had requested it.

Dr. Mei Ling Chen, the President of the Council of Advisors on Science and Technology, listened intently. Nearby, a translator, stationed discreetly out of sight, echoed Josh's words in Mandarin. For Josh, this was a novel experience; hearing his words spoken in another language added a unique dimension to his presentation. Each time he spoke, a brief pause followed, creating a moment of anticipation as the translator conveyed his message.

During these pauses, Josh observed the Chinese delegation's reactions. Their expressions, subtle shifts in posture, and non-verbal cues like nodding, smiling, or frowning provided him with real-time feedback. He worried that the translation might not fully capture the nuances of his presentation, but the attentive demeanor of President Li Wei, educated in the West, offered reassurance. Josh focused on the President's gaze and body language, finding comfort in his engaged and responsive presence.

As Josh continued his presentation, President Li Wei's alarm became evident. The gravity of the situation grew with each slide, and the implications of a potential resumption of North Korean nuclear testing on Changbai Mountain became starkly clear. Li's eyes widened, his brow furrowed, and his jaw clenched tight. He nodded politely, signaling agreement or comprehension, but as the severity of the information dawned on him, his posture grew rigid.

By the time Josh concluded his presentation, forecasting the catastrophic impact of a Changbai Mountain eruption on China, the surrounding region, and the world, he observed a profound shift in the President's demeanor. The once composed leader now appeared deeply unsettled, placing his hand over his mouth in a gesture of mounting concern. Signs of anxiety were unmistakable: shallow breathing, frequent sighs, and rapid, darting eye movements.

The room was heavy with tension as President Li Wei processed the alarming information. He stood and requested an unscheduled break. "Too much tea, I'm afraid," he offered with a strained smile, attempting to mask the gravity of the moment with a hint of humor.

As the delegates dispersed for the break, Josh felt a mix of relief and apprehension. His presentation had clearly struck a chord, and now he could only hope that the ensuing discussions would lead to meaningful action and collaboration between the two nations.

Soon, the summit resumed. This time, Secretary of State Henry Caldwell took the spotlight. The focus shifted from President Li

Wei, known for his concentration on domestic issues, to his counterpart, the seasoned diplomat Minister Li Wei Xiang. Like the President, Minister Xiang shared a Western education and a penchant for pragmatic solutions. Caldwell knew he needed to offer him just that—a solution.

Secretary Caldwell, looking directly at Minister Xiang, began his presentation with a calm yet authoritative demeanor. He laid out the bold plan his deputy, Paula, had assembled. The presentation started with a focus on denuclearization, followed by a proposal for two mutual security pacts: one between China and North Korea and another between South Korea and the U.S. Caldwell argued that these security pacts were the only diplomatic measures capable of persuading North Korea to suspend the nuclear testing that threatened to endanger Mount Changbai and jeopardize China's future.

Minister Xiang and President Li Wei leaned forward in their seats, their attention riveted as Secretary Caldwell continued his argument. He emphasized that these security pacts alone would not be sufficient. Caldwell proposed a phased reduction and eventual withdrawal of U.S. military forces in South Korea, contingent upon the suspension of nuclear testing and the removal of nuclear weapons. A gradual pullback of North and South Korean forces from the Demilitarized Zone (DMZ) would accompany this. As he spoke, China's top officials jotted down his key points, recognizing the significance of his proposals.

Caldwell closed his presentation by outlining a proposed one trillion-dollar economic package aimed at ensuring regional stability and prosperity. The room was thick with anticipation as he concluded. Breaking the silence, President Li Wei questioned, "And who will pay for this?"

"We will, Mr. Chairman," Caldwell replied, using the more formal title for the Chinese president to convey respect and gravity.

"We?" President Li Wei asked, seeking clarification.

"The United States of America and the People's Republic of China, with contributions from the Republic of Korea (South Korea) and Japan," Caldwell explained. "We all share a mutual interest in peace on the Korean Peninsula."

The Chinese delegation fell silent as the weight of his words sank in, each delegate contemplating the bold vision of a cooperative future that Caldwell had laid before them.

Secretary Caldwell's presentation marked the end of the formal portion of the summit. President Paul stood and invited his Chinese counterpart for an evening walk around Heavenly Lake. The idea for the walk had come from Secretary Caldwell, who appreciated the historical symbolism it might evoke. He hoped it would be reminiscent of iconic U.S. presidential walks with foreign leaders, such as President Ronald Reagan's meetings with Soviet leader Mikhail Gorbachev during the Cold War. President Paul was eager to distance his counterpart from Ding Xuexiang, the Director of the General Office of the Communist Party of China, whose role as President Li Wei's gatekeeper might interfere with the ultimate message Paul intended to deliver.

As they strolled along the serene trails winding around the lake, President Paul turned to President Li Wei and inquired about his thoughts on the presentations. The tranquil setting contrasted with the intense discussions of the day, creating a moment of candid reflection.

"Do you believe in the scenario Dr. Cooper offered?" President Li Wei began, his tone probing yet thoughtful.

Deep inside, President Paul felt a surge of anger and frustration. He wanted to respond, "Of course I do. Dr. Cooper is telling the truth, and you should know, considering you arranged for North Korea to kidnap and torture him to verify it." But he held back, opting for diplomacy.

Instead, he responded, "I found Dr. Cooper's presentation sound. Besides his insights, the presentation reflected the views of our entire intelligence community." Paul knew this was a lie. He had directed the Director of National Intelligence to keep the information controlled, not even sharing it within their own ranks.

President Li Wei nodded thoughtfully, his expression inscrutable. "Thank you for the presentation, President Paul. I understand it contains sensitive intelligence information. I appreciate your willingness to share it with us. It speaks well to the state of trust our two nations have enjoyed."

President Paul acknowledged the sentiment with a slight nod, understanding the delicate balance they walked. The evening air was crisp, and the sky and cloud's reflection on the lake added a sense of calm to their serious conversation. As they continued their walk, both leaders were aware of the significance of this moment—a step towards potential cooperation or an apocalyptic eruption of Changbai Mountain's volcano.

The two leaders continued their walk around Heavenly Lake, the view breathtaking. The jade-colored lake mirrored the shifting hues of the white clouds and blue sky, casting a magical glow over the landscape. It created an otherworldly backdrop that made President Paul feel as if he were walking through a dream. Perhaps he was, he mused.

President Li Wei's voice broke the serenity. "Mr. President, what makes you think I will sign this framework?"

President Paul had expected this question. Drawing on his experience as a poker player, he played the ace he had kept tucked up his sleeve. First, he reiterated the key points of the proposal, emphasizing the mutual benefits and the path to regional stability. Then he asked his counterpart to imagine a world where North Korea realized the catastrophic potential they held—knowing they could trigger Changbai Mountain to erupt, not with the force of a ten-kiloton nuclear explosion, but with a power a thousand times more devastating.

"You wouldn't!" the Chinese President hissed, his voice barely containing his alarm.

"Sign the agreement, Mr. Chairman," President Paul concluded, his tone unwavering.

The surrounding air seemed to grow colder as the weight of the conversation pressed down. Nearby, the jade waters of Heavenly Lake remained calm, contrasting with the storm brewing in their dialogue. The Chinese

President's face was a mask of contemplation and unease. He gazed out over the lake, where the sun's reflection cast a golden path across the water.

After a long, tense silence, President Li Wei finally spoke, his voice measured but resolute. "For the sake of our future and the safety of our people, I will consider it."

President Paul nodded, understanding the significance of this tentative commitment. They continued their walk, the air now filled with the promise of cooperation and the daunting task of ensuring peace on the Korean Peninsula.

Marine One delivered the American delegation to Air Force One with characteristic precision and efficiency. Once airborne, President Paul gathered Josh and Secretary Caldwell to express his gratitude for their hard work and dedication before excusing himself for the evening. Following the President's lead, Josh settled into his seat, exhaustion overtaking him as he slipped into a deep sleep for the twelve-hour flight home.

Nine hours later, a steward gently shook Josh awake.

"Dr. Cooper, it's time to prepare for landing."

"Landing?" Josh mumbled, disoriented from sleep. "We're not suppose to land in Washington D.C. for another three hours."

As he rubbed his eyes and looked out the window, the setting sun painted the sky in hues of orange and pink. To the east, the majestic silhouette of Mount Rainier came into view, marking the Cascade Mountains east of Seattle. Josh's heart soared as he realized the significance of this sight. True to his word, President Paul had directed the Air Force crew to fly directly to Seattle instead of Washington, D.C.

A wave of emotion washed over Josh as he recognized the familiar landmarks. The sight of Mount Rainier was more than just a geographical marker; it was a symbol of home, family, and the life he had momentarily left behind for the summit. The fatigue from the journey seemed to lift as anticipation and relief filled him.

As the plane began its descent, the sprawling city of Seattle came into clearer view, its lights twinkling in the twilight. Josh felt a deep sense of gratitude toward President Paul for this considerate gesture. He knew that, for now, he was finally going home.

The anticipation of reuniting with his family brought a smile to his face, and the worries of the past weeks seemed to fade away. Josh took a deep breath, savoring the moment, as Air Force One touched down smoothly on the runway. He was home, ready to embrace the familiar warmth and comfort of his loved ones.

REVIEW

I hope you enjoyed your time at Changbai Mountain.

I want to take a moment to thank you for supporting me and other independent writers. Your support means the world to us.

If you have a few minutes, please leave a review on Amazon. Your feedback helps us continue to grow and improve.

OTHER BOOKS BY JOHN PRITCHETT

Asteroid Apophis: Lord of Chaos masterfully combines elements of science fiction, political drama, and suspense. The discovery of the asteroid Apophis sets off a chain of events that involves a diverse cast of characters. As the threat of an impending collision looms, these individuals must navigate a complex landscape of political maneuvering and scientific exploration.

The intricate details and the rigorous efforts to track and understand Apophis will captivate science fiction enthusiasts. Those intrigued by political dramas will appreciate the intricate portrayal of the White House's crisis response, showcasing the President's decisive actions and the coordination of efforts to avert disaster.

The narrative builds suspense with the asteroid's unpredictable behavior and the urgency of the President's response. Readers who relish thrilling scenarios and character-driven stories will be drawn into the motivations and challenges faced by each character as they confront the potential catastrophe.

For those who value scientific accuracy, the novel offers a realistic portrayal of astronomical observations, telescope technology, and the dire consequences of an asteroid impact. Asteroid Apophis: Lord of Chaos is a must-read for anyone fascinated by space exploration and the intricate dance between science and politics.

Footsteps: A Son's Journey is a deeply engaging and emotionally resonant narrative that delves into themes of personal introspection, family dynamics, and the protagonist's quest to confront long-buried emotional trauma. As the story unfolds, readers are drawn into a world of suspense and vulnerability, where suppressed grief over a father's death and the impending remarriage of the mother create a powerful emotional backdrop.

The revelation of the father's tragic death on Mount St. Helens serves as a pivotal moment, compelling the protagonist to face the emotions and memories they have long avoided. This turning point fuels a compelling character arc, as the protagonist grapples with internal conflicts, the fear of losing their father's memory, and the decision to confront the past.

Themes of guilt, regret, and the complexity of grief resonate throughout the story, making it relatable to readers who have experienced loss. The protagonist's journey toward healing and their realization of the importance of sharing their pain with their mother adds depth to the narrative, offering a poignant exploration of family bonds and personal growth.

With a well-paced plot, emotional depth, and relatable themes, Footsteps: A Son's Journey is a captivating read for those who appreciate stories of personal transformation, family relationships, and the intricate process of healing from grief.